tHE tRaiL to you & Me

I0744837

THE TRAIL TO YOU & ME

Copyright © 2022 by Stone Ridge Books

The following is a work of fiction. Any names, characters, places, and incidents are the product of the author's imagination. Any resemblance to persons, living or dead, is entirely coincidental.

ISBN 978-1-953388-07-0 (paperback)

All rights reserved. No part of this publication may be reproduced, scanned, or transmitted in any form, digital or printed, without the written permission of the author.

Illustration: Warren Muzak

Desing & Formatting: Stone Ridge Books

www.mandilynnbell.com

www.stoneridgebooks.com

the trail to you & me

MANDI LYNN BELL

BOOKS BY MANDI LYNN BELL:

Meet Me at the Summit

Let the Rubble Fall

The Trail to You & Me

SIGN UP FOR MY NEWSLETTER

Be the first to know about new book releases,
see behind the scenes content, and more!

https://bit.ly/AuthorMandiNewsletter

CHAPTER 1

"I'm sorry, we aren't looking to hire any new instructors right now." The young woman hands my résumé back without giving it a glance.

"Well, do you mind if I leave my résumé with you in case anything opens up?" I offer, my fingers gripping the paper, arm still stretched out in front of me. This is the third yoga studio I've visited today, and they've all ended the same: whoever is working at the reception desk greets me with a smile, I introduce myself and hand over my résumé, and half a second later, my résumé is handed back to me.

"We aren't hiring right now," she repeats.

Behind me, I hear the door open, and two women holding yoga mats walk in, their hair tied up in knots as they approach the reception area.

"Hi, welcome to River Lane Yoga! Do you have your membership cards?" The woman working the reception area moves to look around me, and I know that's my cue to go.

If I were a dog, I'd be walking out the door with my tail

tucked between my legs. Lucky for me, I'm just a broke college student who spent $2,000 on a yoga certification course without anything to show for it.

I've wanted to be a yoga teacher since high school. My parents divorced my freshman year, and no matter how amicable they tried to make the situation, it left me grasping for some sense of control or peace. My mom brought home every self-help book she could find, and I couldn't stop myself from getting sucked in. The first thing we tried was meditation, but then meditation turned to yoga—my preferred and only form of exercise. I've never been the type of girl to frequent the gym, but yoga doesn't feel like working out; it's self-care. Plus, if doing yoga means I can tell my doctor I work out five days a week, then that's just a bonus.

My mom did yoga with me nearly every day until the novelty of it wore off. Since then, I've tried roping just about everyone I know into doing yoga with me, but it's mostly been a solo mission. The dream is to make money teaching yoga, but until then, I have to settle for dragging unwilling friends into my amateur yoga classes in my apartment living room.

Becoming a yoga instructor is just one part of the five-year plan I created after high school.

Year one: Dive headfirst into college courses to learn everything I can about starting and owning a business—and, of course, graduate in three years instead of four. Why? So I can save myself two semesters' worth of campus fees and be able to get started on my career that much sooner.

Year two: Get my yoga instructor certification. Finish all two hundred hours that are required to become certified, and also get CPR certified.

Year three: Get a job as a yoga instructor so I can start building clientele. Finish and graduate college. A halfway decent GPA would be nice, but it's not required.

Year four: Start my own yoga studio, where I'm in charge of my schedule, décor, classes, and everything in between. I already have a Pinterest board where I've planned it all out.

Year five: Marry the love of my life and live happily ever after.

So far, year five is the haziest. I'm not sure when I'm supposed to meet the "love of my life," but I'm sure it will all work out. Unfortunately, with my dating history, year five is starting to look the most far-fetched, but I have faith Mr. Right will show his face sooner or later.

I graduated high school two years ago, fully convinced my five-year plan was destined to happen, but everything fell apart pretty quickly.

I grew up with two sets of parents: my biological parents and my best friend's parents. Marly and I were joined at the hip when we were little, so much that our parents basically shared custody of us, handing us off for weekends and coordinating family events so Marly and I didn't have to be separated. The only time we didn't hang out was when she went hiking and backpacking with her dad. She always tried to drag me along, and I went occasionally when she guilted me into it, but I assumed she enjoyed herself more when I wasn't complaining every five minutes. Despite our preferences in how to enjoy nature—I believe it's nicer to look at than experience firsthand—

Marly and I were inseparable.

Things got complicated after Marly's parents died in a car accident our first semester of college. Whatever fantasy world Marly and I had built together came crashing down. We went from moving into our first dorm room together to packing our bags and trying to wrap our heads around what had happened.

I stayed enrolled in college, desperately clinging to my five-year plan, but Marly dropped out. I went from taking eighteen college credits my first semester to only six. Between trying to make sure my best friend was okay and grieving the loss of parents that weren't even my own, my life was a hurricane that first year of college.

My own parents watched from the sidelines, having no idea how to help while Marly and I tried to navigate an impossible situation. My mom toyed with the idea of having us both take a year off together, but I didn't entertain the idea. I needed *some* part of my life to stay normal, and I refused to give up on my dreams before they'd even gotten a chance to get started.

It wasn't my parents who'd died, but I felt responsible for Marly that first year. It felt like if I didn't keep her head above water, no one would.

It was like a part of Marly had died in the crash as well. The Marly I grew up with was adventurous and daring, but most of all, she loved life. After her parents died, she was a shell — physically present, but she was floating off somewhere, losing herself the longer time when on.

It was hard enough to lose two people I considered a second set of parents, but then to see my best friend suffer was harder than I could ever have imagined. On top of it all, I was afraid to show my own grief in front of Marly. I didn't know if seeing me cry would make her spiral, so I tried my best to keep it together.

It's been two years since Marly's parents died, and life is finally starting to feel normal again—for both of us. Marly moved across the country for a fresh start and to be with her boyfriend, and I've caught up on my college classes—or at least I'm trying to. Each semester of college, I pack on more and more classes, trying desperately to convince my advisor that I can handle the extra workload. I even maxed out on the amount of summer classes I could take. No matter how many extra courses I add on, I'll still need to do twenty-one credits my last two semesters to graduate in three years.

It's my last summer before my twenty-one-credit semester starts, and the thought of what lies ahead makes me want to curl up in a ball and cry.

My saving grace is yoga. When my life around me is chaos, yoga is the one way I can turn it all off. When I step on the mat, a sense of peace starts to roll through my limbs. With each second that passes, my mind quiets until all that's left to focus on is the way my body moves and flows with each pose.

Last month I took my certification course for yoga, studying the philosophy and methodology and working with other instructors to learn from them as well. Taking the course was a huge burden off my chest because it meant my five-year plan was back on track. What they don't teach in the course, however, is how to get a job. Yes, they tell you the theory behind getting your first gig as an instructor, but actually doing it? That's a totally different story.

It was my mom's idea to start driving around, giving my résumé to different yoga studios, and while I was skeptical that it would work, I was still disappointed to be turned down every place I visited. Today was no different.

I throw my keys on the counter when I get to my mom's house for dinner. Her back is to me when I walk in, and she's leaning over the oven as she sautés vegetables. I haven't lived at home since high school, but my mom likes to lure me back every now and then with a free hot meal.

"How'd it go?" Her long hair is tied up in a bun atop her head. It's naturally a dark auburn, almost identical to my own color, but hers has been colored a lighter shade to hide the gray at her temples.

"No luck," I say, sitting on the barstool at the kitchen island. I pull my résumé out and scan it again, wondering what it is that makes people turn me away before I even get a chance. Résumés definitely don't seem like the norm for applying to be a yoga instructor, but what else am I supposed to do?

"You'll find a place in no time. Maybe see if the gym down the street is hiring," she offers.

My 200-hour certification is staring at me like a blinking red light on my résumé.

"They probably only want to hire instructors with 500-hour certifications." I push away from the counter in a huff, having no idea how I'll be able to find the time to take the next course alongside my summer classes and job—or how I'll pay for it. The 200-hour certification was expensive enough.

"I thought you were going to wait for that certification until after you had some experience teaching?"

"I was, but if no one's going to hire me . . ." I trail off, pulling my phone out to look at my schedule for the summer. My screen is a rainbow of schedules and commitments I've made for the next two months. I'm absolutely maxed out.

While most college students are enjoying their summer break, I'm playing a constant game of catch-up. I'm enrolled in two summer classes; one is this month, and the other is next month. Both classes sound relatively simple. There are no lectures, just reading assignments. Each week I have an essay due, and that's it. It feels like highway robbery given how short the class syllabus is, but after looking at my tuition bills, I'm reminded I'm not the one being robbed.

"What?" my mom asks, glancing over at me as she pulls the vegetables off the burner.

"I'm seeing if I have time to take the next certification between summer classes and work."

"Don't you think you should take it easy?"

"I want to be an instructor," I say, still scanning through my schedule. I signed up to work almost every day, which proved to be a grave mistake on my part. I needed the extra cash to pay for the instructor certification, so when my coworkers asked me if I could cover their shifts while they went away on lavish vacations, I said yes and imagined how the closest thing I'll get to a vacation this year is reading about how the weather cycles impact the atmosphere in my textbook.

"I know you don't want to, but what if you dropped the

summer classes? Then you'd have time for the certification."

I put my phone down, frowning. We've had this conversation almost every week now. Each time I come over, we start talking about what I've been up to. If I dare bring up my busy schedule, my mom starts trying to tell me to drop a few things, live a little. I never thought I'd see the day when my mom told me to not work so hard.

"Mom, please," I say, rolling my eyes.

"I'm just saying, Lori. You need to give yourself a break." She pulls chicken out of the oven, setting it to the side on the counter. "Go visit Marly in Colorado. You could both use the girl time."

I flew out to see Marly for her birthday a couple months ago, and the visit was great. She's happy. Not just happy. *Thriving.* She's out there living her dreams, becoming a photographer and exploring the outdoors with her boyfriend every weekend. Seeing her in her element, moving on from her grief, was not only a relief, but it gave me my own sense of hope that I could do the same. But when I came back, I fell painfully behind on some of my reading assignments. I had to beg one of my professors to let me retake a test I'd failed. Since then, we've only been able to text, call, and video chat.

When I don't say anything, my mom continues. "I know you've always had the plan to graduate early, but that was before Jill and Eric died."

I recoil. "I'll be fine."

"I'm just saying, you need to give yourself a little grace. You had to grieve the loss of two people who treated you like their daughter." Her voice catches, and when I look up, her face is red. Marly and I weren't the only ones who were grieving.

My parents loved Jill and Eric. When things started to turn sour during the divorce, my mom dropped me off at Marly's house so my mom and dad could sort things out without me witnessing.

"I just need to get through this first year," I tell my mom, trying to plaster on my best smile.

My mom stares at me, unconvinced. "I'm just saying . . ." She shrugs. "You're young. You should be spending your summer going out on adventures. Go to the beach. Take a day off from work."

I get up and grab our plates from the cabinet. "I'll make time for adventures after I've finished all my classes," I say, knowing full well the most adventurous part of my summer days will be my drive to work.

My mom takes a plate when I offer it to her. "Where you got your drive, I have no idea. When I was your age, I was too busy dating to even realize I'd missed the deadline on an assignment."

I roll my eyes, smiling. "I still date. Just not successfully."

My mom is smiling now too, scooping portions onto her plate. "Just don't get too caught up in college, okay? Graduating in three years or four years, it's still something to be proud of."

"Three years." I grin. I'm not willing to give up on my goal just because it's getting hard.

CHAPTER 2

My best friend lives across the country. We've gone from seeing each other every day to seeing each other whenever one of us can afford a plane ticket.

Part of Marly's grieving process was going on the road trip. I'd worked with her family to coax her into going on the trip, and it was exactly what she needed. What I didn't anticipate was that this spark that brought her back to life would be the same spark that would pull her away.

"Can you hear me now?" she says, adjusting her laptop for our weekly video chat session. After her cross-country road trip, Marly found herself in Colorado, falling head over heels for a guy who lived there. She's unofficially moved to Colorado to be with him, while I'm here in New Hampshire where we grew up.

I want to say I'm jealous, but the thing Marly and her boyfriend bond over is their love of climbing mountains. And that? That I'm not jealous about.

When she's with him, she's back to her old self, so even if

she's hundreds of miles away, it's better than having her here and miserable.

"Yup!" I say, turning a lamp on next to my laptop so Marly can see me better. "And I'm glad you figured out your tech issues because I've got a problem for you to solve."

"Oh boy," Marly says, half rolling her eyes.

"So, I'm trying to get a job as a yoga instructor since I have this lovely new certification." I hold the certificate toward the screen. It looks like a regular piece of paper with a foil seal in the corner. For $2,000, I expected something a little fancier, but this is as good as it gets.

"Oh, it came in!" Marly says, leaning forward to get a closer look.

"Yeah, it arrived in the mail a couple days ago. So, I thought the summer would be the perfect time to go to yoga studios and see if I can get a job. I went in, showed them my résumé and all that, but no luck. I'm thinking the issue may be that I only have the 200-hour certification, not the 500-hour one."

"Did they say that's why?"

"No, they didn't tell me anything besides 'we aren't currently hiring.' " I make a face and roll my eyes. "But I don't have time to get the 500-hour certification until I quit my waitress job. And I can't quit my waitress job until I get a job as a yoga instructor. And to be an instructor, I guess that means I'll need to start the 500-hour course sooner than I thought. I want to try to do it this summer, but with work and summer classes, it's not going to happen."

Marly cocks an eyebrow. "I thought you said you only

needed two hundred hours to start teaching?"

"You do, but just because it's the minimum doesn't mean that's also the minimum for the yoga studio hiring me."

"Well, maybe they just really aren't hiring." Marly shrugs.

"I know, I know," I say, letting my head drop to the back of my desk chair. "But I'll need to do the 500-hour certification eventually. I might as well do it now."

"Okay," Marly says, pausing to think. "I thought you said the summer classes were super easy?"

"They are. But they still take up a lot of time even if they're easy."

"What if you quit the waitress job?" she offers.

My frown deepens. "Then I won't be able to afford the certification course."

"Cut back hours?" she tries, giving me a sad smile.

I lean forward, burying my face in my hands. "I already told everyone I would work their shifts for them so they could go on vacation." I groan. It's starting to feel a little hopeless.

Another voice comes in on the video chat. "Marly, did you still want to go bowling with Trent and Chelsy tonight?" Marly's boyfriend walks in from behind and pauses for a moment when he sees me on the screen. "Oh, sorry."

"Hi, Dylan." I wave.

It's hard to ignore the way Marly's face lights up when she hears Dylan's voice. She turns automatically when she sees him, and I'm not sure if she's aware of how her gaze follows him when he's in the room. It's not in an obvious way, but after knowing Marly so many years, even the tiny shift is clear. They've been dating for almost a year now, and while their relationship started off a little rocky, it's safe to say they're in the honeymoon phase of dating.

"Yeah, once Lori and I finish our video chat."

Dylan gives me a quick smile and wave before exiting the room, and when Marly turns back to me, her face is still vibrant and grinning.

"I'm not going to lie, I'm a little jealous," I admit.

It takes Marly a moment to realize what exactly I'm jealous about, but once she does, she blushes and quickly tries to compose herself, attempting to hide her smile.

"It's your own fault," she says.

"For what? Being single, or you having a boyfriend?"

"Both, technically," she says, referring to how if I hadn't been so pushy about her going on the road trip, she never would have met Dylan. "But you're guilty of going on one date, finding something to dislike, and then refusing to give anyone a second date."

"I have standards," I say, laughing.

"What about that Johnny guy you dated a couple months ago? You were crushing on him all semester, and then when you finally went on a date, you never saw him again."

"He chews too loud."

She gives me a face, and I know my answer is unacceptable.

"Marly, you know how I am about that!"

"I know. I know. You have self-diagnosed misophonia." She laughs quietly. "Okay, what about that guy you went out with senior year of high school? Sean? You wanted him to ask you to prom."

"His deodorant didn't last past school hours." I scrunch up my face just thinking about it. He smelled fine at school, but he had football practice before our date and didn't feel inclined to shower or freshen up. It was all downhill after that.

"And Andrew? Which class was he in? Algebra?"

I roll my eyes. "Are we just going to go through every guy I've ever dated? I see the pattern: no second dates."

"I'm just saying, in order to get a boyfriend, you'll need to get past the first date." She shrugs. Easy for her to say; she's already got the guy.

"When I can score a first date, I'll let you know," I say. I can't even remember the last time I ran into a guy who seemed date-worthy. There are plenty of guys in my college classes, but they usually say stupid jokes, which is an immediate turnoff.

"You'd meet guys if you worked less and got out of the house more."

"Out of the house? I'm never home."

"Where are you, then? Work?" She smirks.

"You know, I meet plenty of cute guys when I'm waiting tables. But any cute guy who's at a restaurant is there because they're out on a date and therefore already spoken for."

Marly smiles, and even though it's been a couple months since we've seen each other in person, the video chats make it feel like we're sitting in each other's bedrooms, sharing the latest gossip like we used to do in high school.

"So, you meet lots of cute guys, then?"

I laugh, shaking my head. "There's plenty of them to go around," I lie.

"When one of the guys asks you out, let me know," she says, rolling with the lie.

"I will!" I say, hedging her bet. "And maybe I'll even go out on a second date."

Marly widens her eyes in mock surprise. "Now we're talking."

CHAPTER 3

the truth? I hate my job. I don't just hate it because it takes up too much of my time for too little pay; I hate it because I'm genuinely terrible at my job. I'm a waiter at Angela's Kitchen, a local Italian restaurant, and if I'm being honest, I applied to the job because I knew I'd get free food and it was one of my favorite restaurants. Joke's on me; now I never want to come here in my free time, and when I eventually quit, I'll be too ashamed to ever show my face again.

I started in April, and it's July now. I assumed I would get better, but some days I theorize I've only gotten worse, like the first week was just beginner's luck.

I'm good at memorizing orders. It's the only pride I can take in myself. I've always joked that I'm not a good student, I'm just good at memorizing. Taking orders isn't the issue. Remembering I have tables that need their orders taken? Well, that's the real problem. It usually takes a coworker tapping me on the shoulder to remind me I forgot an entire wing of the restaurant exists.

"Table eight," Allison says as she rushes past me, her arms full of food.

"Shit," I say, turning to look at the table behind me. Six men are huddled in a booth, most of them engrossed in conversation, but two sit off to the side, murmuring to each other, frowns deep—probably wondering where their waiter is.

I finish processing another table's credit card and drop it off before going to table eight, wondering how long they've been waiting. Someone's already brought water for everyone at the table. Allison, maybe? I'll have to thank her later.

"Hi, sorry for the wait. My name's Lori, and I'll be your waiter today. Can I start anyone off with drinks other than water?"

The men perk up when they see me. They're not the usual crowd we get. Most customers are dressed up for a night out, or even just casually dressed. But these men are wearing shirts that look like they'd be better off in the trash bin with how worn they are. It probably looks worse next to their shaggy hair and beards. They're all clean looking, so I can't accuse them of that, but their clothes have seen better days. And haircuts are long overdue.

We aren't a fancy restaurant by any means. We're the place parents bring their screaming toddlers in a sad attempt for date night. But if we were a fancy restaurant, these men would certainty have been told to turn around and come back when they're wearing something more appropriate.

"Another round of bread," a man who looks around my dad's age says, holding up the empty breadbasket.

"Sure thing." I smile.

"Can we get three servings of mozzarella sticks to start off?" another man says, his beard the longest out of everyone sitting at the table.

I go around the table, taking everyone's drink orders. I can't get a read on the table. Typically, there's a general feeling I get from each group: family night out, girls' night, first date. But this table of men is . . . odd. The best way I can describe them all is scruffy, with beards and hair in desperate need of grooming, but they're all so different. One man is quiet and gruff. Another is loud and much too eager to talk. Two are younger, closer to my age, but the rest are older. It's a bizarre mix, but they all seem friendly.

"I'll get those right out," I say, smiling as I walk away.

I'm running around, trying to stop at each of my tables and make sure no one needs me, when the man with the long beard puts his hand up to wave me over.

"Are you guys ready to order?" I ask, pulling my notepad out.

"Of course we are; we've walked twenty miles today!"

An older gentleman in the corner chuckles, mostly to himself. A younger guy sitting at the corner of the booth cringes and turns to me.

"Sorry," he says, grinning sheepishly. "We're thru-hikers. Some of us forget what civilization is like." The guy turns to glare playfully at the bearded man, who's digging through the fresh breadbasket I brought them.

The guy who just spoke turns away, but my eyes linger on him. His brown hair looks like it's supposed to be cut shorter but is grown out, scruffy around his ears. He has a beard just like the rest of the men at the table, but his is the tamest, though still unkept.

"Thru-hikers?" I ask. The words sound familiar, but I can't place them right away. The men perk up, eager to talk.

"The Appalachian Trail. We started in Georgia, and we're heading to Maine. Should get there by September if we stop sightseeing every time we see civilization," a guy wearing a bandana around his head says.

"Grey, you gotta admit, eating out is way more fun than eating another PB&J."

"I just wanted to shower." Another man shrugs.

"Screw the shower, I just wanted a mattress."

"Warm food," another says, holding up a breadstick.

"Oh!" I say, realizing what they're talking about. "Yeah, we get hikers in the area all the time."

Marly is an avid hiker, and she knows more about the Appalachian Trail, but I know the basics. I live only a couple miles from where the trail intersects with town, so it's impossible not to know about it. Backpackers on the trail are either section hikers or thru-hikers. Either way, they're hiking a long trail with only what's on their backs. Thru-hikers are easy to spot because they look and smell like they haven't showered in days. It explains why everyone looks like they need a haircut, though they're missing the special perfume thru-hikers normally wear, so they probably found a hotel or hostel to shower.

"So, then you're aware we'll eat our body weight in food?" one of the guys says with a hearty laugh.

"I expect no one will need doggy bags." I smile, and the

group chuckles.

I go around the table, taking everyone's orders. They each order at least one entrée, usually with two or more sides. It's a massive amount of food, but I won't be shocked if they eat it all without an issue.

"Do you want me to get the menus out of the way?" I ask.

"No way! We may need a second round!"

I smile. "All right, then. I'll be back out with your appetizers shortly."

"Thank you," the younger guy on the end says, his words soft compared to the rowdy group around him.

A few minutes later, I'm back at the table with the three helpings of mozzarella sticks, and their eyes lift immediately to the food, but they don't break the conversation they're having.

"I woke up, and my shoes were frozen and frosted over. I normally make a hot meal when I first wake up, but I couldn't get myself to inch my way out of the sleeping bag. I was hoping someone else would wake up first and offer to boil water for me." One of the men laughs.

"Chip, what about that one time your tent flooded?" one of the older men says to the younger guy sitting on the end. He makes a face, unamused.

"Took days for that thing to dry out." He glances over to me as I set the plates of food down. "Thank you."

The men dive into the food, all hands coming out to eat. Their conversation continues, comparing stories of the trail, none of it making the journey of hiking the Appalachian Trail sound fun.

"What's up with table eight?" Allison says when I'm at the

kiosk checking out another table.

"They're AT thru-hikers," I say.

"Rowdy bunch," she mumbles, leaning against the wall, eyeing them all. "The cute one on the end keeps staring at you."

I turn to look, but when I do, they're all either engrossed in their food or talking to one another.

"Not right now," Allison says, grabbing me to turn my gaze away. "Whenever you're at the table, his eyes are glued to you."

"Well, I'm the waiter. Who else is he going to look at?"

Allison rolls her eyes. "No, like, in a cute way."

I peek over at the guy again. It's not that he isn't cute; he is. He's got that scruffy lumberjack look going on, with the beard, flannel shirt, and messy hair. It's much better than the homeless hiker look that the rest of the guys at his table are sporting, with beards growing out in all directions and clothes that look well past their expiration.

"He's cute. Just not my type." I walk out to the kitchen to check to see if another round of food is ready. Allison walks with me.

"What's your type? *I* think he's adorable!"

I glance over at her. "Do *you* have a crush on him?"

"No. And besides, he's not interested in me. He's interested in you."

I shrug. "He's been living out of a tent for the past couple months. He's probably interested in any female willing to talk to him."

Allison lets out a frustrated grunt, grabbing a plate of food for one of her tables.

"You're supposed to make my eight-hour shifts more enjoyable," Allison says, giving me a playful grin.

"I can get you his number," I offer.

"You're impossible." Allison laughs, her arms full as she makes her way back to the dinner area.

When the food for table eight is ready, Allison helps me deliver the multiple plates to the rowdy group. They're all mostly shouting over one another, excitedly sharing stories.

"Order's up!" one of them exclaims when he sees me and Allison approach. We lay out the food, filling every inch of the table with dishes. They settle down once the food is in front of them, already digging in before I can finish putting the last plate out.

"So, what do you think about a game night?" the one wearing the bandana says, picking up the meatball grinder he ordered.

"I'm good," one of the men says.

"Oh, don't be an old fart!"

"He wants to get an early start to get away from you, Grey." The bearded man laughs.

"I'm down for a game night," the younger guy sitting on the edge says.

"Are you into game nights?"

It takes me a moment to realize the man in the bandana is talking to me. I pass another plate of food down the table and blush when I realize they're all looking at me, waiting for my answer.

"Uh, yeah."

Allison passes out the last plate of food, but she lingers,

grinning as she waits for the conversation to play out.

"You should join us! Chip over here needs someone to play on his team." He points to the younger guy sitting on the end, who turns positively scarlet. I glance at Allison out of the corner of my eye, and when I turn to her, she's beaming. I give her a face, and she walks off, probably ready to go gossip to the rest of the crew.

"What do you say? Any good at Pictionary?" someone asks.

All eyes are still on me, except for the guy sitting on the end. He keeps his eyes trained on the table.

"I could probably carry the team to victory," I say, trying to end the conversation while also satisfying their fun.

The table bursts into laughter, so I know I said the right thing. Most of the men turn back to their food.

"Do you guys need anything else?" I ask.

The guy sitting at the end of the table looks up.

"We're all set for now," he says, trying to redeem himself after the entire table ganged up on him.

A few seconds later, when I'm far enough away from the table, Allison grips my arm to stop me.

"I told you!" she whispers roughly.

I can't help but laugh. "Is that your version of flirting? Because if it is, you need to get a little more action in your life."

Allison gives me a smirk before returning to her work.

The night rushes by, and I pass by table eight occasionally to check on them and make sure they don't need anything else. They've quieted a lot, the task of eating keeping their mouths occupied. I eye the guy sitting at the end of the table, wondering if Allison was right, but if she is, it's impossible to tell from my point of view. He looks up whenever I walk over, but he never does much more than smile.

"Did you guys want to do dessert?" I ask when it seems like they've cleaned their plates.

A few guys perk up and lean forward to grab the menus from where they put them off to the side of the table.

"I'll do the brownie sundae," the one wearing a bandana says.

"Make it two," the one with the long beard pipes in.

"Can I get the cheesecake?" says another.

I go around the table, taking their orders, until I get to the guy sitting on the end.

"I'm all set," he says.

"Chip wants to look good for the ladies," the burly man sitting next to him says, giving me a wink, causing everyone else around the table to let out a soft chuckle. Chip—which is a name I've never heard outside of *Beauty and the Beast*—seems to dismiss the idea. I thought they called him Chip before, but I just assumed I'd heard wrong.

"That'll be right out," I say.

A couple minutes later, I go to the table again to drop off their desserts, and the group is tame this time around. Chip can barely manage to make eye contact with me, which only further confirms Allison's suspicions—that and the relentless teasing from the rest of the guys at the table.

"Did you turn him down or something?" Allison says, coming to stand beside me when the night starts to calm. We both get off from work in less than an hour. Her eyes are trained on table eight, her source of entertainment for the night.

"No," I say, following her gaze. The group is still telling stories. They're less animated than they were before; perhaps the energy is finally dying down. Chip's smile is gone, but he watches his friends, never fully engaging in the conversation. "His friends were poking fun at him though."

"About what?"

"Something about wanting to look good for the ladies." I giggle, and Allison's eyes nearly burst out of her head.

"What?" she says with a laugh.

"Shh!" I signal her to quiet down when a few customers close to us turn and look.

"I was right!" she tries to whisper but fails.

I shake my head, laughing. "Yes, congratulations. After working here for three months, you've mastered the art of telling when random strangers are flirting."

"It helps the shift go by faster, okay?" She walks off to check on one of her tables, a little pep in her step after being proved right. And I can't help feeling a little smug myself, even knowing the flirting won't go anywhere.

Within a couple minutes, I'm wrapping up table eight, giving them their check and processing their cards. When I glance over next, they're all getting up to leave. I smile, a little relieved to have such a rowdy group gone.

Once the table clears out, I make my way over to clean up. I'm removing some of the empty plates when someone comes up behind me.

"Sorry about them."

I turn to see Chip, his hands stuffed into his pants pockets.

"They can be a rowdy bunch, but I promise they're all good guys."

"Oh! It's all right. You guys kept the night interesting. Makes the shift go by faster."

He smiles in a sort of crooked way that brings emphasis to the deep blue color of his eyes, which I hadn't noticed before. Allison is right: he's cute—in his own way.

"I don't know how much of your shift is left, but they weren't kidding about game night if you want to join. A whole bunch of us will be hanging out at the hostel down the street. Guys and girls, so not creepy. I promise."

He says the words so quickly that I laugh a little at his nervousness. I glance at the clock on the wall behind him. There's only fifteen minutes left before I get off for the night.

"I'd love to, but I have to . . ." I have to go home and figure out how to take the 500-hour certification course, but all I can hear is Marly's—and now also Allison's—voice in the back of my head telling me that I need to say yes.

"It's fine. We just like to hang out as we pass through the area, get to know the locals," he says before I can finish my sentence. He smiles, and I soften up to him.

"No," I interrupt him, then hesitate. "My shift ends in fifteen minutes, but I warn you, it's possible I'm actually the worst Pictionary partner you'll meet."

He grins. "I think we can manage."

My smile mirrors his. "I guess we'll see if you regret adding me to your team."

His smile lights up. "What's your number? I'll text you the address."

He pulls out his phone and types my number, adding me as a contact. He's gone before I've realized much of what I just agreed to. When I turn toward the kitchen with my arms full of dirty dishes, Allison's grin is wide.

CHAPTER 4

I should be more freaked-out about driving to a random address where I know I'll be greeted by a group of strangers. If my mom knew where I am right now, she'd be appalled—or already calling the cops. While I'm cautious—I googled the address to make sure it's actually for a hostel—I'm also optimistic. I met a cute guy, and we flirted. There's no harm in taking it a step further and spending time with him. Tomorrow Chip will walk off into the woods again until he gets to Maine. No harm, no foul.

So, here I am, tired, slightly sweaty, and about to hang out with a bunch of strangers. My mom should be proud of me getting out of the house to do something besides work.

What Chip doesn't need to know is that before I left work, I used my iPhone to share my location with Allison so she can watch where I am and call 911 if I end up anywhere that isn't my apartment or the hostel.

The hostel isn't far from the restaurant, only a couple blocks down the street. It's an old colonial-style house that looks like it could be a bed-and-breakfast. It's two stories with white siding and gray shutters. The front entrance is a porch that stretches across the entire width of the building. It'd be beautiful if not for the excessive amount of clothing hanging out to dry on the porch and some of the windows.

I park my car next to the only other vehicle in the driveway and make my way toward the front door, knocking when I get to the top of the steps.

"Did you get locked out?" A girl around my age opens the door, her hair damp like she just got out of the shower. When she sees me, she pauses, seeming confused. "Sorry, I thought you were someone else. Are you staying here tonight?"

"Uh, no," I say, trying to look behind her to see if there's any sign of Chip or any of the other guys who were at the restaurant. "Chip told me to meet him here."

"Oh! He's up in his bunk. I'll go grab him."

She disappears down the hall, and I make my way inside, shutting the door softly behind me.

I've never stepped foot in a hostel, so I'm not sure what I expected, but this isn't it.

It's more like a home than a hotel, with mismatched couches across the main living area and photos hanging on all the walls. Every photo is a different hiker, and I can tell they're hikers from the layers of grime and sweat on their faces and the huge bags on their backs. There's a desk off to the right with a laptop and notebook that's being used as a sign-in sheet. Off to the left is a fireplace where a bunch of hikers are gathered around, one of them with a guitar he's playing softly. Across from them is another small group playing a game of cards. The Appalachian Trail—or AT—logo is made out of two-by-fours and hanging on the back wall as decoration. Directly underneath it is a bookshelf stuffed to the brim with books of all sizes.

"You made it!" Chip says, coming down the hallway.

"This is what a hostel is?" I ask, my eyes still wandering around the room. I didn't expect the hostel to feel so much like a college dorm, with activity in every corner.

"Yup! Home sweet home! For the night, that is. Come on, I was just heading out to help with the bonfire out back." He gestures for me to follow as he makes his way back down the hall. We pass a staircase that leads to the second floor, and then the hall opens up to a huge kitchen, where a few more people are scattered about.

"How many people are staying here tonight?" I ask. More people show up the closer I look.

"Tonight? I think twenty or thirty. I haven't had a chance to ask yet."

"Where do you all sleep?"

"Upstairs. There're a couple rooms, and they're all stuffed to the max with bunk beds. It can be a little rough if someone snores, but it's better than a tent."

We walk past the kitchen, and Chip opens the door that leads into the backyard, putting his hand gently at the small of my back to guide me forward.

It's louder once we get outside. All the men from the restaurant are there, plus a group of women huddled together around a campfire. The group varies widely in age, but they all talk and laugh like they've been friends for a lifetime.

"Well, look who arrived!" the man in the bandana shouts when he sees me.

Chip turns to me with a grin when we walk toward the group. "I'll introduce you to everyone," he says in a low tone.

The entire group turns to look at us, which should make me even more freaked-out, but they clear the way for us, offering a seat in one of the patio chairs next to the firepit. There's a small campfire going, giving a small glow to everyone's faces. The smell of the burning wood unlocks a deep sense of nostalgia from all the campfires I had growing up.

"Everyone, this is Lori." Chip turns to me, his hand still on my back as he guides me to a chair. "Lori, this is Grey, Rye, Woodchuck, Tin Cup, Dusty, Mountain Goat, Monarch, Kodak, Twin Peaks, Trip, Night Owl, Shake, Bigfoot, and Jersey."

Each person gives me a small wave as their name is called, and I try to keep track of everyone, but as soon as Chip stops talking, I've already forgotten who's who.

"Hi," I say, perhaps too softly, still wondering what their names are; those can't possibly be their real names.

"You don't have to remember who's who," Chip says softly, leaning down close to my ear. "But you should know me. I'm Chip."

I smile despite being so flustered. The chairs are angled loosely around the fire, flames bouncing off just enough light to see everyone's faces.

"Shall the games begin?" says the man with the bandana on his head. I think Chip said his name is Grey.

The group shifts into a flurry of energy. As promised, we play Pictionary using a giant whiteboard and markers that were in the hostel. The group is just as loud here as they were at Angela's, but now, being a part of the group, I can see why. The energy is contagious, radiating off everyone and growing exponentially until it erupts into laughter. Despite knowing none of these people until today, I find myself getting lost in the laughter and shouting along with them. After watching them banter long enough, I'm able to catch a few names as well.

"Chocolate chips?" Twin Peaks says, watching Rye draw on the board. He wobbles his hand to signal "sorta."

"Cookie dough!" I shout.

"Yes!"

The group cheers, and with that, our team wins, and the other half of the group is less than enthusiastic.

"Oh, come on!" Mountain Goat sighs.

The groups break up, and the shouting turns to murmuring as a few people leave to go inside the house.

"We're heading in for the night. Will you be leaving with us tomorrow?" Dusty says, hand on Chip's shoulder.

"I don't think so. I might do a zero day. I'm sure I'll catch up on trail though."

"Sounds good," Dusty says, then follows a few others into the house.

Once the game area clears, there's only us and two other women left outside with us. They walk in and out of the house to put things away. Before I know it, it's just the two of us sitting at the fire, the night sky broad over our heads.

"What's a zero day?" I ask, turning to Chip.

"Zero miles, so taking a break."

I nod, realizing the AT thru-hikers have an entire world of their own that I never knew existed. "What do you do on zero days? If you're not hiking?"

He shrugs. "Anything that seems fun or nothing at all." He kicks his legs out to stretch them. "Sometimes you need a day to just do *nothing*."

He leans back in his chair, closing his eyes, looking perfectly at ease. The thought of doing nothing for a day makes me jealous. I can't remember the last time I had a "nothing" day. It feels like ever since college started, it's been a whirlwind of trying to fight for something as it gets farther and farther away.

At this point, even the thought of waking up and walking in the woods, away from all my stress and problems, sounds better than what I've been up to lately.

"So, do you all hike as a big group?" I ask, daring to imagine what life must be like for Chip, packing up a tent and walking in the woods for miles. On the one hand, I can imagine it to be utter torture. But on the other hand, the thought of literally walking away from all my problems is almost thrilling.

"No. I hike solo for the most part, but Dusty and Tin Cup sometimes hike together. I run into them a lot and end up hiking with them occasionally." He shrugs.

"What about everyone else?"

"I've seen a few of them on the trail before. Like Twin Peaks. I've run into her about five times now. Then Mountain Goat. He's someone I see a lot, same with Rye and Monarch. I just met Kodak today. She's going south, but most of us are heading north."

I nod my head, still a little fuzzy on the details.

"What?" he asks.

"You guys just act like one big family."

His grin is wide. "Because we are. When you're living on the trail, no one is a stranger."

"Except for me," I say, lifting an eyebrow.

"No, you're the least strange of them all."

I laugh when he smirks at me.

"What makes someone wake up one day and want to hike the entire Appalachian Trail anyway?"

Chip's face softens, and he goes serious. "I guess it's different for everyone. Some people just like to hike. Or it's a bucket list item. Other people are here to figure life out. Escape stress. Start anew." He shrugs.

I let myself imagine dropping everything and, for just a couple of months, focusing on nothing other than walking north.

"I can imagine the appeal," I mumble. Chip looks over like he isn't sure he heard me correctly. "Of course, the lack of modern amenities puts a damper on the whole situation."

Chip grins. "Going back to the basics is the only way to humble yourself."

"Why are you hiking the AT?" I ask.

He leans back. "I guess I fit under the category of 'start anew.' Nothing was going right, so instead of trying to fix things, I decided to do the Appalachian Trail and get six months of me-time to think about my life and what I want to do next."

His words hit home, a little too familiar to my own situation, but I'm not ready to give up yet.

"Six months?"

He shrugs. "More or less."

"Couldn't you start anew without having to hike thousands of miles?"

He hesitates. "I'm sure you've heard the saying, 'It's about the journey, not the destination.' "

I nod.

"It's like that, I guess. When you're on the trail, you spend a lot of time alone, so there's a lot of time to think. It's not just the physical part of hiking the trail; it's the mental part."

"So, what's the hardest part of being on the trail?"

He locks eyes with me, and the question is suddenly too personal. "Trying to figure out what happens when it's over."

I want to ask what he means, but he looks away.

"So, the trail is one big mental and physical battle?" I say, trying to keep my tone light.

He smiles. "That's the idea."

"Cheaper than therapy, I guess."

"You can come along if you want." He says the words playfully, but I'm almost certain he's serious.

I can't help but laugh. "To be honest, I'd rather stay here and serve tables all day than sleep in a tent." But even as I say the words, I can feel my will crumbling into something that's almost jealously. If only I could drop everything and escape into the woods—not to hike or camp, just to hide for a few days until my problems solve themselves.

"It's not all tents." He gestures to the house.

I glance inside, where there're fewer people than before, everyone starting to go to bed for the night to prepare for a long day of hiking in the morning.

"How does it work anyway? The hostels?"

"It depends on the hostel. For the most part they're just a place where you can sleep and regroup. You know, shower, laundry, food. Sleep on an actual mattress."

I nod, trying to picture what it would be like having your tent become a more familiar place to sleep than an actual mattress.

"Do you just walk to the nearest hostel? Like, are they all along the trail?"

"Some of them are within walking distance of the trail, but not all of them. Most of the time I call to get a ride if it's not close to the trail. No need to hike the extra miles if I don't need to."

"So, what's your plan for tomorrow if you're not hiking one of these massive mountains?" I gesture to the horizon in front of us, where I know somewhere there's a mountain peak looming in the sky, even if I can't see it.

"Head into town, stock up on food. I could leave tomorrow afternoon, but I think I might just stick around for the day and relax."

"No sightseeing?" I'm used to my town being full of tourists all summer long, but maybe when you're hiking the Appalachian Trail, New Hampshire is nothing special.

"I was more thinking I'd give my poor feet a break, but what did you have in mind?"

I pause, only now realizing what I said. "I have to work

tomorrow."

He laughs softly at my response. "It's fine, Lori." He leans back and looks up at the stars.

Most nights it's too cloudy to see the entire night sky, but tonight it's crystal clear, the stars speckling the sky.

Chip sinks into his chair, the silence a soft blanket around us. I'm shocked by how comfortable I am around him, and it makes me brave.

"My shift ends at six thirty tomorrow if you want to do some sightseeing," I say.

He turns his head, his face just a soft glow as the fire in front of us begins to die down.

"North Conway has some fun shopping areas," I offer.

"Mm." He nods his head. "I'll get myself a commemorative shot glass to carry all the way to Maine."

We both laugh.

"Okay, well, what do you want to do?" I ask.

"I was thinking a grocery store run, and then we can figure out the rest later."

I grin at the idea of going grocery shopping together. "New Hampshire is known for its grocery stores. I'm in."

Smiling, he leans forward to get out of the chair and offers his hand.

"What?" I ask, still sitting.

"I walked twenty miles today, and if you don't leave now, you'll be forced to carry me to bed."

He extends his hand farther, and I take it, laughing as he pulls me up. Once I'm standing, we release hands, but the memory of his hand in mine is still here. He leads me to the fence that encircles the yard and opens the small gate to lead me to the front yard where my car is parked.

"So, I'll see you tomorrow, then?" he asks, standing by the door of my car.

I unlock it, a wave of nerves brushing over me, unsure of what to do. I've gone on plenty of other dates; some of them ended in kisses, some of them didn't. Never once have I been nervous about it. It was only awkward when a guy tried to kiss me and I tried very hard to avoid the kiss.

This is different. I went into the date thinking I'd never see him again. This was supposed to be a throwaway date, a fun story to tell. *Hey, remember that night I hung out with that random hiker I met while waiting tables?* Yet I've somehow made plans to meet with him tomorrow.

"Sure," I say quietly.

Chip pulls my car door open, ushering me inside. Whether he senses my nerves is impossible to tell. What I can tell, however, is how perfectly unbothered Chip is, which brings about a new round of anxiety. Does he even like me?

I shift anxiously, standing between Chip and my car. And because of my nerves, I can't seem to stop myself from talking.

"Why'd you ask me to come tonight? Or do you ask out all your waiters?"

He smiles in a way that makes me feel like he's been waiting for me to ask that question all night.

"When you're alone all the time, not everyone is a stranger. Even though you may not know someone really well, you can tell pretty quickly whether you'll get along with someone."

"So, you thought you and I would get along really well?"

"That," he says, hesitating with a grin. "And I thought you were cute."

Before I can respond, he walks away, leaving me standing at the side of my car, wondering who I just met.

CHAPTER 5

"So, did you guys kiss?" Allison asks me as soon as I walk in for my shift the next day.

I'm not able to stop myself from laughing when she greets me. "It's not like that."

"No?" Allison says, following me as I drop my bag off in the break room.

"It was a whole bunch of people with weird names sitting around a fire playing Pictionary. There's not much to report."

"Weird names?"

"Yeah, like Big Bear, or something like that." I shrug. "It's a hiking thing, I think."

"So, no kissing, then?" she tries again.

"Not yet."

"Yet?"

I grin, leaving her in the break room, jaw dropped, as I make my way back to the dining area to start my shift.

My feelings toward the date are muddled. It's always fun to go out, but Chip certainly isn't the type of guy I normally find myself gravitating to. When I imagine the type of person I want to date, it's always tall and clean-shaven. Not to say Chip isn't any of those things, but he gives off mountain-man vibes more than anything else. Then there's the beard, and it's not that I have a problem with beards. It's just that it's so . . . scruffy. One trip to the barber, and Chip would probably be a heartthrob.

Chip not being my type makes things easier though. It was freeing to go on a date knowing we'd probably never see each other again. I don't have to worry about how to act or look, because it's all going to end the same way no matter what. He's going to start walking toward Maine, and I'm going to drive back to my apartment.

My shift goes by faster than it usually does, the constant blur of people coming in and out making it easier to let the hours tick by. When my coworker Ron comes in at six thirty for his shift, he takes over my tables, and I'm free for the day. I grab my bag from the break room, noticing a text from Chip waiting for me.

Pick me up from the hostel? I've got plans for us.

I need to go to my apartment to change before picking Chip up, but I text him saying I'll be there soon. When I pull up, he's sitting on the front steps. It's definitely Chip, but I have to do a double take.

The beard isn't gone, but it's been trimmed down to be clean and modern. His curly hair has been trimmed as well, the sides cut close and the top left just long enough for the curls to sit neatly on the top of his head.

He smiles when he sees me, getting up to meet me at the side of my car. I roll my window down, a pit of nerves in my stomach as my eyes linger over him.

"So, I promise I do have fun plans for today, but can we run a quick errand first?" he asks, leaning into the car, his hands resting on the edge of the window. I have to pause to take a few seconds to compose myself.

"You clean up well," I almost half mumble, eyes glued to him now.

"Is that a yes?" He laughs, watching me try to pick my jaw up off the floor. "I walked to the barber for a haircut, but I still need to stock up on food. Am I good enough to take out into the public now?"

"Yes. Get in."

He backs up and crosses to the other side to the passenger seat, which gives me just enough time to pull myself together.

"So, where to?" I ask when he opens the door.

"Wherever the closest grocery store is."

I make a face—I assumed he was joking last night—but I put the car into reverse and pull out of the driveway.

"So, how was work?" he asks, his voice casual and comfortable, like we've known each other for years.

"Good. How was sleeping in the same room as fifteen other people?"

"Better than the tent." He shrugs.

"You know, my best friend is a hiker," I say, thinking of all the times Marly tried to drag me out with her.

"What type of hiking?" he says, curious.

"She's done all the 4,000-footers in New Hampshire. Now she's living in Colorado."

He seems pleased by the answer. "Mountains here weren't big enough, then?"

"Something like that. Plus when you meet a cute guy, you're much more inclined to move across the country."

He raises an eyebrow like he's going to make a comment about it, but then lets it go.

"So, do you hike?" he asks.

I almost laugh at the suggestion. "No, definitely not. I mean, I've gone, but I don't like it."

"Hmm," is all he says.

"What?"

"No one likes the hiking part. It's the other parts that people like: the view, the company, the sense of freedom and feeling like you're on top of the world. I'm convinced that anyone can like hiking if they just focus on the right thing."

"Hard to focus on the right thing when you can barely breathe."

He laughs. "Fair enough."

We pull up to the grocery store, and I can't help but feel a little lost as we make our way into the store, Chip leading the way.

We walk through the produce section quickly before Chip makes a beeline for the cereal aisle, or as I like to call it, the junk food aisle. Along with every sugary cereal you can imagine, it also has granola bars covered in chocolate, pretending to be healthy.

Chip takes his time working through the aisle, grabbing a box of every kind of junk food I ate as a kid.

"This isn't what you eat as meals, is it?" I ask as he puts a box of miniature cakes into his basket.

"Meals, snacks, whatever tastes good."

"Shouldn't you be doing something healthier, like a sandwich?"

He moves on to the next aisle, where there's bread, and grabs a packet of wraps.

"I can only bring what fits in my bag, so it can't be fragile or refrigerated."

An endcap on one of the aisles has a giant bag of M&M's, and he grabs it, dropping it into his grocery basket.

"Isn't that unhealthy?"

"Some would also argue burning over three thousand calories in one day multiple days a week is unhealthy."

I trail close behind him, watching him put item after item into his basket, none of which have much nutritional value.

"How's this?" He grabs a jar of jelly.

"That brand has a lot of added sugar. Try this one." I pick up another jar and hold it out to him, but he smirks and places the original one in his basket.

"I've been taking my vitamins," he says, grabbing peanut butter next.

"Really?" I say, genuinely surprised.

"No." He smirks, walking past me and making his way toward checkout.

"Aren't you concerned about your health?"

"My biggest concern is getting in enough calories every day to replace everything I'm burning," he says with a light chuckle.

I want to say more, but I stop myself. What I say doesn't

matter; he'll be gone tomorrow.

Once Chip is done checking out, we head back to my car, where he throws his things in the back.

"Now where are we going?" I ask, buckling up.

"Cathedral Ledge. I've got the GPS coordinates on my phone."

"What's Cathedral Ledge?"

"Don't you live here?" he asks, shocked.

"Yeah, but I'm not a tourist. I don't do all those sorts of things. And you're not taking me on a hike, are you? Because I didn't sign up for that."

He laughs quietly, plugging his phone into my car so I can hear the directions over the speakers.

"It's not a hike. We're driving to the view."

I scan his face to make sure he's not lying before I back out of the parking lot.

The drive is a bit farther than I expected, but Chip is an open book, sharing stories of everyone he's met on the trail and everything he's seen and done so far. For someone I've known less than twenty-four hours, it feels like things should be more awkward between us—that, at the least, there might be an awkward pause between conversations. But we both talk back and forth, laughing with each new story Chip comes up with. An outsider looking in would probably assume we're lifelong friends, not two people who met for the first time yesterday.

"So, Dusty and I were about a half mile away from where we were supposed to sleep for the night, and this guy must have fallen. I think we ran into him right after it had happened, but he hit his head and was bleeding pretty good."

"Oh my god. Was he okay? Did you have to call 911?"

"No, he was able to walk without much help from us. We ditched camp that night and took another trail that would lead us to the trailhead where a car could take him into town. Now his name is Stitch."

"Stitch?"

"Yeah, because he had to get stitches to fix the cut on his head. A couple days later he was back on trail, right where he left off. When you're hiking the AT, you kinda go on a journey. You don't come out the same person you were when you started, so you get a trail name to go with the journey."

"What's your name?" I ask. We're almost to Cathedral Ledge, but the road is getting narrow and winds upward. Chip failed to include that the drive would be straight up a mountain.

"You know it," he says.

"Your trail name is Chip, but I'm talking about your real name." I want to glance over at him, but I keep my eyes forward as I make a sharp turn upward.

"Focus on the road." He laughs, amused by my reaction.

I keep quiet for a moment, careful as I turn and inch the car up the mountain. If it weren't for Chip—or whatever his name is—I probably would have given up and decided the view wasn't worth it, but whenever I do manage to glance over, he's got a big grin across his face.

"I just thought that when you introduce yourself to someone for the first time, you might use your real name," I say, keeping my tone calm as my car fights for its life up the mountain.

The road levels, and after another smaller turn, a makeshift parking lot opens up. There's a ton of cars parked off to the sides of the road, and I start to wonder why people are insane enough to drive all this way.

"I don't know the real names of everyone you met yesterday." He shrugs, then opens the door and lets himself out.

Despite me being the local and him being the tourist, he's the one who leads the way and walks us toward the view.

"Doesn't that bother you, not knowing people's names?" I ask.

He shakes his head. "Not one bit."

After we walk away from the rest of the cars, the trees disappear, and they're replaced with a wide expanse of sky. Below our feet is nothing but solid rock that leads up to the edge of a cliff.

The viewing area is massive, the smooth rock stretching out far enough that even though dozens of people are enjoying the view, it doesn't feel crowded. A fence lines the mountain-edge, making it impossible to get too close to the drop. Off in the distance, mountains stretch as far as the eye can see, but I can also make out houses, fields, and lakes.

"Not a bad view," Chip mutters. His hand is at my back, guiding me forward until we reach the fence. I lean forward, resting my forearms on the metal bars of the fence. Chip does the same beside me, his elbow grazing mine.

It's about half an hour before sunset, so golden hour is at its peak around us. The air is hushed as everyone leans into the railing, taking in the view. The expanse of the White Mountains opens up in front of us. Tonight the sky is perfectly clear, and the mountains off in the distance seem to go on forever, a subtle gradient of yellow and orange streaking the sky.

I've lived here my entire life, so I'm accustomed to the views of the mountains surrounding me, but golden hour brings them to life in a way I've never noticed before. Everything glows with an edge of orange, nature practically screaming to be seen and heard.

"I lied," I say. Chip glances over to me, an eyebrow raised. "I've been here before."

He fakes disappointment. "And here I thought I was showing you something new."

"My parents used to bring me here when I was little. That's Echo Lake." I point to the small body of water off to our right.

"What mountain is that?" Chip asks, pointing to the one closest to us.

"Oh, I have no idea. The only one I can point out is Mount Washington, and that's because it has a museum and weather station at the top."

"Huh," he says, looking off to the mountains in front of us. "What?"

"I was just hiking Mount Washington. I missed the museum."

"You'll have to re-hike it," I challenge.

"Will you go with me?"

I freeze, his gaze on me now. That's when I notice how close we are to each other. He only has one elbow on the railing now, leaning to the side, his body angled toward mine.

"No," I say so quickly I can't stop myself. "But not because of you. The hike."

The corner of his mouth lifts into a smile, and my face goes hot and red.

"So, what's your real name?" I try again.

"That's classified information."

I try to hide my grin. "Why?"

"It's on a need-to-know basis." He shifts and angles his body back to the metal fence, no longer facing me.

This time I turn to face him.

"Well, I need to know. How am I supposed to write up a police report when I realize you're actually some convicted felon who has a warrant out for his arrest?"

He smiles but keeps his gaze trained on the horizon, pleased with himself. "I can assure you, I'm not that."

"Well, then who are you?"

"I'm Chip."

"I'm Groot. Now what's your real name?" I say, my voice getting loud enough that a small family looks over.

"So, you're a Marvel fan?" Chip says, finally turning to look at me, but now I wish he hadn't. The sun bounces off his skin in the perfect way, making this entire moment seem like something out of a romance movie, but instead of kissing, we're arguing about what his name is.

"Yes. And now you know ten times more about me than I do about you. I'm Lori. I live here. I work as a waiter at Angela's. And I've seen all the Marvel movies."

We're both leaning against the fence now, our bodies facing each other. The sun is beginning to tuck into the horizon, filling the sky with shades of orange, yellow, and pink, but instead of staring at the view, I'm staring at someone I didn't know until yesterday.

"I'm Chip." He grins. "I live in Maine. I don't currently have a job because I'm hiking the Appalachian Trail. And I've also seen all the Marvel movies."

I frown, but a smile is threatening to break through.

"But what's your name?" I say, softer now, a laugh almost escaping my lips. It feels like an inside joke, like I'm not meant to know his name. Even if he leaves tomorrow and I never see him again, it will always bother me that I never learned his real name.

He looks down, smiling to himself, and when he looks up again, he leans closer until we're only inches away.

"If I tell you, then the mysterious thing that makes you stick around will be gone."

"I doubt that," I say, my voice low.

"Well, I don't want to risk it."

I stare at him, hundreds of names going through my head, wondering which one might be his and what it is I'll have to do to find out the truth. My annoyance at wanting to know his name only seems to fuel his amusement, because he seems to pride himself on my ignorance.

I lean forward, closing the distance between us before I can think twice about it. I kiss him, not because I want to know his name, but because, if I'm being honest with myself, it's something I've wanted to do since he walked me to my car last night. If I take Chip by surprise, he doesn't show it. He kisses me back like it's something he's been waiting for me to do all night. His fingers wind through my hair, knotting at the back of my neck, pulling me to him. Our lips melt together in a way that only draws me closer to him.

Out of all the first-date kisses I've had, none of them have been like this. Kissing him shouldn't feel this natural. It should be awkward and clumsy; this is anything but.

Chip is the one to pull away, just enough to be able to look at me.

"You want to know my name that bad?" he asks, his fingers still laced through my hair.

"You're certainly making me work for it," I say, my head still spinning a bit from the kiss.

"What if you hate my name so much you decide you don't like me?" he teases, loosening his hand and brushing my cheek before pulling away.

"It can't be worse than Chip."

"What's wrong with Chip?"

"Because when I tell my friends about you, they'll think I made out with a snack item or a Disney character."

He laughs and pulls me to his chest, sandwiching me between him and the bars of the fence.

"You're not going to tell me, are you?" I say.

There's just a sliver of the sun left in the sky. Before we know it, it will be gone.

"Now where's the fun in that?"

CHAPTER 6

We stay out long past everyone who came to see the sunset. Even when the sun is gone, Chip and I linger on the cliff, watching as the color fades from the sky and is replaced with a deep blue.

"So, you leave tomorrow?" I ask quietly.

We've moved to the middle of the large rocky area and are sitting on the cool ground of the stony surface. In mid-July, the air is humid, even with the sun down, but sitting on the rocks makes the night comfortable. We're sitting side by side, but I find myself leaning toward him, leaving only a tiny gap between us.

"Yeah. Can't drag my feet too much, or I'll never get home."

"You said you live in Maine?" I ask.

"Born and raised."

"That's a long walk home," I joke, but his eyes seem far-off, as if he's thinking of something else.

"Yeah."

There's more to his story, and I start to wonder what he meant yesterday when he said he's hiking the Appalachian Trail to get a fresh start, but the details feel too intimate.

"So, why Chip?" I ask. He looks up, seeming confused. "Why is your trail name Chip?"

He smiles at the question. "A chipmunk broke into my food supply when I first started out. The bastard opened every bag of food, and I had to go back into town to restock everything. No one will let me live it down."

I let out a deep, heavy belly laugh, which I haven't experienced in a long time. I'm not sure if it's the night as a whole that led to this moment or if the explanation feels too random, but I fall into the laugh, leaning on Chip's shoulder.

"You're named after a chipmunk?" I say, trying to compose myself.

"I'm just glad you didn't ask that question before we kissed. That would have ruined the mood."

I try to hold in my laugh, but he's beside me, laughing along with me. I move to scoot closer, and when I do, he wraps his arms around me, pulling me to his side. I lean into him; whatever nervousness was there earlier in the day is all but gone.

"I'm a little jealous, you know," I say, looking up to the sky. For each minute that passes, another star appears in the sky, dotting the dark blue expanse.

"Of what?" Chip says with a low chuckle. "You have me under the impression that hiking the Appalachian Trail is the last thing you want to do."

"That's probably true," I agree. "But I like the theory of it, I guess. I can't imagine dropping everything to walk in the woods. It seems kind of freeing."

"It is," he says softly. "Whatever stress is going on, you get to forget about it when you're in the woods. You just focus on surviving and putting one foot in front of the other."

I let out a single laugh. "You almost make me want to join you."

Chip turns to look at me. Even in the darkness, I can make out the grin on his face.

"Not too late," he says.

I shake my head. "Can't."

"Why not?"

I make a face as if it's obvious.

He corrects himself. "Besides hating hiking with a burning passion, why not?"

"I don't *hate* hiking."

"So, then what's the problem?"

My thoughts waver. I let myself imagine it for a moment, dropping everything and walking off into the woods. If it were up to me, I'd fly to Europe, but the woods seem like a good plan B. But even daydreaming about it, I can feel my stress rise. I'd fall behind in class—or worse, I'd miss an entire semester's worth of credits. I'd have to quit my job, and without a job, I'd have to move back in with my mom. And what about becoming a yoga instructor? Where does that fit in?

Just as quickly as the dream appeared, it's gone.

"I've got too much going on," I tell Chip.

"That's the perfect reason to go."

I shake my head. "I'm already super far behind."

"Behind on what?"

I shrug. "Life."

He raises an eyebrow at me, grinning in a way that makes my stomach flip. "I highly doubt that."

I want to correct him, tell him all the reasons I'm painfully behind where I want to be in life, but I don't.

"Here's what I've learned so far on the trail," Chip says, shifting to sit up. "You can spend months, years, or your entire life caring about something that you think will make you happy. But if the journey to get there doesn't make you happy, then what's the point?"

I let myself sit in his words. I know what he's saying is true, but my mind keeps wanting to come up with retorts, reasons not to listen.

"Is what you're doing right now making you happy?" I ask.

"I'm happier than I've been in a while," he says with a small grin.

I look away, but I can feel his eyes on me. Crickets chirp in the distance as the night settles in, and I start to notice for the first time how I dread saying goodbye to this stranger.

"Back to trail life tomorrow?" I ask, unable to ignore it any longer.

He nods his head, but slowly, almost like he wishes he could delay it a little longer as well.

"Do you need a ride back to the trail?" I ask.

"I'm going to leave at six a.m., I think. The hostel has a shuttle—"

"I'll take you," I say before he can finish. And then it occurs to me how long we've been out here. "Do you have to get back soon?"

He takes his phone out and I see that it's 10:07 p.m.

"Would you think I'm lame if I said I should be in bed by now if I want to get an early start?"

I pull away and stand up, already missing the warmth of his body. I offer a hand. "Seeing as I'm also going to be waking up early tomorrow? No."

§

The ride back to the hostel is quiet, mostly because driving down the mountain in the dark proves to be even more nerve-racking than driving up it in the daytime.

I drop him off at the hostel, handing over his grocery bags before giving him a small wave goodbye.

When I get back to my apartment, it's a slap back to reality. My yoga mat is set up in the middle of the floor from when I was trying out a new vinyasa flow. My notebook is on the ground, the page still open to where I was taking notes. My laptop is on the dining table; I was unsuccessfully trying to find places to apply to. These are all things I was supposed to be working on after my shift at work, but I guess that'll be a problem for tomorrow.

When I get into my room, my college textbook is on the nightstand where I left it earlier this week, yet another reminder of something I'd forgotten. There's a paper due in two days, but if I put a couple hours aside, I'll be able to finish it in no time.

Tomorrow I'll be back on track. I'll drop Chip off, have a fun story of that time I dated an AT thru-hiker, and then be back in the zone.

§

My alarm goes off at five a.m., because despite knowing I'll never see Chip again, the vain part of me can't help but want to get all dolled up to see him one last time.

It's ridiculous to worry about, because Chip's seen the worst version of me: the tired, sweaty work version. I shower so my curly hair will behave itself, dousing it in enough product to keep even the unruliest head of hair tame. I change into a pair of shorts, my favorite summer tank top, and a cute fitted hoodie.

It's still dark by the time I pull up to the hostel, and I'm stepping onto the porch when the door opens and Chip steps out.

"A few people are still asleep," he says in a whisper.

When he closes the front door behind him, I'm able to fully see him for the first time. He's wearing a pair of shorts and a T-shirt that look like they've seen better days, with dirt and sweat stains etched permanently into the fabric—or at least I assume that's the case and he isn't actually wearing dirty clothes.

His backpack is a whole other monster. It's tied around his waist like a permanent part of his body. The bag is a bright orange, with patches of dirt and mud coating it. There are flip-flops, water bottles, and other things hanging off the outside pockets, the bag practically splitting at the seams because it's so full.

"Hi," I say quietly, a little shocked at the sight of the bag. I'm not sure what I thought he'd be carrying, but it wasn't this much stuff. I've seen Marly backpack before, but she never had that much on her, though I don't know if she's ever done a trip that was more than a night or two.

Chip smiles like a kid in a candy shop as he follows me to the car.

"Here, you can put the bag in the back," I say as I open the trunk. Chip pulls the backpack off his shoulder and drops it in with a soft thud.

"Ready to go?" he asks me, even though he's the one hiking.

We both get in the front, and Chip gives me the directions to the spot he needs to be dropped off. By the time we get to where he left off, the sky is just starting to get some color. I pull into a small parking lot surrounded by woods. Somehow, I'm not the only car here. In fact, there are four other cars scattered in the small lot, but their drivers are long gone and already hiking.

Hikers are absolute lunatics.

"Guess you're not the only one up this early," I say softly.

We move around to the back of the car, and I pop the truck, pulling his bag out for him. I intended for it to be a nice gesture, but when I grab the bag, not only do I realize how heavy it is, but that it also smells. I'm not sure how I didn't notice it before, but it reeks of body odor.

"Oh my god," I say, holding it as far away from me as I can, which doesn't go well since it's so heavy.

Chip takes it as it begins slipping out of my hands and slings it over his shoulders. He clips the waist buckle first before clipping the chest strap.

"It's always a little heavy after a resupply. I weighed it this morning, and it's about twenty-nine pounds."

I almost expected it to be heavier after holding it, which only makes me realize how much arm strength I don't have.

"How far are you hiking today?"

He starts to walk toward the entrance of the trail on the opposite side of the parking lot. I follow him, and we take slow steps away from my car.

"Fifteen miles if I'm lucky. The terrain in New Hampshire is rough, so it's hard to keep up the miles when there's so much incline."

Chip gets to the entrance of the trail, but he lingers, turning back to look at me. I keep a few paces away. The difference between the two of us is impossible to ignore now.

The smile Chip has been wearing all morning fades just a little.

"So, do I get to know your name now?" I ask, my hands clutching my car keys, looking for something to hold on to. I don't expect him to answer. I just want to see his smile return.

The corner of his lip twitches. "Will you be joining me for a walk in the woods?" He gestures to the path, where the woods are still dark. The sky lightens with each passing moment as the start of a new day rolls in. The thought of walking in the woods, even if the sun comes up, makes me nauseous. But a tiny part of me envies the way Chip can just walk away and the only thing he has to worry about is getting from point A to point B.

"I don't think so," I say.

"So, it's not a definite no." He smiles, seeming happy with that answer.

I let out a low laugh. "I wouldn't hold your breath."

He glances away from me, looking out into the woods before

turning back.

"Thank you for everything," he says, his words more serious now.

"Of course," I say, even though it feels like I should be thanking him for letting me escape the stress of my life, even if only for a couple hours.

With one last smile, he takes his next steps into the woods. It's oddly nostalgic, watching him walk away. I barely know him, but the goodbye is more serious than that. When I step towards my car, I have a tiny twinge of regret, wishing he didn't have to leave.

"Lori?"

I pivot, a knot of excitement in my stomach when I hear my name. He's far enough away that I can just barely see him in the low light of the morning.

"My name is Caleb."

My smile is wide when I hear his name. "That's a much better name than Chip."

CHAPTER 7

It's been three days since I dropped Caleb off, and it's been a brutal slap back into reality. When I was with Caleb, my stress was momentarily put on pause, but since he left, I'm right back to where I started—or worse. Between applying for jobs, practicing yoga, working, and doing my summer classes, it feels like I'm always behind.

Worst of all, my daydreaming of Caleb isn't any help. Just my luck that the one guy I find mildly interesting is the one I'll never see again.

Caleb is everything I'm not. He's laid-back and ready to wander off into the woods without a care in the world. How stressed do I have to be to be jealous of someone sleeping in a tent?

I've almost deleted his number from my phone because I keep getting sidetracked by the thought of texting him. Every time I'm distracted, I think maybe texting him will get it out of my system. But then I remember he's living in the woods and probably doesn't have a cell phone signal anyway. Even worse, I sit waiting for him to text me, maybe with an update of where he is now or how it's going. But no messages ever come, and I tell myself that's probably a good thing. I'm already distracted enough.

If he lived in New Hampshire and wasn't trying to backpack across the country, maybe we'd have a chance. Instead, he was a summer fling, and I should be happy with that.

I grab my textbook from my nightstand and try to focus on the weather patterns in North America. I spend about ten minutes trying to read the same sentence before grabbing my phone. It takes a couple rings before Marly picks up.

"Hey, Lori," she says. "What's up?"

"I'm spiraling," I say quickly.

She hesitates for a moment. "How so?"

I let out a heavy sigh. "I didn't want to tell you before because I didn't want to make a big thing out of it. I went out with a guy. We had a thing. Now he's gone, so it's supposed to be over. That's why I wasn't going to tell you, because it wasn't going to go anywhere. But now I can't get this guy out of my head, and there's no point in dreaming about it because we're too different and he's gone." The words rush out in one final breath.

"Hold on," Marly says. "Slow down. You met a guy? Where?"

I laugh a little. "At work. Just like you said I wouldn't."

"Well, this is good, isn't it? What's his name?"

I hesitate, thinking of how I only learned his name right before he left. "Caleb, but he also goes by Chip."

"Chip?" Marly asks, as confused as I was when I first heard his name.

"Marly, he's hiking the Appalachian Trail."

The other end of the line is quiet for so long that I think our call must have been disconnected, but I check my screen, and she's still there.

"Marly?" I ask.

"The guy you met at work is hiking the Appalachian Trail?" she asks.

"Yeah, and that's the problem. I don't think I'll ever see him again."

"And you *like* him?"

"Yes, and *that's* the problem!"

Even though we're on the phone, I can almost picture the look of shock on Marly's face. "Did you know he was an AT hiker when you met him?"

"Yes." I sigh.

"So, you knew he was just passing through the area?"

I groan. "It was supposed to be a fun date so you could stop pestering me about not having a social life. Everyone else gets to have summer flings. Why can't I have a summer fling without getting emotionally attached?"

Marly lets out a soft laugh. "I don't know. You usually don't like people enough to go on a second date."

"What do I do?" I ask, my stress starting to boil over.

"Did you guys talk about staying in touch?"

"No, we never talked about anything that would happen after he started hiking again." My emotions spiral further. "What if he does this all the time? What if he dates a different girl every time he stops in a new town?"

"Lori, calm down," she says, her voice level.

I take a few deep breaths, urging my thoughts to cease.

"I doubt he's some serial dater," she says, and I try to let her words sink in until she continues. "Did you guys have sex?" she asks suddenly.

"What? No."

"Well, you said summer fling, so I wanted to be sure. And if you think he's some serial dater of the AT, then he'd probably do it for more than just a date."

I frown, a little insulted that she'd think Caleb was that kind of guy. "He's not like that."

"So, you like him?" Marly asks.

I don't say anything, biting my lip.

Marly takes my silence for the usual reluctance I give her when I don't want to admit something.

"What about him do you like?"

I close my eyes, trying to contain a nervous laugh.

"Besides him being the most genuine person I've gone on a date with?" Oh, god. When did I start to sound this cheesy? "I'm mostly just in total awe of him. Not just for hiking the Appalachian Trail—which I'm sure is hard enough—but for having this laid-back attitude about life. When we were hanging out, it was like I could literally feel myself relax around him."

I hear a soft laugh.

"What?"

"You're more impressed by his ability to live carefree than you are by his ability to literally walk thousands of miles."

"Is that bad?"

"I don't think so. He helps balance you out, I guess." She pauses before hitting me with a new question. "Did you guys kiss?"

I don't say a word, but my face heats up and goes red.

"You did, didn't you?" Marly asks when I don't respond.

"I couldn't help myself!" My voice goes up an octave, which only makes me sound guiltier. "He wouldn't tell me his name, so I thought if I kissed him, that would be enough to convince him to tell me."

Marly starts laughing. "You went on a date with him without knowing his name?"

"Well, I knew his trail name, but I wanted to know his real name."

Her words are breathy as she tries to contain her laughter. "Okay, so, did it work?"

"Not at that exact moment, but when we were saying bye later, he said his name was Caleb."

"And you like Caleb," she says calmly.

"I do, but I shouldn't," I say.

"What's wrong with liking him?" she says, confused.

"Because I'll probably never see him again because he's hiking the Appalachian Trail, which just sounds awful. But even if it weren't for that, he lives in Maine."

"Is he cute?" she asks.

"Why does that matter?"

She laughs. "Because if he's getting you worked up so much, he must be cute. I just want to confirm."

"He's cute, but he's not my type," I say, repeating the same thing I told Allison. Then I remember how he looked when we went to Cathedral Ledge, and my stomach flips. "But then he got a haircut and his beard trimmed, and then I went all weak in the knees."

"He has a beard?" Marly says, shocked. "I've never pictured you with a beard guy. I've always pictured you falling for some business guy who wears suits all day."

"Exactly!" I shout. "Caleb's not my type."

"Not your type," she says in a sarcastic tone. I can practically picture her rolling her eyes.

"What do I do?" I ask again, desperate now.

"Why don't you text him?" she offers.

"He's backpacking. He probably doesn't have his phone on. Or if he does, who says he'll get a signal?"

"You'd be surprised by how much someone backpacking uses their phone. And worst-case scenario, it may take him a day or two to see the message."

"So, I have to send a message and then *wait*? For days?"

"Yup."

I let out a sigh, burying my face in my hand. "What would I even say?"

"The truth, maybe? That you miss him and want to see him again?"

"No. Definitely not that," I say.

"Then just tell him you're happy to pick him up or bring him supplies if he needs it. AT hikers always need rides into town. I'm sure he'd love that."

"I don't want to sound weird," I say, mulling the options

over in my head. They all seem pretty abysmal.

"It's not weird, I promise."

We're both quiet for a minute until I hear Marly laugh softly, almost to herself.

"What?" I ask.

"I was just thinking you must really miss me if you're falling for a guy who's basically the male version of me."

I roll my eyes, pressing my hand against my face. "Just what I need in my life: someone else to drag me outdoors when indoors is looking perfectly comfy."

Marly lets out a hearty laugh.

CHAPTER 8

It's a slow night at the restaurant. There're only four tables of people, with no signs of any crowds coming anytime soon. Ron is the other waiter on staff tonight, and we've been sharing the tables, but we mostly find ourselves looking for busywork around the restaurant. I'm sweeping one of the back corners when my manager, Mary, finds me.

"It doesn't look like things are going to pick up tonight. You can take off early if you want."

The words make me perk up instantly. "Sure, I'll just finish up."

I finish cleaning up and wave goodbye to Ron and the kitchen staff, then head out the door before Mary can change her mind. It's a huge relief to have what feels like a few additional hours in my day.

When I get back to my apartment, I pull my laptop out so I can work on one of the papers due for my summer class. I stare at the blank page, my mind wandering in circles before I give in and pull out my phone.

I don't want to text Caleb. What I want to do is erase any memory of him from my mind and focus on myself again. But here I am, acting like a schoolgirl absolutely obsessed with her crush.

I type out about a dozen text messages before finally settling on one.

Hope the hike is going well! If you need a ride, let me know.

I hit send before I can regret my decision. About five minutes later, I'm still staring at a blank screen on my laptop, but now I'm overthinking the text message I just sent. I did exactly what Marly told me to, but I can't help but feel weird about the whole thing. How often does he need rides back into town anyway? The offer probably sounded creepy.

If there were an unsend button, I would have used it by now, deleting the message before Caleb had the chance to see it.

I try to spend the remaining hours of my night being productive, but every time I sit down to work, my mind wanders off to the date I had with Caleb and how perfect it felt. I want to scold myself for getting so wrapped up in a guy.

Eventually, I finish writing my paper and hit submit on the online portal for the class, relieved to have at least one thing off my plate. I'm getting ready for bed when a text chimes in on my phone.

Do you make a habit of picking up strangers on the side of the road?

It's 10:35 p.m., not super late by any standard, but after talking to Caleb, I thought he'd be long asleep by backpacking standards.

Only if they're cute. I hit send before I can chicken out.

His response comes quickly. *Hope I meet your definition of cute ;)*

Does that mean you need a ride? I type out, grinning at my phone. *And what are you doing awake? The sun's been down for hours. Shouldn't you be passed out?*

Sleeping at a shelter tonight. We're having a fire.

Meeting more strangers?

A tiny pit of jealousy forms. Maybe he is just super friendly to everyone he meets. Could there be another girl he met at the campfire tonight?

Lots of strange people here, he types.

The response doesn't answer anything for me, which is perhaps worse.

A minute or so goes by, where I wonder what to write in response, but then another text comes in from Caleb.

I won't be heading into town again until I reach Grafton Notch in Maine. Want to meet me there?

I pull up a map on my phone to see where that is. He's only an hour away. Driving an hour to see a guy isn't too bad, is it?

When I don't respond right away, Caleb sends another text.

I can get a ride from somewhere else too. No pressure.

My fingers start typing before I can think of my response. *No, I'll pick you up. When?*

I pull my digital calendar up on my laptop, eyeing the next couple days I have off. I have one more shift to work tomorrow, and then I'm free for three days. I'm supposed to be using that time to search for a job and do another writing assignment, but one day with a guy would be good for me.

Another text comes in.

Tomorrow?

This should be my cue to give up and concede that fate doesn't have my back. I'm not meant to date Caleb. I'm working a ten-hour shift tomorrow to cover for one of my coworkers attending a wedding.

I want to tell Caleb yes, that I'll be there to pick him up, but my full calendar stares back at me.

I can't tomorrow, I finally type back.

It feels like this was my last chance to see him again. Tomorrow he'll call someone else for a ride, and then he'll hike even farther north, the distance between us growing.

That's fine. I'll get a ride somewhere else.

The conversation ends there, and my hope deflates. Caleb must have gone to bed, because I never hear from him again — not that night or the next day when I'm working my ten-hour shift.

§

I spend the next couple days trying and failing to get work done, wondering if I should have called in sick to give Caleb a ride. He never texts me back, and while Marly reassures me it's because he has to conserve the battery life of his phone, I convince myself it's because he's forgotten I exist.

However, as I'm finishing a paper for my summer class, his name pops up on my phone — still saved in as Chip. It rings twice before I pick up.

"Hello?" I answer.

"Lori? Hey, you know how you said to let you know if I

need a ride?" His voice is nervous on the other line.

"Yeah. Is everything okay?"

"I took a fall. Tweaked my ankle a bit. A few scrapes and bruises. I'll be fine, but I need to rest for a day or two. I can call someone else to come pick me up if it's too out of the way."

I hear rustling on the other end of the line, maybe even the voice of someone else in the background. There's more rustling with a hushed "ow" under his breath.

"No, it's my day off. I can come get you. Where are you right now?" I abandon my laptop and go to my room to pull on a sweatshirt and find shoes.

"Uh, I was on my way to the Sabbath Day Pond Lean-to, but I'm going to turn back. I crossed a road a mile or two back. I'll meet you there."

I feel like I should know what he's talking about, but I don't.

"Can you text me an address of where to go?" I ask, searching for my keys. My eyes scan the counter and dining table before I notice the keys hanging on the hook by the front door, just like they're supposed to.

"I'll text you the GPS coordinates," he says, his voice sounding relieved. "No rush. It's going to take me a while to get there." He cusses under his breath as he moves.

"I'll be there soon." I hang up, gripping my keys and heading out the door. As I'm walking through the parking lot, a text comes in from Caleb with the GPS coordinates. I start the directions and silently swear to myself when I see I'm over two hours away from where I need to pick Caleb up.

Be there in two hours, I text quickly. No response comes in from Caleb, but I try not to worry about it.

I try to drive as fast as I can, hoping he isn't waiting too long for me to show up. By some miracle, I have a second chance to pick Caleb up, but it feels like I'm failing just by how long it's going to take me to get there.

During the drive, a nervous pit forms in my stomach. At the thought of seeing Caleb again, my mind runs through dozens of scenarios, all of them ending with me running into his arms.

All my nerves are on edge, so I try to calm myself down and focus on the mission at hand: making sure Caleb's okay.

I know I'm close when the busy highways turn into small back roads. Eventually, I turn onto a dirt road that's just wide enough for one car, and then Caleb is there in the distance. His backpack is on the ground, and he's sitting on it. He's wearing shorts, revealing legs covered in mud, with a small collection of blood at the knee.

Another hiker is waiting with him, standing by his side and offering a wave as I pull off to the side of the road. There's no parking lot this time. If I didn't know any better, I'd think we were just on some random dirt road, but behind Caleb is a small wooden sign pointing left to a wooded trail that's barely noticeable unless you're looking for it.

I get out of the car, jogging to where Caleb and the other hiker are standing.

"Sorry. I didn't realize how long it would take," I say.

"It's okay. If I knew how far of a drive it was, I would have tried to find another ride," Caleb says.

Once I get closer, I notice how different he looks from the

last time I saw him. His hair, while still cut the same, now sits on the top of his head in a greasy, sweaty way, hair clinging to his skin around the temples. Almost his entire body is covered in mud, but I'm not sure if that's from his fall or just living in the woods. The man standing next to him looks to be a little older. The man's hair is long and pulled into a tangled man-bun on top of his head. Though he also looks like he's covered in a healthy layer of dirt, he isn't anywhere near as dirty as Caleb.

"I'm Jolly." The other hiker waves to me. "I was just keeping Chip company until you got here, but I have to head out so I can set up camp before dark. You guys all set?" He turns to Caleb.

"Yeah, I'm all good. See you on the trail," Caleb says.

Jolly gives a quick wave and proceeds down the small wooded path before disappearing. He leaves us in an air of awkwardness.

"So, what happened?" I finally ask.

Caleb moves to stand with a low grunt, putting most of his weight on one leg while keeping his left hovering slightly over the ground.

"I was walking through a muddy part of trail and fell. It would have been fine if that was it, but then I fell again because my shoes were slippery. Figured that was my cue to call it quits for the day, plus I knew a trail angel who was eager to see me." He gives me a smile that's been burned into the back of my brain.

"Trail angel?" I ask.

"Yeah, someone who gives you food or a ride or helps you with your hike in some sorta way."

"Do you have lots of trail angels on speed dial?" I laugh,

trying to say it as a joke.

I move to his pack, which is on the ground, lifting it and putting it over my shoulder. I'm immediately greeted with the smell of BO. I make a face, and Caleb lets out a small chuckle.

"Just my favorites," he says, watching me move around my car and throw the bag into the trunk.

We both get into the car, and it only takes a couple seconds for me to realize how bad Caleb smells.

"Oh my god, Caleb, is that *you*?" I say once I close the car door. I'm not sure whether to laugh or cry over the smell. Under normal circumstances, I would have tried to keep my complaints to a minimum, but he smells bad. Not fresh-out-of-the-gym bad, but days-upon-days-of-bad-body-odor-smell-crammed-into-one-tiny-car bad.

"Sorry," he says, voice sheepish. "I try to jump in a river or lake whenever I can find one, but it doesn't remove the smell the same way a shower would."

"When was the last time you showered?" I ask, unable to help myself.

"At the hostel in Conway."

My body almost recoils when I hear his answer.

"That was almost a week ago!" I force myself to laugh it off, but I'm going into panic mode. Did I miss how different we are when we first met? Between his witty comments and charms, how did I miss that he's the type of guy okay with not showering regularly? "I thought you went into town a couple days ago. Didn't you shower?"

"I've been on trail since I last saw you." He shrugs.

"You didn't need to resupply until now?"

"I didn't need to go into town for a few more days. I mostly wanted to see you since you offered." He tries to contain his guilty smile.

I let out a sigh mixed with a laugh, covering my face with my hands. I'm on the verge of a mental breakdown. What in the world have I gotten myself into?

Here I am, in the prime of my life. Not prime as in *good*, but prime as in *stressed*. It's summer, yet I manage to work more than forty hours a week, I have two summer classes, and I'm trying to get started as a yoga instructor. But despite all that, I dropped everything on my day off—when I should be writing a paper—to pick up a guy I've been crushing on who smells *awful*.

Maybe this is what I needed—to see Caleb one more time, but the real Caleb. Not the Caleb who's trying to woo me, but the thru-hiker Caleb. The Caleb who lives an entirely different life than me.

Maybe this will make letting go of him that much easier.

"So, where are we going?" I ask when I decide it's time to get things moving so I can go home.

CHAPTER 9

It's not that I don't want to help Caleb, because I do. I've driven all this way, so if I'm going to help him, I might as well do my full duty and make sure he's okay before we part ways. I don't want to leave him stranded somewhere, plus once I open the windows in my car, the smell isn't too bad.

"You sure you don't want me to take you to an urgent care or something?" I ask, watching him limp as he gets out of the car.

"Yeah, I just need to clean up and ice my ankle. I don't even think I sprained it." He puts a little weight on his left foot and winces. "I might get a brace too," he says, giving up the tough act and limping again.

I let Caleb lead the way as he wanders down the aisles of CVS, collecting an armload of first aid supplies and junk food.

"If you're hungry, we can pick up dinner," I say, hoping he'll put the giant bag of M&M's down.

"Sure, but this is part of my resupply." He tucks the candy under his arm, and I try to stop myself from saying anything further. Caleb checks out, limping his way back to my car, bags in hand.

"Where to now?" I ask as we both get in the car again.

"I booked a Super 8 while I was waiting for you, so you can drop me off there. If we see a fast-food place on the way, do you mind just pulling over so I can get something? I can pay for your meal too if you want."

I can't hide the disgust on my face. "We are not eating fast food."

"Okay, then we can order pizza?" he tries again, clearly not understanding the issue.

I put the car into reverse and back out of the parking lot.

"If we're going to eat, then we're going to a restaurant where the meals aren't going to be a greasy, fried mess." I glance over to Caleb, who's staring at me with a smirk, his hair still oily and untamed. "But first we're going to the hotel, and you're going to shower."

§

It isn't necessary for me to stay. I did what I promised: I picked Caleb up, helped him pick up first aid, and brought him to his hotel for the night. My job is done, but I can't leave knowing the moment I'm out of sight, he'll break out a burger, hell-bent on giving himself a heart attack someday.

So, here I am, sitting on a stiff mattress at a Super 8, scrolling through my phone while Caleb showers. I'm looking for places to eat nearby, and luckily, there are plenty of options, all better than the fast-food locations Caleb pointed out on the drive to the Super 8.

"All right, am I decent?"

Caleb steps out of the bathroom, steam rolling into the room with him. He's wearing the same pants and flannel he wore when we went on our date in Conway.

"Is that your only outfit?" I eye him.

"I've got a total of three outfits: super hot hiking outfit, super cold hiking outfit, and this." He gestures to himself. "My out-on-the-town outfit."

I laugh. "Come on. Let's go eat."

We end up at a steak house, which I hope will be a nice change of pace for Caleb after eating nothing but junk food for the past week. He's indecisive going over the menu before finally settling on a steak dinner with a side of fries and mashed potatoes.

"No veggies?" I ask after we both place our orders.

"The potato is a vegetable, so I'm actually having two sides of vegetables while you're only having one." He gives me a smirk.

I ordered barbeque chicken with a side of steamed broccoli and mac and cheese.

"Potato isn't a vegetable. It's a starch."

He shakes his head, smiling. "Google it. It's a vegetable."

I roll my eyes, laughing. "The plant may be a vegetable, but on the food pyramid, it's starch."

"I thought people didn't even use the food pyramid anymore."

He raises an eyebrow to challenge me, and I shake my head. If I were having this conversation with anyone else, I'd probably be annoyed by now, but it doesn't feel like an argument with Caleb. He smiles too much for me to be mad. Instead, the friendly banter only makes me feel like he's someone I've known for years, not days.

He takes a sip of his soda, trying to hold back a smile at my annoyance. And there it is again, that spark he has when he smiles that makes my heart want to cave in on itself. He's across from me at the table, but I urge myself to look anywhere else and to stay focused.

"Thank you, by the way," he says, and I look at him, just out of instinct, and then instantly regret it.

Whether Caleb knows what he's doing or not, his eyes soften, and it takes everything in me to stay seated across from him. I want to reach my hand out, or even brush my foot up against him just to be sure he's real. No guy is ever this . . . sincere.

"For what?"

"For coming to rescue me. Was it really a two-hour drive?"

His eyes are locked in on me, and I'm frozen under his gaze.

"Yes," I say quietly.

He frowns and looks down, releasing me from his gaze. "I'm sorry. I shouldn't have called. There were other people. I should have tried them first."

"Caleb, it's fine," I say, my voice soft.

He looks up at me with what I can only describe as adoration. The corner of his lip twitches, and for a moment I want to close the distance between us and kiss him.

"Who had the streak dinner?" A server comes over with our food, and I'm thankful for the distraction. Perhaps I would have been better off not eating dinner with Caleb, cutting off the relationship when it was at an all-time low.

"Me," Caleb says.

The server hands Caleb his food, then places my meal in front of me. I use the moment to try to recenter myself.

You don't like him. You're both so different. He's cute after a shower, but he stinks the rest of the time.

I almost laugh at how ridiculous I sound.

We're both quiet as we eat, and while I have no idea what's going on in Caleb's brain, my brain is working to untangle itself.

I should have just taken him to Taco Bell. I could have dropped him off at the hotel without another regret. We haven't even finished our meal, and I can already tell I'm a glutton for punishment.

"So, besides you being a waitress, living in North Conway, and being a Marvel fan, I don't know much about you," Caleb says as we're finishing our plates.

After the silence between us, the question almost comes as a shock. It takes me a moment to come up with the answer. "After I graduate college, I want to open my own yoga studio."

His eyes light up. "You're a yoga teacher?" he asks.

"Sorta. I'm certified, and I taught classes in order to get my certification, but I don't have a job yet."

He nods. "Is it hard to get started?"

I can't help but feel a bit defeated just thinking about it. "That's what it's looking like."

Caleb smiles as if he's trying to counter my mood. "A lot of people on the AT do yoga. Nothing formal, just some stretches and poses to keep things limber. I only do it when there's a group of people doing it, but if you ever need students, I know where to find them."

I smile, trying to imagine all the hikers stretching out after a long day, huddled around their tents. "Just walk down the wooded path, and there they are?"

"Yup."

"No wonder I've been struggling." I feign surprise. "I've been looking in the wrong place."

"Hundreds of students are waiting for you out there."

I raise an eyebrow, unsure if he's joking. "Hundreds? Is that how many people hike the AT?"

He shrugs. "I think around three thousand people hike it every year, but only a quarter of those get to the finish line."

I shake my head in mock disappointment. "And here I thought you were the only one crazy enough to live out of the woods for months on end."

"I'm not in the woods tonight. I'm at a Super 8. That's the lap of luxury."

"I think the word you're looking for is *dingy*." I make a face.

"I was thinking *cheap*, actually." He chuckles.

We both smile.

"Honestly though, I'm sure hikers would love to take a yoga class from a real teacher rather than five minutes of stretching."

My face goes red. I don't even consider myself a real yoga teacher yet.

"You really want me to like the Appalachian Trail, don't you?"

"It's magical." He shrugs, then shifts to a more serious tone. "The trail transforms you, even if you don't finish. No one walks away the same, but everyone walks away better than they started."

I'm about to say something, joke around to break the seriousness in the air, but the waiter comes by with the check, and the moment is gone. I reach for it, but Caleb beats me to it.

"Let me pay," I offer. "You're living out of a backpack."

He's amused by my offer. "A gentleman never lets a lady pay."

CHAPTER 10

"I promise you, no matter how gross you may think freeze-dried food is, anything tastes good after hiking all day," Caleb says, his voice a comfort as the sun begins to set. We pull into the parking lot of the Super 8, the streetlights flickering on.

"No way will you ever manage to get me to eat it." I shake my head.

"If you're hungry enough," he says.

"That's the thing. I'd never be hungry enough because I'd never do the hiking part."

When I glance over to Caleb, he's smiling, the grin mischievous like he's just made it his personal mission to take me on a hike.

"Come on, didn't you say your best friend is a hiker? You're telling me you've never gone with her? Not even once?"

I turn in my seat to face him, the center console a clear divide between us. I should be telling him I have to go, that I need to start driving home since it will take me two hours to get back, but I don't.

"I do, but only for special occasions," I say.

He grins, an open invitation. "I can work with that."

I open my mouth, eager to respond with another quip, but nothing comes to me. Instead, I end up laughing and try to ignore the way my face turns red.

"What?" he says.

"I can't handle you," I finally say.

His smile widens. "What do you mean?"

"You" —I point to him—"and the way you just show up out of nowhere, trying to woo me before retreating into the woods, never to be found again."

"But you did find me again."

I let out another hearty laugh. "If I'd known the condition you'd be in, I'd have arrived with a bucket of water and dish soap to keep up the illusion."

The smile on his face falters the smallest bit. "Trust me, if showers were an option on the trail, I'd do it."

The air is still between us, neither of us knowing where the conversation leads to next. The glowing yellow-and-red sign of the hotel shines into the car as the sun goes down, making everything around us glow in warm shades of the setting sun.

When I look over to Caleb, his gaze is cast out, toward the hotel doors, both of us thinking about our goodbyes but having no idea how to handle them.

"Why did you ask me out?" I break the silence.

He looks toward me, his brow furrowed. "Didn't you want to eat before you head home?"

"Not that." I shake my head. "I mean last week when I was

your waiter at Angela's."

He pauses, blinking and looking around at everything but me.

"Because you joked around with all of us so easily. We were this big obnoxious group, but you joined in with us like you were part of it. Even though you were working and just trying to get through your shift, you had this sort of magnetism. I wanted to know more about you." He shrugs. "So I asked you out, because at the least, I thought it would be fun to hang out a little more. And then when you were at the hostel, it felt like I already knew you." He lifts his eyes, finally looking at me. "You didn't feel like a stranger."

"You said that already," I say quietly. "You said on the trail, no one feels like strangers."

"We're not on the trail," he whispers, and that's when I realize how close we are. We've both angled ourselves in our seats to turn toward each other. The gap between us is minuscule, but the tension in the air bolts me in place.

Every nerve in my body is on edge. I can see the way he watches me, the way his eyes roam over every inch of my skin.

"I have to go home," I say, more out of panic than anything else.

My words slice through the air, the moment broken. Caleb pulls back, looking away, and I instantly regret saying something.

"Sorry," he says quietly. He shifts in the car, looking around like he's left something behind, then takes a deep breath and opens the side door, stepping out.

"Caleb," I say, getting out of the car with him.

His hand lingers on the car door as if he's afraid to let go.

"Will I see you again?" I ask, my voice so quiet I'm not sure if he heard me.

His eyes flick up to my face. "I want to," he says.

I wait for him to say more, but he's silent.

I take a careful, measured breath. "But you have to leave tomorrow."

"Maybe you can visit me again." He smiles, which makes it harder to say what I need to.

"I don't know if I can drive up here again. I don't have a lot of days off this summer." The logical part of my brain is already reprimanding me for making the drive today. How much time have I wasted by spending the entire day with Caleb? I could have been writing a paper or doing more job searches.

"That's fine," Caleb says, but the corners of his lips turn down, and I know he's just as disappointed as I am.

We're at an impasse.

I force myself to smile even when I feel tears start to form. It takes everything in me not to close the final distance between us and fling myself into his arms.

"It was good seeing you again," I say in an unsteady voice, but I have a hard time meeting his eyes.

Caleb closes his car door, and I turn back to my car, getting ready to leave. Before I have the chance to look up again, Caleb moves to where I'm standing, his arms circling my waist. The hug is familiar, safe. I can feel Caleb's breath at my temple when he talks.

"Maybe we'll figure something out later."

I pull away just enough to look at him. His eyes have a tiny burning hope, like he's already excited for the next time we're going to see each other, but I have no idea when that'll be—or if we ever will. Questions form in the back of my mind, but I'm too afraid to ask him, afraid I won't like the answers.

It's easier to assume this is it. Make as clean of a break as possible.

It's just a summer fling—at least that's what I keep telling myself.

CHAPTER 11

S eeing Caleb made things worse. The visit didn't quell the feelings or prove them wrong. All it did was prove I'm falling for Caleb, no matter how much I tried to convince myself I wasn't.

I told myself I'd never see him again because it's easier to part ways than to always wonder when I'll see him next. Caleb is a distraction, and that's the last thing I need amid everything else. What I need is to focus on writing my next paper for class and searching for more yoga studios that are hiring.

The next day, my plan is to stay so busy and occupied that thinking about Caleb isn't an option. I'm rereading the essay I spent five hours on when a FaceTime notification pops up on my laptop. I look at the clock and see the time.

"Oh, shoot," I say, rushing across the room to grab my charger from where I left it on my nightstand.

Marly and I have been doing weekly video chat sessions since she moved to Colorado, but because of everything with Caleb—or trying to be so busy I don't have time to think of

Caleb—I'd forgotten about it completely.

I plug the computer in and hit accept on the call. After a few seconds, Marly's face pops up on the screen.

"Well, look who decided to finally answer," Marly says.

"What do you mean?" And that's when I check my phone and see the missed texts from Marly, double-checking that we were still good for our weekly video chat. "I'm sorry, it's been a day."

"Isn't it your day off?"

I bury my face in my hands, rubbing my eyes. "Yes, but I've been working on my summer class, trying to get a month's worth of work done in one day, and . . ." I pause, knowing I don't want to open this can of worms. "Boys suck."

Marly raises her eyebrows in surprise. It's been a while since I've had my own boy drama. I don't typically date a guy long enough to create drama or have enough feelings for drama, but here we are.

"Chip?" she asks.

"Caleb," I correct.

"Right. Sorry, trail names are easier to remember. But what happened? I assumed you guys had your magical night and then he disappeared into the cosmos like all the other guys you've dated." She grins, teasing me as I roll my eyes.

"No, I followed your advice and texted him."

The smile disappears from her face. "Really? Wait. So, did you see him again?"

"I texted him to let him know I could give him a ride into town if he ever needed it. Then he called me saying he got hurt on the trail and needed a ride into town, so I drove two hours and picked him up."

"Very heroic," she comments.

"Marly, you never told me how bad thru-hikers smell."

She laughs; I'm sure she can imagine how that encounter went.

"It comes with the territory. There's no helping it."

I shake my head, unable to get the memory of the smell out of my head. "I don't think you understand. I didn't know a human could smell that bad. Like, this wasn't gym stink; this was lifelong-no-baths stink. I was ignorant enough to pick up his bag, and it was the stuff of nightmares."

She's still laughing at me as I tell the story. "Okay, he smelled bad, and so did his backpack. Where's the drama there? Did you refuse to give him a ride?"

"Of course not! If anything, I was thankful for the smell because it made it harder to like him, which is what I needed. If I'd just dropped him off at the hotel, I'd probably have moved on with my life by now."

"So, what happened?"

I pause, not willing to admit how easily I was won over. "I took him back to a hotel, and he showered and became all cute and sexy again."

Marly nods her head, trying to contain her smile. "That is a problem."

"So, then we went out to eat—"

"Again? That's, like, three dates with one guy."

I glare at her, and she smiles guiltily.

"Anyway," I continue. "We went out on this date, and it was great, which is bad. I was supposed to either get him out of my system or realize we're not a good match."

"So, does this mean you kissed him again?"

"No," I say, wishing I had. If I'm going to put myself through this type of torture, I should at least make it worth it. "But we almost did."

She raises an eyebrow, curious.

"We were talking in the car, and then things started to get hot and heavy, and I got nervous, so I just blurted out that I had to start driving back."

"And then you just left?"

"Sorta. He was saying I could come visit him along the trail again, but I told him I wouldn't be able to because I'm too busy. He said we could figure something out, but how can we do that when I'm the only one who can drive? What's the point?" I start getting worked up as I talk. I've managed to keep it together so far, but I'm breaking at the seams.

Marly's eyes go soft by the time I finish speaking. Despite all the dates I've been on, never once has a boy made me cry.

"If he asked you to pick him up again, would you?" she asks.

I shake my head, but I know it's not the truth. "I don't know. Probably."

"Is that a bad thing?"

"Marly, I'm so behind—" I start, but she stops me midsentence.

"You're not behind." She says the words so firmly that it makes me pause. "You are further ahead than most people our age. You hold yourself to an impossible standard, so go easy on yourself."

"I know, but—"

"No," Marly says.

Suddenly, I'm aware of how our roles have reversed. How many times was I the one trying to talk sense into Marly?

"The people who walk into our lives are important." She pauses, letting me feel the full impact of the words. "So, who is Caleb to you? What is it about him that would make you drop everything to go see him?"

I bury my face in my hands. "Because despite how different we are, I can't stop thinking about him. No matter how stressed I am, being around him makes me happy. I feel like I can daydream with him around."

Marly gives me a knowing smile. "You really like him," she says.

I wipe my hands down my face again. "Of course I do. Why else would I drive two hours to pick up someone I barely know?"

"So, now what?"

I drop my hands, snapping my gaze back to the screen. "I don't know. That's why I'm talking to you. You're the one with a boyfriend. Tell me how it works."

"You keep going on dates?" She shrugs, the answer unenthusiastic.

"Well, that's going to be difficult since he'll be hiking the Appalachian Trail for the rest of the summer."

"Then wait until he finishes?"

"He lives in Maine. How am I supposed to date a guy in Maine?"

"What part of Maine? We're only an hour away from the border. Maybe he's closer than you think."

"And if he's not?"

"Then you move to Maine to date a guy, just like I moved to Colorado to date a guy." She laughs, but I glare back at her, unamused.

"I like where I live."

Marly frowns again, putting the jokes to the side. "If you guys are meant to be, it will all work out."

I let out an exasperated sigh. "I wish he didn't look so good after showering," I mumble.

Marly laughs softly. "Worst case, you join him on the trail, fall in love, and live happily ever after," she says, trying to lighten the mood again.

I shake my head, not even allowing myself to imagine it.

"You people are crazy."

CHAPTER 12

My resolve to forget about Caleb crumbled the second I started the video chat with Marly and only grew worse as time went on. After we hung up, I finished some final touches on my essay, submitted it online, and then tried unsuccessfully to read the next chapter of my textbook. Instead, my mind worked in circles, thinking about everything Marly had said before I gave in and texted her.

Text him, she says after I send her too many long self-pitying text messages.

What if he doesn't respond?

He'll respond.

I pull up the chat I have with Caleb, but I can't get myself to type anything. What would I even say?

Another text comes in from Marly when she doesn't hear from me.

Or just go see him. You obviously like him too much to stay away.

But it isn't that simple. For one, I have no idea where he is. And two? Even if I did know where he is, I'm not sure I *want* to see him again.

I'll just go stand at a random spot in the road and wait for him to show up. I add in a rolling eyes emoji.

Text. Him.

I let out a puff of air. *Fine.*

I pull up the conversation with Caleb again and type out the simplest thing I can think of.

How's the hike going?

I take a screenshot and send it to Marly. She responds with a thumbs-up emoji. I toss my phone to the side in an attempt to focus on my work again. I'm reading the world's most boring textbook when I hear my phone chime as a text comes in. Caleb's name is on the screen.

A little stalled at the moment. Are you still offering rides? I'd love to see you again.

I'm almost ashamed of how quickly my mood shifts. My eyes glaze over everything except *I'd love to see you again.*

I am. But you know my conditions, I type out, immediately falling back into our banter.

Cute? I hope I still fit the bill ;)

I can't help but smile.

Only one way to find out. Where are you?

The response comes within seconds.

Right where you left me. Ankle was worse than I thought and needed to heal up.

My first reaction is betrayal. All this time I thought he wasn't texting me because he was hiking and didn't have cell phone signal. But he was just sitting in a dingy hotel room?

But then that emotion is replaced with anger at myself because this entire time he was sitting in a dingy hotel room and I was wasting time by moping all day.

I can come by in the morning? I type.

That's it. My one and only offer. Take it or leave it.

Can't wait to see you.

My response is immediate, the smile creeping over my lips, impossible to hide.

§

The next day, I have a shift scheduled for four p.m., but I told myself I'd drive to see Caleb first thing in the morning and then drive back just in time for my shift.

I pull up to the Super 8 at seven and let myself up to the hotel room, making my way toward the same place I was a few days ago. I only have to wait a couple seconds after knocking before Caleb answers the door.

"You're here early." He greets me with a smile and ushers me in. "Welcome back to my temporary home."

It's cleaner than I expected. The bed isn't made, but all his things are packed away, back in his backpack. When Caleb moves to sit on the bed, I notice he's in his hiking clothes again, ready to leave. His ankle must be healed enough to go back.

"So, what's wrong with your ankle?" I say, eyeing the foot he was limping on the other day.

He sits on the bed and kicks his foot out as if he's trying to let me examine it.

"Not much. It's just a little tender. Figured I'd give myself one more day to rest before I submit myself to another twenty miles."

"Does that mean you'll be hiking tomorrow?" I ask, my gaze lingering to the way his bag is packed up like he's ready to leave today.

"Actually, the plan was to get back on trail today, but if you want to spend the day together—"

I put my hand up to stop him. "No, it's fine. I can't stay long. I have a shift that starts at four." At the mention of leaving, his face drops the slightest bit. "Why didn't you text me yesterday to let me know you weren't going to be hiking?"

His face wavers for a moment, as if he's confused. "I thought you were busy."

I open my mouth, about to deny it, but the truth is I was busy. I needed almost the entire day to write that paper. I should be home right now reading the chapter in my textbook I didn't finish because I was too busy worrying over Caleb.

And that's the problem, isn't it? Caleb makes my motivation go out the window.

"I was." I frown, moving to sit beside Caleb on the bed.

His gaze lingers on me, and we sit in the air that's formed between us, wanting to move forward but having no idea how.

"What town do you live in? In Maine?" I say just to fill the silence.

He frowns. "Ashland."

"Where's that?"

He lets out a sad laugh. "About as far north as you can get."

Whatever hope I had in my heart sinks. How many hours of driving would it take to get from North Conway to Ashland? Five? Maybe more?

I shake my head and laugh to myself a little.

"What?" Caleb asks.

"Leave it to me to fall for a guy who's a hiker and lives in another state."

This is the first time I'm saying my feelings out loud, but at this point it's less like a confession and more of stating the obvious.

"The hiking's only temporary. I don't plan on living out of a backpack for the rest of my life."

I let out a stiff chuckle. "That's good." But the words don't comfort me. He's closer to me living out of a backpack than he'll be when he's back home in a few months. "What's the plan when you get home?"

Caleb looks like I've just asked him to recount the periodic table from memory.

We've talked endlessly, but only about my life or his life on the trail. I don't know a thing about his life before the AT.

"I don't know, to be honest. Your life's on pause when you hike the AT. And usually the person you come out as is different from the person you go in as—life-changing journey and all that." He laughs nervously and shifts a little.

A question forms in the back of my mind—about us, about where we are at the end of all this—but it's too serious to ask. I count in my head, checking my math. We've only seen each other four times—encounters that add up to just a small handful of hours. It doesn't seem right to ask Caleb what will happen to us at the end of his hike.

"Do you need to restock before you head out?" I ask.

Caleb seems as relieved as I am to move on to a different subject. "No, I did all that yesterday."

He gets up, throwing his backpack over his shoulder and offering me his hand. Caleb checks out of his room, and we keep our hands linked as we walk to my car.

Caleb gives me the location of where he needs to be dropped off, and I let him tell me his favorite stories from hiking. His voice is exasperated while he recounts tales of walking in the rain and cold weather. Every part of it sounds unappealing, but Caleb recalls it with a sort of badge of honor. He's not mad about the time he got stuck in a thunderstorm three miles away from the nearest shelter — he retells the tale like a proud army veteran.

"Why don't you just take the day off when it rains?" I finally ask.

"It rains all the time. If I take the day off every time the weather is less than pleasant, it'll take me years to finish. It's not supposed to be fun."

I glance over, perplexed. "I assumed if you're spending five months in the woods, then you thought it was fun."

Caleb lets out a loud, hearty laugh. "Oh, none of this is fun."

I blink, waiting to hear the punch line. "Then why bother?"

He pauses, taking a deep breath. "I guess . . ." He runs his hand over his chin, brushing through his beard, which still looks tamed. He must have stopped at the barber yesterday as well. "I'm testing my own determination. I just need to prove to myself that I can do it. If I can do this, then I can do anything."

In an odd way, hearing Caleb talk about the AT makes me see it: the thing that makes us similar. Despite all the ways we're opposites, determination is the thing that threads us together. Our goals couldn't be more different, but our drive to accomplish them is clear.

"It's right here," he says, pointing to where I need to pull off to the side of the road. "Do you think you could show me some stretches before I leave?" Caleb asks, unbuckling, his hand on the door.

"What do you mean?"

"I wasn't joking when I said people would love to have a yoga teacher on trail. I know you don't want to hike, but if you teach me a few things, maybe I can pass it on." He gives me a small innocent smile, and I cave in to the request.

"Sure," I say, unable to refuse.

We both get out of the car, and I turn around, trying to figure out what I'm working with. My car is parked on the side of the road. The road itself isn't very wide, but it's a dirt road, so I doubt we'll see anyone else. The space between the road and the edge of the forest is narrow, but it's mostly smooth trampled dirt, which is better than nothing. We don't have any yoga mats, blocks, or blankets, but I suppose Caleb won't have any of that while he's hiking either.

"Okay, come here," I say, gesturing Caleb over. He comes to stand in front of me, and I put my hands on his shoulders, moving him into place. There are a few rocks and branches along the side of the road, but I place him in a small clear patch.

"Mirror me and just listen to what I say, okay?" I glance down at my jeans and blouse and realize this may not be my most graceful yoga class.

I decide to do a basic sun salutation, starting off in mountain pose—standing tall with my arms straight at my sides. I reach my arms up, extending the stretch, and then lean into forward fold. From there I shift to plank, then cobra to pull my chest up, downward dog, and then back up to mountain pose.

I move through the poses carefully, describing each move step-by-step as I go. I explain the slow and steady breaths of the moves as I make them myself. I watch Caleb, a perfect student. He isn't as balanced as he shifts into each pose, but he ends in a strong stance.

We run through the same poses twice until we meet back where we started and stand in mountain pose.

"How was that?" I ask.

Caleb grins. "Much better than what we've been doing." He walks toward the back of my car, opening the trunk so he can get his bag.

"So, how far do you think you'll get today?" I ask, lingering at his side as he pulls the bag on.

"Not too far. I want to make sure my ankle's okay before I start doing long days again. The next shelter is in four miles, so I might just go that far and then get an early start in the morning."

"That's it?" I ask, a little surprised by how short of a distance he plans to cover.

"Not every day can be a twenty-mile day." He grins.

"Anyone can do four miles in a day." I shrug.

"Even you?" His eyes meet mine, the challenge clear, and I know I've walked right into his trap.

"I could do four miles," I say, trying not to let my gaze wander down the wooded path.

"Prove it." Caleb's smile widens.

"I have to be at work at four," I say, thankful for the excuse now.

"Okay, then not today. When's your next day off?"

I don't say a word; I know when my next day off is, but I don't dare tell him.

"Come on, you're telling me you're working every day for the foreseeable future?"

"No, but usually I spend my days off doing just about anything besides walking in the woods."

"It's just four miles," he says, using his best smile against me.

"How would that even work? Would I walk four miles and go home?" I'm testing the water, and I know I shouldn't. I shouldn't even consider entertaining the idea, but here I am.

He sees my point of weakness and jumps on it. "Just four miles. Two miles out. Two miles back. I'll even let you drive home to the comfort of your bed if you want, but you're more than welcome to stay the night."

"I'm not sleeping on the ground." I shake my head.

"You can use my sleeping pad. Or we can sleep in the shelter. It's a building, so even better than a tent." He smiles as if he's talking about a five-star resort.

I entertain the thought of backpacking with Caleb, but I don't get far. The only things I can bring to mind are bugs, rocks, and no toilet.

"I'm all set," I say.

He frowns but doesn't seem surprised by my answer. He shifts on his feet for a moment before stepping forward to close the small distance between us, wrapping me up in his arms. The movement takes me by surprise, and I stumble into him, putting my full weight against his chest. His arms are tight around me, a comforting grip around my waist.

"Thank you again," he says when he pulls away.

"Can you text me when you set up camp for the night?" I ask before I can chicken out. "So I can know you did fine with your ankle."

He smiles like this simple question has made his day. "I don't always have a cell phone signal, but if I do, I will."

"Thank you," I say, smiling at the thought of at least knowing I'll hear from him soon.

"Text me if you change your mind about joining me." He grins, and I roll my eyes, laughing.

Without another word, he walks toward the trees and starts down the path.

My mood shifts as he walks away. The instant I'm out of his reach, the air is cooler. What if I don't see him again? He gets farther away, his orange backpack a bright spot in the green woods.

Four miles. That's all it would be. Four miles and one night sleeping in the shelter.

I could use a little romance in my life, and what good is romance without adventure?

"Caleb!" I shout, telling myself if he doesn't hear me, I should turn around and go home.

But he does hear me.

"Yeah?" In the distance, he turns to face me again.

"I think I could survive one night out in the woods."

CHAPTER 13

I spend the two-hour drive home regretting my decision. For two hours, I'm able to wrap my head around what I've just agreed to, and for two hours, I try to think of any way I can back out.

Backing out would be easy. It was near impossible to find a date where I had two days off in a row to meet up with Caleb along the trail, so instead we chose one day I had off, and I promised I'd be able to find someone to cover my shift. All I'd have to do is text Caleb I couldn't find coverage. I can just refuse to ask any coworkers to cover my shift, and the problem will solve itself. But less simple than that is knowing that if I back out, I don't know when I'll see Caleb again, and that fact doesn't sit well with me.

Maybe I'll ask just one person. If they say they can't take my shift, then it isn't meant to be.

When I get back to my apartment, I have just enough time to shower, change, and send Marly a text before I have to leave for work.

SOS. I've somehow agreed to go backpacking for one night. Save me.

Once I send the text, I'm back in my car, driving to work. There isn't a response from Marly yet, so I rush into Angela's and begin my day.

It's busy tonight, the busiest it's been in a while, but it makes the day go by faster. I'm never able to stand in one place for more than a few seconds. I take orders, remove dirty dishes, deliver desserts, and ring up checks — all in an endless cycle of tasks.

I work the closing shift, and as the dinner rush comes and goes, the night grows quieter until the last customers walk out the door. I'm helping clean up for the night when Allison walks by with the trash that needs to be taken out to the dumpster.

"Hey, Allison," I say, grabbing her attention.

She pauses, letting the bags drop to the floor with an exasperated thud. "What's up?"

"Would you mind covering my shift for me Thursday?" I checked the schedule in the break room earlier today and didn't see her name on it yet, so I knew it would be possible. Knowing Allison, she probably already has something planned for that day. I'm not sure if I'm relieved or disappointed over the possibility.

She cocks her head to the side, thinking. "Yeah, I can do that. I think I was just going to catch up on the show I'm binging."

I should be happy, but all I feel is dread. "Thanks," I say, plastering on the best smile I can.

"Sure thing!" Allison says, voice chipper as she picks up the bags and brings them out to the garbage.

With a groan, I turn back to the tables, cleaning them off and trying not to imagine what I'll be doing in a couple days.

The last minutes of my shift drag on, and part of me begins to regret asking Allison to cover my shift. There's no excuse to back out now.

When I get back to my car, I find a missed call and multiple texts from Marly.

What are you talking about?

Are you going to go HIKING?

With Caleb?

The texts are from a couple hours ago, but I type up a quick response.

Caleb must have hypnotized me when I wasn't looking.

I start the car and make my way toward home, but it only takes a few minutes for Marly to see my text and call.

"What's going on?" she says as soon as I answer.

"I've messed up." If I were at home already, I'd be retreating to my bedroom so I could suffocate myself in a pile of pillows until I passed out.

"You're going backpacking?" Marly says, voice shrill.

"Don't say that," I mutter.

"What would you like me to say?" she says, laughing now.

"Literally anything but that. Tell me I'm just going for a nice leisurely walk in the woods and at the end of the day, I get to retreat back to an amazing clean bed that's overflowing with pillows."

"Lori, you are in deep, deep trouble."

I can tell she's trying to hold back from laughing, and I want to cry. "Help me."

"Okay, deep breaths. What happened? How did you get talked into backpacking?"

"He was just teasing me because I said four miles of hiking was easy, so he challenged me to do it, and . . ." I try to think back to what happened. How did I get myself into this? "He's cute, Marly," is all I can come up with as an excuse.

"I'm sure he is, but that doesn't explain how you got to this point." Though I can't see Marly, I know she's probably shaking her head, thinking of what I've cornered myself into.

"The issue is that when he walked away, I realized I didn't know when or if I would see him again, so I panicked and said I'd do an overnight trip with him."

"It could be worse," Marly says, taking in my words. "Four miles is short. Even you can do four miles."

My face goes flat. "Thanks."

"You know what I mean."

"So, what do I do? How do I get out of this?"

"I have an idea if you're willing to hear it," Marly says as I pull into the parking lot for my building.

"I'm all ears." I park my car and settle into the seat, closing my eyes, ready to hear whatever solution Marly has come up with.

"What if you just do the hike?"

My eyes snap open. Whatever dreams of relaxation I had are gone. I don't respond right away, sure that I just heard her wrong, but I run Marly's words over in my mind multiple times, and each time she's saying the same thing.

"I can't," I say, the words coming out as a squeak.

"Why not?"

"Because I love being clean. And even better, I love sleeping on a mattress."

Marly's laughing again. "You'd be surprised by how comfortable sleeping pads can be."

"Marly, I promise you, I can't do this." It feels like I'm begging now.

"When did you tell Caleb you'd go with him?"

I cringe, regretting the answer I gave him before he disappeared into the woods. "In two days."

"That's perfect!" Marly says, not matching my mood at all.

"In what world is that perfect?"

"Because it gives you enough time to prepare, but not so much time that you try to back out."

"I'm trying to back out right now."

"Did he say what you need to bring? Do you need a tent?" Marly says, ignoring my last comment.

"He said we're going to stay at one of the shelters, so I won't need a tent."

What do you even bring to go backpacking anyway?

"Perfect! You can borrow some of my stuff. Are you home?"

If Marly notices any of my apprehension, she's ignoring it.

"I just pulled into the parking lot. Why?"

"Let me know when you're inside. I'll stay on the phone."

With a strong surge of reluctance, I push my car door open and make my way across the parking lot and into my building. I take my time getting to my door, already fearing whatever plan

Marly has.

"Okay. I'm in my apartment." I sigh as the door closes with a soft click.

"Good. Okay, you know how you're still holding on to some of my parents' things in the hall closet? Open the box with the REI stickers on it."

I switch my phone to speaker and set it on the floor while I dig through the closet. Marly has a lot of boxes full of her parents' stuff. While most of her parents' belongings went to relatives and a storage unit, some of Marly's favorite things stayed in these boxes. She's supposed to bring the boxes to Colorado someday, but until then they're hiding in my hallway closet for safekeeping.

"Okay, hold on. I think I've got it," I say, pulling out a box that was hidden in the back.

I open it to reveal an arsenal of hiking supplies, most of which I have no idea what they are or what they're used for. But there's a few familiar things, like a backpack, boots, a few maps. Some things look like they might be sleeping bags rolled and bagged into tight balls.

"I thought you took all your hiking stuff with you to Colorado?" I ask, sifting through the box. I open one of the bags and pull out a tightly bound blanket that uncurls in my lap.

"I did. That's actually all my dad's stuff."

My hand freezes on the sleeping bag. "Marly, I can't use your dad's stuff."

"Yes, you can."

"Why should I use it when you don't even use it? What if I

break something?"

"I don't use it because I have my own stuff. And if you break it, you break it. My dad would have loved to see you venture into the great outdoors. It would have been his honor to offer up his gear."

My face goes hot thinking of how Marly's dad would have reacted to seeing me try to go backpacking to be with a guy. He would've had a fit! He was always teasing me about not going on hiking trips with him and Marly.

I pull the backpack out of the box, recognizing it from the photos Marly had plastered on her wall growing up of the hiking trips they went on together. The bag is huge, a bit longer than my torso. It's a moss-green color, with endless pockets, buckles, and straps hanging all over the place. The backpack looks more complicated than it should be.

I've never used any backpacking supplies before, but having seen the backpack in Marly's photos for so long, the familiarity is a tiny bit of comfort.

"I'd be mortified if he knew what I was about to do," I say, laughing quietly.

"He'd be cheering you on," Marly says softly.

It feels strange to get choked up thinking of Marly's dad, but I know he was more than just a parent of a friend. He treated me like I was his daughter too.

I let out a shaky breath. "Okay, tell me how all this works."

CHAPTER 14

I give up on the idea of getting out of the hike. When I'm on the phone with Marly, she makes me test out all the gear I'll need, including setting up the sleeping bag and pad in the middle of my living room. I don't dare lie on the sleeping pad, afraid that if I do, I'll realize how uncomfortable I'll be and back out.

Much to my dismay, the two days of work I have to finish go by in a blur. The day before the backpacking trip, Caleb sends me a list of everything I need to pack.

It's easier to pretend I'm not joining him on the trail, but the packing list is a harsh reality.

Can't wait to see you tomorrow, he texts the night before I have to leave to go back to Maine.

I want to be excited, but every fiber in my being is telling me to run. Despite my hesitance, I somehow find myself waking up at five a.m. on my day off to begin my three-hour drive to the spot where I'll start hiking with Caleb. The drive gets longer and longer with time, serving as a reminder that the more time that passes, the farther away Caleb gets.

When I leave my apartment, I pause at the doorway, giving everything a once-over, knowing in a couple hours I'll be missing everything about this place—especially my bed. Then, before I can give it too much thought, I make my way toward my car and begin the drive.

I crank up my music as loud as I can, trying to drown out my nerves as I drive down the highway on autopilot.

Caleb told me where to meet him, but when the GPS tells me to turn right into a dirt parking lot, there's no sign of him. I pace around my car for a bit, panic already setting in.

"I'm never going to let myself crush on a guy again," I mutter. I pull my phone out to call Caleb, but I have no bars. "Oh my god." I drop my hand in defeat, and it takes everything in me not to cry. I stand outside my car, eyeing the front seat and wondering when I should call it and make my way home.

"Lori!" a familiar voice shouts.

I turn and find Caleb walking out of the woods, a huge grin across his face. He picks up his pace and closes the distance between us, wrapping me in his arms.

I'm so thankful to see him—to see anyone. I'm just thankful for the human contact. It's after a few seconds that I breathe in the air and smell the BO. I'm the one to pull away, putting just enough distance between us that I can't smell him.

Dear God, what have I gotten myself into?

"You all packed up and ready to go?" Caleb says, eyeballing me.

I'm wearing shorts and a tank top, but I brought a spare change of clothes and sweatshirt. Marly helped me pack, stopping me from bringing additional outfits even though I swore I'd need at least three changes of clothes if I had a hope of feeling even slightly clean.

"I think so," I say, surprised by the sound of my own voice when I speak.

I go into the trunk of my car and pull out the backpack.

"Mind if I double-check?" he says, gripping the bag.

"Sure."

He unclips the top of the bag and starts pulling my things out. I don't have much besides my clothes and sleeping things, but Caleb checks it all, and I'm thankful when he doesn't insist on looking through the little bag that contains all my clothes. Against Marly's advice, I packed three pairs of underwear, though now that I think of it, I have no idea how I'm going to change in front of Caleb.

"First aid kit?" he asks.

"It's in here." I point to the smallest outer pocket on the bag.

"Perfect. I have one too, but it's always good to have your own in case we get separated."

My eyes go wide at the thought of being in the woods alone.

"I'm letting you know now, if you leave me in the woods for even a second, I'm going to cry." My voice makes a nervous squeak when I speak.

Caleb laughs, but I don't think he knows how serious I am.

"Looks like you've got it all," he says, zipping everything back into place.

"What would you have done if I forgot to pack something?"

"I would have suggested we find a hotel to sleep in tonight."

"I wish you'd told me that last night when I went over the packing list three times."

"Have you been fitted to the bag?" He hands it back to me.

"What?" I ask, taking it. The bag doesn't weigh nearly as much as Caleb's, but it still feels too heavy to be carrying around all day.

"Put it on. I'll show you."

I shrug the bag onto my shoulders, already regretting every decision that's led me to this point. I buckle the hip and chest straps, leaving them on the loose side so they don't squeeze me too tight.

"So, you want the weight of your bag to rest on your hips, not your shoulders." He moves around me as he talks, tightening some straps at my back. "How's it feel?"

"Fine, I guess."

He stands in front of me and tightens the hip strap as much as it can go before also tightening the chest strap.

"How about now?"

I'm about to complain that it's too tight, but the weight shifts so the bag is no longer pulling my shoulders back; instead, it rests on my hips, making the weight manageable.

"Better," I say.

"Good. Is your car locked up? And the car key is in a safe place?"

I point to one of the pockets on the backpack, where my keys are clipped into a strap and the pocket is zipped closed.

"Okay, let's get to walking." He offers his hand, and I take it eagerly.

It's not the first time I've gone hiking with a backpack on, but it is the first time my backpack has held more than water and snacks. It's surreal to walk away from my car and embark into the woods knowing I won't be returning to it until tomorrow.

Once we're on the trail, Caleb releases my hand, ushering me to lead the way. There's a sense of disappointment when his hand leaves mine.

"I don't know which way to go," I say softly.

He points to a white strip painted on a tree. "This is a trail blaze. The white blazes are for the Appalachian Trail. Just follow those, and you're going the right way. I'll let you know if you're going the wrong way."

I begin walking, completely out of my element. The path isn't smooth dirt like I imagined. Each step, I need to look down just to make sure I don't trip over a rock or tree root.

"So, we're only doing four miles, right?" I ask, stepping over a boulder sitting in the middle of the trail. How am I supposed to look for the white trail blaze when I need to keep my eyes on the ground just so I don't trip?

"I was actually going to ask you about what you wanted to do. Because we have two options. The first is to do two miles to the next shelter, sleep there, and then backtrack two miles to the parking lot for a total of four miles."

"Okay," I say, thinking that's probably about as ideal as things are going to get. All of this is my fault after all. Now that I'm wearing a backpack, four miles is starting to feel like the longest distance of my life.

"Then the second option is that we do fifteen miles to where we sleep at the second shelter. The second shelter is supposed to be a little nicer, and then the next morning we only have to walk one mile to get to another parking lot. Then you can hitch a ride back to your car so there won't be any backtracking."

I stop in my tracks. I did not sign up for this.

"Lori?" Caleb comes closer, and his hand is on my arm.

"I don't know if I can do that," I say, trying to put on my best brave face, but even I can hear the fear in my voice.

He watches me closely, and I wonder if it's too late to turn around. I have no shame in calling it quits a couple feet into the trail and driving home to my clean bed.

"It's okay. We don't have to," he says, but I can tell he's disappointed. How much am I messing up his hike by making him do one section of the trail twice just so I can tag along?

"Maybe I can decide when we get to the first shelter. I'll see how I'm feeling," I say, because I can't manage to tell him how terrified I am.

He smiles. "Sounds good."

We move forward, and I continue in the lead, my head glued to the ground, constantly keeping my gaze trained to my feet so I don't trip.

"Am I going slow?" I ask when it feels like we've been hiking for hours.

"No, you're fine."

I glance behind me, and he's smiling, completely unfazed even though his bag weighs at least three times more than mine. Meanwhile, I've started huffing and puffing, quickly realizing yoga is not a form of cardio.

"I need a quick break," I say, unclipping the straps on the bag and letting it fall to the ground. Even though I thought the waist straps on the bag made it lighter, the instant relief I feel when the bag isn't resting on my hips anymore is astounding. "How long have we been going?"

Caleb checks the watch on his wrist. "About a half hour. We're making good time though."

I groan. How has it only been half an hour? "How far do you think we've gone?"

"The tracker on my watch says three-quarters of a mile, which is pretty good."

I frown, unable to maintain composure. "Caleb, you're real cute and all, but I don't think this is gonna work out."

I sit on a large boulder on the side of the trail and fully embrace the pity party I've rightfully earned. It feels like I'm covered in sweat, and my feet? They're sweating too, which I didn't know was possible. If Caleb smells bad, I must smell worse, because the sun is out today, and humidity is ready to drain every ounce of energy out of me.

Caleb lets out a soft chuckle, coming to sit beside me. "You're doing really good," he says, wrapping an arm around me.

I lean into his body, having no idea who's sweatier now— me or him.

"I'm really not. I'm probably slowing you down."

"I'm not in a rush," he says, kissing the top of my head. Any other day I'd think that was cute, but today I'm just self-conscious about how sweaty my hair is.

I let out a strained laugh. "That's good, because I'm not

going anywhere anytime soon."

He laughs again, rubbing my back.

"You guys okay?" A man and woman come from behind, slowing down when they see us. Their backpacks are just as big as Caleb's, and they each have hiking poles in their hands. They look just as worn and ragged as Caleb does—clearly fellow thru-hikers.

The couple look to be in their mid-thirties. The woman's hair is braided, but the baby hair around her face sticks out in every direction, making me wonder if my hair looks just as bad.

"Just taking a break," Caleb says as I smooth my hands over my hair. I pulled my hair back into a tight ponytail, but I can feel some of my curl coming loose and frizzing out all over the place.

"Is this your date?" the man says, glancing at me and then giving Caleb a knowing smirk.

Caleb turns red. "This is Lori. Lori, this is Fawn and River Ranger."

I give them a gentle wave.

"You going all the way to Little Bigelow?" Fawn asks.

"No, I think we might end up at Horns Pond tonight." Caleb shrugs.

"Bummer. She's going to miss the views."

"What views?" I ask.

"If we go a little farther, there's a mountain with some great views ahead, but that's past the first shelter," Caleb says.

"We have to get going," River Ranger says. "We have a shuttle picking us up at the next parking lot and don't want to miss our ride."

"Have a good hike!" Caleb says before they disappear into the trees.

"You know them?" I ask once they're out of sight.

"I ran into them back in New Hampshire, and we've been playing leapfrog ever since. They passed me today, but since they're going into town, I'll probably pass by them again soon enough."

"So, I'm your date?" I tease, smirking when his face turns red again.

"It was the easiest way to explain the situation. It didn't seem like you were coming along for the outdoor experience. If it isn't a date, I'm not sure why else you're subjecting yourself to torture."

This time it's me who turns bright red.

"Do you want a snack?" he asks, fishing a granola bar from his backpack.

"No," I say, grabbing my hair tie and pulling it out. I regret the choice almost instantly.

Before my hair was just frizzy, but now it falls around my shoulders in messy, unruly curls. I can sense Caleb's eyes on me as I work through my hair, trying to braid it back so it can maybe look a little better. I opt for a single French braid down the middle, pulling the hair and frizz back. When I finally finish and tie the end off, I run my hands over the sides of my head. To my dismay, I can still feel hair sticking out in every direction.

"How bad do I look?" I ask, turning to Caleb, who's just taken a big bite from his granola bar. His mouth is too full to respond, but he lets out a muffled giggle.

With a groan, I start rummaging through my bag. Marly told me to pack a bandana because it would be a great multiuse tool. She said I could use it as a sweat rag or soak it in a cold stream and tie it around my head to keep me cool. She also said it might come in handy to clean things off. She had a long list of reasons to carry the bandana, but most of it went over my head. I doubt she intended me to use it as a fashion accessory though.

I pull the bandana from where it's stashed in one of the small pockets on the backpack. The cloth is a deep blue color, and I fold it until it's long and thin. I wrap it around my head as a makeshift headband, tying it at the top of my head in a way that I hope resembles a cute fifties look.

I run my hands over the sides of my head again—this time I don't feel frizz or as many flyaways.

"Cute," Caleb says when I finish.

I give him a playful grin. "Thank you."

I get up, grabbing the backpack off the ground and hoisting it over my shoulders and buckling myself in. If only Marly could see me now.

"You didn't want to take a longer break?" Caleb asks, getting up and grabbing his own bag.

"Nope. We've got a view to see."

CHAPTER 15

I'm hopelessly optimistic. I told myself if I can ignore the pain and annoyance of walking in the woods, I'll be able to go on long enough that we'll get to see the view and sleep at the second shelter, and then Caleb won't have to hike the same section of the trail twice because he has to walk me back to my car.

But truth be told, my body is not meant to hike in the woods.

"We're almost there," Caleb says behind me when I let out an exasperated huff.

"Don't say that unless you mean it," I say with a groan.

"We passed a sign that said a half mile a while ago. We should be there any minute."

I barely hear what Caleb's saying before I see the shelter. There's a break in the trees off in the distance and what looks like a few small log cabins. I start running, absolutely joyful over seeing something that somewhat resembles civilization.

When I officially reach the shelter, I have to stop, because my eyes settle in on the cabins, which aren't actually cabins at all. Cabins have four walls; these buildings have three walls, leaving one side exposed to nature. There's nothing inside the building. It's just a shelter from wind and rain.

"Is this it?" I say, trying to take it all in. This can't be it. There has to be an actual building with four walls somewhere else. How is everyone supposed to sleep in something that doesn't have four walls?

"This is the place!" Caleb says, coming up from behind me. "What do you think? Do you want to have lunch? You can pick out a spot in the shelter if you want." He starts walking toward one of the buildings.

"We're supposed to sleep in that?" I ask, following behind Caleb.

"Either that or we can sleep in my tent. It should be just big enough for the two of us."

I step into the shelter. The logs used for the walls are massive, and I'm sure for someone who sleeps in a tent, this place would seem immaculate, but for someone who's missing an apartment with a full-size mattress? I want to run.

"What about animals? Can't they get into the shelter at night?"

"There's usually a bear box at shelters where you can put your food. Either that or we can hang our food bag in a tree so bears can't get it. I've heard some people have issues with mice in some shelters, but I've never seen them."

My stomach drops. No guy is worth this.

"How much farther until the view?" I ask, desperate for some bit of hope to cling to.

"I think if we keep going, we'll get to the first peak in about a half mile, but the best views are much farther along."

In my head, there's a long string of swearing.

"Okay, let's go," I say, gripping the shoulder pads of my backpack. I turn to keep moving, then pause when I realize I have no idea which direction the trail goes.

"You sure? The hike gets harder the farther we go." Caleb stares at me, looking me over.

The truth is, I don't know if I can handle whatever lies ahead, but right now, I'm way too high-strung to relax enough to sleep here tonight.

"Yeah, I'm fine." The words come out in a rush.

"Okay, well, let's eat lunch first," Caleb says, eyeing me like he doesn't trust my words. He drops his pack onto the ground, opening it and taking out a few things. He sits on a rock in front of one of the shelters and motions for me to sit next to him.

I sit, but the nerves in my stomach make me too nauseous to even think about eating.

Caleb begins to prepare a sandwich, but instead of bread, it's a tortilla wrap. He smears on peanut butter and jelly, then sprinkles on chocolate chips. He rolls it up and hands it to me.

I take it, playing with the wrap in my hand, spinning it around rather than eating it.

"I know it may not be nutrient dense, but you'll need the calories if you want to keep going." He says the words lightly, but I don't look up. "You okay?"

I let out a nervous laugh. "I'm very much out of my element," I admit, and that's when a tear comes down my face. I wipe it away before Caleb can notice.

"We can head back if you want. I can bring you back to your car, and you can go home and sleep in your own bed tonight. Or if you're too tired, I can pay for a hotel room for you or something."

I shake my head, trying to smile. "It's fine. It's just . . ." I try to think of the words. "I miss my bed already."

He wraps his arm around me, pulling me to his side. I feel myself release, like I've been building tension inside my body all day, getting tighter and tighter, until all at once, it's released like a spring. I let out a shaky breath, but I don't dare cry.

Caleb kisses the top of my head again, and this time I don't worry about what I smell like or how sweaty either of us are. I lean into his body, taking the one small piece of comfort I have left.

We eat in silence, but Caleb never lets his arm drop from around me.

"You know, when I first started hiking the Appalachian Trail, I cried like a baby," he says, breaking the silence.

"I doubt that," I say, taking a bite of the tortilla wrap he made me.

"Oh, trust me, it wasn't pretty. The first few weeks on trail are rough. I mean, the first few days were fun, but then it hit me that I'd be living in the woods for the next couple months. I realized I had no idea when I'd sleep in my actual bed again and that it was just going to be me and the trees for a long time."

I try to picture it, Caleb buckling under the pressure of it all, but I can't.

"I think that's the hardest part of being a thru-hiker. It's not the physical part; it's all mental. Physically, I know hiking from Georgia to Maine is hard, but it's possible whether you're hiking twenty miles a day or five. Anyone can do it if they want. What sends hikers home is the mental part. Even when you hike with a group, you're still spending a lot of time by yourself. I spend hours every day alone with my thoughts. Even when I spend all day talking to someone, at the end of the night, I'm in my tent alone, usually without cell reception. It gives you a lot of time to think. To get to know yourself. And you have to ask: Do I like myself? Do I like the person I've become? And if the answer is no, you spend the entire time on trail becoming that person you dream of being."

I pull away just enough to look at Caleb. "Do you like yourself?" I ask.

"I've got some room for improvement."

"Well, just so you know, I like you," I say.

He smiles gently at first, but then the smiles grows, and he shakes his head, breaking our gaze. "You're one of a kind."

He gets up from the rock and packs our food back into his bag. I help put things away and put my own backpack on, trying to focus on Caleb instead of the hike ahead.

"Ready to go?" he asks, heading back in the direction we came from.

"Is that how we get to the first mountain?" I ask.

"Yes, but that will be more than four miles. I thought you'd want to go back to your car. I meant it. We can turn around, and I'll get you a hotel room or something."

It's tempting—to let Caleb lead me back toward what feels

the most comfortable—but I bite back my fear, clutching the straps of the backpack.

"You can't give me a big speech about how hiking is all a mental battle and then try to make me give in."

He smiles and shakes his head. "You're not hiking the AT. This was just supposed to be a fun trip."

I take a deep breath, urging myself to be brave. "So, let's go have fun."

CHAPTER 16

apparently, everything we hiked before was the flat part of the trail. It didn't feel flat at the time because I was constantly stepping over roots and rocks, but the farther we go, the more I realize how much worse it can get.

It takes no time at all for the trail to change drastically. As soon as we leave the shelter, the trail goes from somewhat annoying to walk on to absolutely miserable. The trail turns into boulder-like steps, and I struggle to lift each leg high enough to pull myself upward and farther along. If I thought hiking was just a leg workout before, I was very wrong. I find myself reaching my arms out, gripping rocks to help pull myself up and over boulders.

"Is it supposed to suck this much?" I say, stopping long enough to catch my breath.

The only consolation is that Caleb seems to be as sweaty and out of breath as I am now. In fact, he lags behind a bit, but that's probably because he's carrying a lot more weight on his back.

"Growth happens when you're uncomfortable," Caleb mutters.

"I liked those motivational quotes a lot more when I was reading them from the comfort of my couch," I say, hoisting myself up another steep section. I can hear Caleb's laughter behind me.

For the entire morning we've been hiking together, we've been able to keep up conversation, exchanging stories to make time go by faster, but the steeper the trail gets, the quieter we get. Finally, when it feels like the trail will never stop going up, a break in the trees opens up, and it's enough to push me forward.

"I think I found it!" I shout, running ahead, surprising myself with my own speed.

I've gone hiking with Marly a handful of times, so I'm no stranger to the incredible views you can get at the top of a mountain, but it doesn't lessen the impact when I reach the summit. I have no idea what mountain I'm even on, but between gasps of air, I find myself in total awe.

It feels a lot like New Hampshire in many ways, the way mountains unfold around us in all directions. The trees are a bright green, coating every surface. What looks like a massive mountain is directly in front of us, a tall triangle along the horizon.

The mountains open up like a rolling ocean of greenery, making it hard to believe I simply walked here. The land is untouched and undisturbed.

Caleb catches up to me, coming to stand beside me. "Welcome to your first summit of the AT." He takes in the view, spinning to see the mountains sprawling out in every direction. He takes his phone out, and I look over his shoulder to see a map pulled up on the screen. "You see that?" He points to a spot on the map.

"Mount Bigelow?" I read the tiny print.

"That . . ." He pauses, pointing to the massive mountain in front of us. "Is that."

My stomach drops out from under me. The mountain looks too far away and steep for us to be able to reach it today.

"We hike to the top of that?" I ask, unable to look away from the summit.

"Yup! We're keeping up a pretty good pace too."

I'm still staring at the peak, wondering how in the world I got myself here today. Me, of all people, wandering around the woods of Maine.

"Do you want to take a break or keep going?" Caleb asks. He pauses to take a few photos on his phone before tucking it back into the hip pocket on his backpack.

"We can keep going," I say, terrified that if I stop too long, I'll chicken out and turn around. Worst of all, we've gone too far to turn around. I've gotten myself in this deep. Might as well torture myself all the way.

I let Caleb lead the way, guiding us back down and into the trees. Once the views are gone and we're back in the dense forest, it becomes easier to breathe again, like I can ignore the impending doom that lies ahead.

The trail continues to slope downward. I take careful steps down the mountain, knowing that for every step down, I'll need to take at least two more steps up to reach the summit of Mount

Bigelow. It feels silly that we have to hike down in order to hike up the massive peak—a waste of energy.

"Most people I run into at this point are hikers I've already met. Except for SOBOs," Caleb says. He's been doing most of the talking, and I welcome the distraction. His voice is the only hope I cling to as we walk forward.

"What's SOBO?" I ask.

"Southbound. It's hikers who hike from Maine to Georgia. NOBO is northbound, Georgia to Maine."

"Does it matter?" My foot catches on a stump, and Caleb turns, putting his hand out to catch me before I'm able to balance myself.

"You okay?" he says, pausing.

"Mm-hmm," I mumble, but I have to take a deep breath to reorient myself.

Once he sees I'm okay, he continues. "It's all about what you're looking to get out of the hike. Most people are northbound because you finish at the summit of Mount Katahdin in Maine. It can feel more symbolic that way. Plus there's a sign that's become iconic over the years for photos when you finish."

I keep walking, ignoring the pain in my feet as we go. I thought going downhill would be easier, but it makes my knees hurt in a way I haven't experienced before. I somehow have to work harder going downhill, all my weight landing on my feet and knees.

Caleb keeps talking until the downhill turns flatter and easier to walk across. The next portion of trail goes on forever, so even though it's not as steep as some other parts of the trail we've done today, we're not getting anywhere fast.

"So, what's waiting for you when you get home?" Caleb asks, his feet effortlessly avoiding the rocks and roots that I've been struggling to dodge.

"A nice hot shower," I say, scared to take my eyes off the ground in case I trip again.

Caleb laughs gently. "I meant in life. I know you're busy, so what work is waiting for you when you get home?"

"Homework, I guess. I'm doing two summer classes to try and get ahead so I can graduate early."

He lets out a soft chuckle. "I'm not surprised."

"I'm a girl on a mission."

"What are you majoring in that has to do with yoga?"

"It doesn't," I say. "I'm a business major."

Caleb glances over his shoulder to give me a smirk. "Business, huh?"

"What?"

"Isn't a business degree the degree people get when they aren't sure what else to major in?"

"Or you want to start a business," I say.

"That sounds a little closer to what I'd imagine for someone like you."

"Someone like me?"

"Yeah, someone who has their life together." He turns to face me as he talks, taking steps backward as he walks. "As opposed to someone like me, who decided to try living in the woods for a couple months because my life isn't together."

I watch as he walks backward, astounded by how he's

somehow able to continue without tripping.

He gives me a flirtatious grin before turning to walk forward.

The banter stops when the trail gets steep again. We go from a brisk walk in the woods to a challenging climb.

If I thought summiting the first peak of the day was hard, I obviously had no idea what lay ahead. I try giving myself small pep talks in my head to keep my motivation up, but I keep getting caught on one tiny detail: this doesn't end today. I'm not just out for a leisurely stroll and then I'll be able go home and shower. I'm sleeping out here tonight.

I slow down. The backpack gets heavier with each step, and the trail only gets steeper the farther we go. I keep telling myself, *This is it, the trail can't go up any higher.* But then we turn a corner, and it continues.

Caleb slows down so he doesn't lose me, and he begins to talk again, perhaps trying to keep my mood up. I don't hear what he's saying; I'm just thankful to hear a voice to reach out to.

"You're doing good," Caleb says after the rockiest section of the trail yet. When I catch up to him, he only pauses briefly before continuing forward.

"I need a break," I say, bending forward to rest my hands on my knees. The backpack shifts with me, making me almost lose my balance and fall forward. I catch myself and stand straight again, trying to breathe.

Every muscle from the waist down hurts. My calves are overworked and desperately need to be stretched out, and my thighs feel like they've been beaten to a pulp.

"You're doing great, Lori." Caleb's voice is gentle next to

me. He reaches his hand out, resting it on my shoulder.

"How much farther?" I ask, trying to ignore how hard and loud my heart is beating.

"Just a little more to get to the top, I think."

I close my eyes, focusing on my breath. When my heart has calmed down to a reasonable pace, I power forward, because now I know it's too late to turn back. It will be just as painful to turn around as it will be to move forward.

I pass Caleb, and he lets me lead the way. I propel myself forward, trying to ignore the ache in my feet and legs.

I'm not sure how much longer it takes, but eventually the trees clear away again, revealing the view stretching above the tree line.

Though we're not at the top yet, I find myself moving forward easier, keeping my focus trained ahead. It's easier to walk above tree line as well. With no trees, there are no roots, which means one less thing for me to trip over.

Finally, the trail comes to a peak. With a final huff of air, I come to a stop.

"Please tell me this is it," I say, tossing my bag off my back, no longer caring enough to have confirmation.

I'm done. This is as far as I'll go.

When I look back to Caleb, he's lagging behind, his eyes scanning the horizon. His phone is out again as he takes pictures of the views. He points the phone at me.

"Smile!" he says.

I try my best to smile, but the instant the phone is put away, I go back to what feels like a deep frown. I find a nearby rock that's too small to be considered a chair, but I sit on it, happy to have the weight taken off my feet. If we were back at my car, I'd kick my shoes off, desperate to be free. But I'm afraid if the shoes come off, it will be that much more painful to get them back on.

When I finally look up, I see the expanse of mountains for the first time. The view is similar to the last viewpoint, but somehow better—bigger. It looks like the trees and mountains go on forever. The vast openness of it all puts an extra feeling of freedom in my chest that revives me a little.

"You practically ran up here," Caleb says, coming to join me. He takes his backpack off, tossing it to the ground next to me. He leans down to kiss the top of my head, and for a moment I savor how natural the motion feels. He moves to sit next to me, and again, I gravitate towards him, even while exhausted.

"I needed to get it over with," I say, laughing in what feels like borderline hysteria.

"A woman with goals. I like it." He puts his hands behind him, leaning back and stretching his feet out in front of him.

"So, how much farther until we get to the next shelter?" I ask, looking around as if the shelter will be around any corner, but of course, it isn't. Above tree line, it's just us and the clear blue sky.

Caleb reaches into his pocket and pulls his phone out again, checking the map on his screen. "We've gone about four and a half miles, so there's about eight miles left."

My heart sinks. I suppose I should've known we still have a ways to go, but I thought we were at least halfway there. Instead, we're only a third of the way through the hike, and my body already feels like it's had every ounce of energy drained from it.

Caleb pulls his food back out, handing me M&M's and a granola bar. On a normal day, I'd probably say no to the candy, but today I take it eagerly, hoping it will spark even a tiny bit of energy.

The longer we sit at the top of the mountain, the more unsettled I start to get, anxiety coating me, layer after layer, only getting worse. I try to imagine putting the backpack on and doing everything I've already done, but two more times.

"Do you want anything else to eat?" Caleb says.

I hear the words, but I feel myself going in a downward spiral.

"Lori?"

I blink, and tears start to surface. My bottom lip quivers, and when I can't hold it back anymore, I get more upset, embarrassment only growing stronger.

"I don't think I can do this," I finally manage to say.

CHAPTER 17

Caleb is holding on to me, and I'm sobbing into his chest. The summer air is hot and humid, making crying feel like my entire body is on fire and overheating. At first, the only thing I'm conscious of is how uneven my breath is, but as I start to calm down, my focus shifts. My hands and face are cradled against Caleb's chest, his arms wrapped tightly around my torso. My breath is hot, and my face is covered in sweat, and when I finally pull away, all I can think about is how much I want to disappear and never have to show my face to Caleb again.

"Here," Caleb says, loosening his grip to hand me a bottle of water.

When I pull back, I realize I'm practically sitting in his lap. I push myself farther away, almost to where I was sitting before, but I stay close enough that Caleb keeps one hand on my back.

I take a few sips, feeling absolutely ridiculous, especially when I look around and see that a few other hikers have reached the summit as well. They stand a couple feet back, giving us our space, but their gazes linger, either out of curiosity or worry.

"What's wrong?" Caleb says so quietly I almost don't hear him.

"I don't think I'm made for the outdoors," I say, trying to laugh, but it ends with me making a quiet whimpering sound.

"Then why'd you want to keep going? We could have stayed at the shelter."

"I wanted to see the view?" It comes out as a question, and Caleb doesn't buy it for a second. I let out a huff of air before admitting the truth. "If we'd stayed at that shelter, you would've had to walk me back to my car."

"So?" he asks, not understanding.

"Then the next day you would've had to re-hike what we'd already hiked."

"Lori, I don't care about that. I'm just happy to be able to see you again. You don't have to do something you hate just because you think it will make me like you. That was already a done deal." He rubs his hand up and down my back.

I smile, leaning into him. "I don't hate hiking."

He gives me a sarcastic smirk. "I'm sorry, was what you were doing a couple minutes ago something you do every time you're happy? Because then I must have gotten my signals crossed."

I hide my face in my hands, laughing while still on the verge of tears.

"When am I going to see you again after this?" I ask. I clearly got desperate if I'm willing to subject myself to backpacking.

"I don't know." He shrugs, hand still rubbing calming circles. "But I'm willing to make it work." He brushes my cheek, tucking hair behind my ear that had started to cling to my face after crying.

It strikes me how odd this situation is. I've always been the type of girl to prepare to go out on dates by doing my hair and makeup. Yet here I am, barefaced, hair in a braid, and probably the smelliest I've been all year. And I'm somehow more comfortable around a guy than I've ever been.

When I met Caleb, I went out with him on a whim, knowing — well, assuming — it wouldn't go anywhere. Now look at the mess I've gotten myself into.

"Caleb," I say, shaking my head. I'm about to say more, but Caleb stops me.

"Can you just live with me in this moment?" he asks, voice soft. "We don't know when we'll see each other next, so let's enjoy today."

"I can't exactly say I'm enjoying today," I admit with a pitiful laugh.

He looks at his phone again and then pauses for a long time before saying anything. "We've got a couple options."

I sit up, hoping one of them might be to call a helicopter to come pick me up and fly me home.

"We've done most of the hard work. The rest of the hike is mostly easy after this."

"Mostly?" I ask.

He shrugs. "Or we can turn around and head back to the shelter we ate lunch at. If we get to the shelter and you want to stay, then we'll set up camp for the night. If you don't want to stay, we'll both head back to your car and see if we can get a hotel room or something so you can sleep before driving home."

I frown, not liking either of the options.

"Is there an option where I can be done walking for the day?"

"I'm afraid not."

I lean forward, resting my head on his chest. He wraps his arms around my body, rubbing his hand up and down my back again.

"Are you okay?" he says in a low voice.

"Just having a pity party for myself," I say.

He laughs gently, wrapping his arms tighter around me. We stay like that for a long time, and I let myself pretend this is option three: stay in Caleb's arms until he carries me down the mountain.

§

As much as I dream of Caleb whisking me off my feet and down the mountain, that isn't an option. Eventually, it's time to decide, and I opt for the decision that gives me the option to sleep in a real bed. I don't want to chicken out and walk back to the car, but I need it to be a possibility in the event I have a mental breakdown.

We make our way back to the first shelter, my backpack heavier than ever. I can't say I'm mad we hiked all the way to the top of the mountain, because it was a great view when I wasn't busy crying.

"Hold on," Caleb says. We're at the first viewpoint we started at today. I was about to hike up and over it without much thought, but Caleb pauses. "That's where we just were."

He points to Mount Bigelow. It's crazy to think a couple hours ago I was standing in this same spot staring at Mount Bigelow, trying to wrap my head around how in the world we were supposed to get to the summit when it was so far away. And here we stand again, except this time we've already been there.

"It's weird to look at how far away it is and know we were just there," I say, looking at the mountain but also watching the look of awe on Caleb's face.

"Seeing the progress is my favorite part. I love looking back and being able to say I was just standing on that summit."

We get back to the shelter sooner than I realize, and there are already plenty of people there, settling into the shelter for the night. When we walk into the small clearing, everyone waves like we're longtime friends, which I suppose might be true for Caleb.

About a dozen people are already here. Some have their sleeping pads set up already, while others have opted to set up their tents in the clearings next to the shelters.

"Hey, Chip! You're going the wrong way!" an older man shouts from a log he's sitting on. He has a long white beard and is wearing a Captain America T-shirt, which makes him stand out a little more from the other hikers.

"I was showing her the trail." He takes my hand as he talks, walking me through the area.

"Who's that?" I say.

"Captain," Caleb says, and I realize I may never get used

to the different trail names everyone has, but at least this one makes sense—he must wear the Captain America T-shirt all the time. "So, do you want to go back to your car?"

I still haven't decided if I want to sleep in the shelter tonight or not. Part of me wants to try, mostly because I know it'll make Caleb happy, but selfishly, I crave the safety of four walls.

I glance at one of the shelter buildings. It's comforting with more people—safer, perhaps. But it's still a building with three walls, not to mention that none of those three walls act as a barrier between people. If we sleep in the shelter tonight, I'll be sleeping on the floor next to someone I've never met before.

On the other hand, walking back to the car would feel like a huge failure. I know Caleb wants me to be happy, but somehow each choice is a lose-lose situation.

"Is it hard to sleep in the shelters?"

He shrugs. "Depends if the people in the shelter snore."

I frown, and Caleb grips my hand tighter.

"Come on, we'll take you back to the car." He begins to pull me forward, but I stay in place.

"No," I say, my eyes still lingering on the shelter.

"I don't mind. I'm not going to make you sleep here if you're not comfortable."

"That's very sweet, and I appreciate it very much, but if I give up now, I'm going to think about this for days on end and be mad at myself for saying I was going to go backpacking and then chickening out."

His eyebrows scrunch up in confusion. "Really?"

"When I say I'm going to do something, I do it." My voice is firm, but I keep glancing back at the shelter, apprehensive.

"It will really bother you if you don't sleep out here?"

I nod.

"More than actually sleeping out here?"

I frown, unsure.

He shakes his head, laughing a little. "You are full of surprises." He glances around. "Would a tent be better?"

Logically, it's probably no safer than the shelter since its walls are made of ridiculously thin fabric, but it gives the illusion of four walls, so that's something.

"Would we sleep in the tent together?" I ask, entertaining the idea.

"Would you rather sleep alone?"

"No," I say so quickly I surprise myself.

He grins, seeming all too amused by my preference that we sleep in the same tent. "Let's go set up the tent, then."

CHAPTER 18

I was going to help Caleb put the tent up, but as soon as he starts to unfurl it from the bag, I realize I've never set up a tent in my life.

We end up picking a spot close to the shelters, which also happens to be next to the designated cooking area, which I didn't know was a thing. All I know is that it seems to be closer to other people, and that feels like the safest bet in terms of location.

"That didn't take long," I say, standing next to the entrance of the tent. It's smaller than I expected. Standing next to it, it comes up to my waist, and width-wise, it looks like it might be just barely big enough for two people.

"When you set up the same tent for four months, it starts to become second nature."

He unzips the entrance and lets me peek in. Inside, it looks even smaller.

"This is for two people?" I ask.

"It might be a little tight, but it should be fine." He reaches into his bag again and pulls something else out, which he begins to unfurl. "You want to get your sleeping pad set up?" he says, blowing into his sleeping pad to inflate it.

I dig through my bag for the sleeping pad I packed and blow mine up as well. By the time I finish, Caleb's is already set up in the tent. He takes the sleeping pad from me and slides it into the tent.

I stand over his shoulder, looking into the small space.

"See? We'll be able to fit, no problem."

The pads are squeezed in, their edges overlapping and pressed to the walls of the tent.

Cuddling it is, then.

"Can I sleep on this side?" I ask, my eye on his sleeping pad when he leans away to grab something else from his backpack.

"Sure, why?" He pulls yet another bag from his backpack, and this time it's his rolled-up sleeping bag.

"So I'm closer to the shelter." I shrug. "Less likely to be mauled by a bear that way."

He grins, laughing quietly to himself as he rolls his sleeping bag out in the other spot.

"Whatever will make you more comfortable."

I want to crack a joke that just about anything would be more comfortable than this, but I'm afraid if I say anything, Caleb will insist on leaving. I've gotten this far. There's no sense in backing out now.

I grab my sleeping bag, rolling it out next to Caleb's. They overlap even more than the sleeping pads, but I try to think of it as a good thing. Worst-case scenario, we get to cuddle tonight.

I cringe inwardly. There are about a million other ways I

imagine cuddling to go for the first time, and they do not involve being sweaty and tired in the middle of a forest.

"Come on. I want you to meet everyone." Caleb takes my hand, guiding me back toward the shelter, where more and more hikers are starting to gather.

The shelters have come alive with people. Some hikers lounge, while others busy themselves preparing food or sorting through gear. Clothes are hanging everywhere—whether left out to dry or air out from smelling, I have no idea. The shelters themselves have hooks where people hang their bags, but a few are still scattered across the ground, their contents spilling out all over the place.

"You staying here tonight?" Captain says.

"Yeah, we've got a tent site set up." Caleb gestures behind us, where the tent is, before turning to me. "Lori, this is Captain. Captain, this is Lori."

"She doesn't have a trail name yet?" Captain comments.

"Not yet." Caleb grins.

"We'll have to figure that out, then."

The two of them launch into conversation, catching each other up on what they've seen the past couple days. Caleb is kind enough not to include my mental breakdown in his review of events.

Caleb starts talking to other hikers, introducing me to everyone as we go. I meet a girl my age who goes by the name Brown Nose, a man a little older than me named Lucky Charms, and a married couple who go by Thing One and Thing Two. The names get passed around so much, I have a hard time keeping track of who is who, especially as Caleb introduces me to more people.

"You hungry?" he says when there's a lull in conversation.

I nod, and we make our way back to our tent to grab food. Caleb picks up an armload of things before starting to walk away.

"Where are we going?" I ask, following close behind.

"The cooking area."

We walk a little ways from our tent to another cleared-out spot where there are makeshift benches and large metal boxes.

"So, before we go to bed tonight, we have to put our food in the bear box so it'll be safe. And we cook over here so the scent of food isn't close to the tent."

I glance back to where we came from, and our tent is still in full view. "The tent's still close though."

Caleb shrugs. "It'll be fine."

He puts everything down and starts assembling some sort of tiny stove, unbothered by the proximity. I glance from the bear box back to our tent, painfully aware of how small the distance is.

Caleb puts ramen noodles in a tiny pot before filling it with water and turning the stove on to boil.

"Ramen for dinner?" I ask.

"We're out of pizza," he says so casually that at first I don't realize he's joking.

As the minutes go by, more hikers join us in the cooking area, boiling their own water to heat up meals and make dinner for the night. Conversations fill the air around me, almost all of them about hiking, making my head spin.

Caleb hands me a bowl of ramen, but he has to tap me on the shoulder a few times before he's able to catch my attention.

"Sorry," I say, taking the bowl from him.

"You okay?" he asks, beginning to boil water again, this time to heat up his meal.

I stir the noodles around, surprised by how amazing it smells. I didn't see him add anything extra to the ramen, so maybe I'm just that hungry.

"Just a little overwhelmed," I say.

When we finish eating, Caleb takes my hand again, guiding me away from the tent and down a portion of the trail we haven't been to before.

"Where are we going?" I ask, my legs protesting at having to go any farther.

"I want to make sure you know where the bathroom is."

I perk up hearing the word *bathroom*, but then I realize I've gone all day without needing to go once. Am I that dehydrated?

Eventually, we come across two outhouse-looking structures, both painted a bright green. Any other day of my life, I probably would have seen the outhouses and gagged, but having a private place to go to the bathroom seems like a blessing at this point.

"These are the privies. They're basically glorified outhouses, but they also work as composting toilets. Inside is a bucket of wood chips. After you go, put a handful in, and you'll be all set."

I blink a couple times before the words settle correctly.

"Wood chips?" I ask.

"You'll see what I mean when you get in there," he says, ushering me forward.

I take a couple steps toward the privy, realizing any sense of mystery in our relationship is officially gone.

When I open the door to step inside, the smell that welcomes me is assaulting. I almost take in a breath and turn around until I remember my only other option is squatting in the woods with my bare butt on full display.

I hold my breath while I go, trying to make my trip inside as quick as possible. When I finish, I notice the bucket Caleb mentioned and grab a big handful before tossing it into the hole, not daring to look too close at where everything is going.

When I open the door and take a step back outside, I immediately take a deep breath of fresh air, walking away from the smell. Caleb smirks at me when he sees my face.

"Not a fan?" he asks.

"Better than the bush, I guess," I mumble, walking back in the direction we came from. Caleb trails behind me, sticking close by, and as he laughs quietly.

We come to a fork in the trail, and I start to go right, back to the tent, but Caleb grabs my arm and leads me in the other direction.

"Let's go this way," he says.

"I'm not really up for more walking," I say.

"I just want to show you something."

I let him lead me away, down a path I don't think we've taken before. The trees thin out until water opens up in front of us.

The small pond is concealed on all sides by trees. Since the water is calm, the trees reflect back on the surface, a perfect mirror. Caleb takes my hand, guiding me to the edge of the water to sit on a rock big enough for the two of us. When I bend my knees to sit, they scream in protest, sore from a long day of hiking.

The rock is an odd shape, making it difficult to sit evenly, but it feels good to have the weight off my feet.

"I thought you'd want to enjoy the last of the views for the day," Caleb says, opening his arms wide to the pond. The sky above the water is starting to turn gold and pink as the sun sets, and the water reflects the beautiful colors.

I'm too tired to come up with a response, so I lean into Caleb's side, resting my head on his shoulder. Caleb wraps his arm around me, the movement feeling all too natural for how long we've known each other, though at this point we've spent enough hours together for it to count for at least five dates. Guess I've got a new personal record.

I can't help but laugh at myself.

"What?" Caleb says, his voice low in my ear.

I shake my head, watching as the pink-and-orange clouds reflect on the pond's smooth surface.

"I normally don't go out on second dates, never mind a date that involves me sleeping in the woods."

He lets out a laugh. "So, you're saying you're not the outdoorsy type?"

I lift my head so I can look at him. "If only you knew."

And then, because our faces are so close, I kiss him. I'm not sure if either of us expected the kiss, but we both welcome it, our bodies leaning into each other. When I pull away, Caleb's grinning. I lean my head back down on his shoulder, shocked by my own boldness. I guess after spending the day being nothing but physically uncomfortable, being with Caleb is the easiest option.

"I'm not really much of an outdoorsy person either." He says the words so casually I assume he's being sarcastic.

"Says the guy who decided to hike the Appalachian Trail. Why live in a house when you can sleep in a tent for nine months?"

"When you're kicked out of the house, tents start looking pretty good."

I pick my head up, facing him. "What?"

He shrugs, looking out toward the pond. "My parents kicked me out of the house. I had a friend who hiked the AT two years ago, so he was joking around, telling me to go hike it so I could 'find myself,' " he says, putting quotations in the air.

"Your parents kicked you out?"

He shrugs off my concern. "We got in a huge argument about college. They said I needed to go to college, I said I didn't. They made me enroll in college anyway, and then I flunked out."

My mouth is hanging open, utter surprise etched on my face. I've been around Caleb so long, it's like this Caleb—hiking Caleb—is everything he is. He's a cute, charming guy who lives in the woods. I knew there was more to his life before the trail, but I never would've guessed he flunked out of college. It's like I was living in a vortex of time. This is Caleb now, the only Caleb I may ever know. But there's a Caleb from before the trail, and he suddenly looks like an incredibly different person.

"How'd you flunk out?" I'm not a perfect A student by any means. I pile on so much work, most days it feels like I'm just trying to survive, but I've never flunked a class.

A pit forms in my stomach as I realize the Caleb I think I know isn't the person he really is. What else is there about him?

"I'm just not good at that sort of thing." He shrugs. "I'm more of a hands-on person. I'd rather work on something than sit and write a paper about it."

"I guess, but sometimes you have to learn the theory behind something before you can do it."

Caleb turns to face me, sarcastic eyebrow raised. "You want me to write a paper before I change the oil in your car? Or should I write a paper about the theory behind building a house?"

"Blueprints are kind of like writing a paper," I say.

"Yeah, well, let me know what classes will accept blueprints instead of essays." He turns away again, watching the water.

"I'm sure if you go to college for architecture, you'd be able to work on blueprints."

He shakes his head, laughing quietly. "Not the point."

My face drops. Silence hangs between us, clear and uncomfortable.

I've spent my entire life getting to where I am now: enrolled in college and trying to start my career. It's impossible to imagine it any other way.

"What are you going to do when you get home?" I ask.

Caleb lets out a long sigh. "I don't know. I was hoping some time alone with my thoughts would give me some answers."

"And has it?"

He turns to look at me. "Just good company so far."

I smile, but I'm more deflated than I was before we started this conversation.

"Do you think you'll give college a second shot?" I ask.

My words garner another deep sigh from Caleb. "No. I'm just not that type of person."

"What about just going back part-time?" I try.

He turns to me again, his brow furrowed. "Why?"

"Because you need to go to college to get a good job."

The look of confusion on his face grows deeper. "No, you don't."

"Yes, you do," I say, words firm.

"You're in college now, right?" he asks, his voice challenging.

"Yes."

"What do you plan on doing when you graduate?"

"Opening my own yoga studio," I say, the words coming out automatically.

"And what do you need the college degree for? You'll own your own business."

"I'm taking business classes."

"Classes don't teach you anything about owning a business. Owning a business will teach you about owning a business."

I go flush with a mix of embarrassment and anger, but I don't say anything, because part of me agrees with him. I let the subject drop, pushing away the doubts I've been having over my own career choices.

The colors start to fade from the sky above us, the trees circling the pond growing darker.

"Should we head to bed?" I ask, my gaze darting around the forest as I wonder what animals might come out tonight. I blink, instantly regretting the thoughts. Why in the world am I sleeping in a tent tonight?

"No, we've got a little time left." He moves to pull something out of his pocket. "I brought a headlamp to get us back to camp."

I stare at the light in his hand, trying to imagine walking through the forest with nothing more than a tiny light as our guide.

I want to ask that we go back to camp now, but even the idea of walking back to the tent is unbearable.

I let out a nervous breath, telling myself not to panic and focus on Caleb rather than everything around us.

"You said you don't like hiking?" I ask, because that at least seems like a very familiar feeling right now.

"It's not that I don't like it so much as it's a lot of alone time. Arguably too much alone time."

"What do you mean?"

"I have a lot more time to think, which was the point of coming out here. I wanted to figure out what to do with myself when I get home, but sometimes you start thinking too much. You don't like the thoughts you're having, and instead of ignoring them and getting distracted by the hustle and bustle of life, you have to deal with it. Out here, there's nothing to do but deal with your thoughts."

The air between us is suddenly serious, the sky growing ever darker.

"Like what?"

"Like what's the point of trying to figure out what I want to do for the rest of my life? Why am I supposed to decide now when things could change? What if I spend five, ten, or twenty years building a career that I hate? And for what, to work forty hours a week doing a job I can't stand until I retire?"

"Don't you think you're a little young to be having a midlife crisis?" I laugh lightly, eager to pull away from the seriousness of the conversation, because I've had similar thoughts; I'm terrified I'm wasting time on a career that may go nowhere. I've built a plan on how I think my life will go, but what if I can't even accomplish the first step? Then what?

He laughs gently. "Like I said, too much time left with my own thoughts. I start wondering what the point of all this is." He brushes his hands forward, gesturing outward to nothing in particular.

"I think the point of it all is to have fun."

He looks at me with a gentle smile. "Are you having fun?" His tone is too serious.

I think back to my life at home, how I've been working nonstop at a job I know isn't fun, taking extra college classes despite feeling hopelessly behind, and trying to become a yoga instructor when I'm constantly treading water.

"Sleeping in a tent doesn't fit my typical mantra of fun," I say, joking.

He smiles and shifts until he's standing. He pulls the headlamp out of his pocket again and puts it around his forehead before offering a hand to help me up.

"Speaking of which." He smiles, but my eyes wander to the

woods at his back, which look darker than ever.

I take his hand, feeling like I'm about to walk into the worst part of the day.

CHAPTER 19

As an adult, I probably should have grown out of my scared-of-the-dark phase. But here I am, clutching Caleb's arm, hoping he doesn't notice how I refuse to allow an inch of space between us. He only brought one headlamp, so I'm hoping he's assuming I need to stick close to him for that reason. In reality, I'm clinging close because if I don't, I might break down into hysterics again.

Being scared of the dark has never been a problem, nor is it something I've had to admit. When I'm at home in my apartment, I have a small light in the corner of my room that stays on at all times. It sits on my dresser and slowly shifts colors—as aesthetically pleasing as it is functional. It also plays white noise, but that's more of a luxury than a necessity.

At home, I just like being able to see *something*. But out here in the woods? It's almost worse to be able to see into the trees with the light. I'm afraid Caleb will pan his light off to the left only to reveal a bear waiting to maul us.

"Do you want to take one last trip to the bathroom?" Caleb

asks when we approach the intersection that would lead us to the privy. As we walk, I can hear other people talking as they settle into their tents for the night. A few headlamps move around in the trees around us, reminding me that we're not alone.

"I'm good," I say, mostly because spending even one more second outside longer than necessary sounds like an awful idea.

We get closer to our tent, and the panic starts to set in again when I remember I'm supposed to sleep in this thing tonight.

"Home sweet home," Caleb says when we finally reach our tent. He kicks off his shoes and puts them under the thin tarp that covers the tent and protects it from the rain. "Put your shoes under the rainfly so they don't get covered by dew in the morning."

I kick off my shoes and move them beside Caleb's. The relief I feel as soon as the shoes are off is amazing, but I'm afraid to take my socks off as well in case my feet are nothing but blisters.

Our backpacks are still sitting outside the tent, but Caleb tucks them under the rainfly as well. He unzips the rest of the tent and then crawls in.

"You getting in?" he says, poking his head out.

"Do you want to get changed into pj's?" I say, feeling silly about the question, but I have zero plans of changing in front of him.

"I usually sleep naked, but today I was going to keep my clothes on."

I wait for the punch line until it hits me he isn't joking.

Caleb has his headlamp pointed at me, so I'm sure he can see how my face goes red.

"Okay, well, I brought pj's." I pull my bag out just enough to grab my clothes.

"Do you want to change out there or in here?" Caleb says, grinning over how embarrassed I am.

"In there," I say, not wanting to be left outside alone for any longer. "Preferably with you out here."

Caleb is still grinning as he gets back out of the tent and motions me inside. I crawl in, immediately aware of how tiny it feels even though it's only me in here. Caleb tosses me the headlamp.

"Turn around," I say, self-conscious of the thin walls of the tent. He shakes his head, laughing to himself, and turns away.

I zip the door closed and place the headlamp on the ground to light up the space. The first thing I try to do is pull my leggings off, which proves to be a nearly impossible task when I'm stuck lying on my back shimmying them off. Luckily, the night has cooled off a lot, so the fabric doesn't cling to me like it did before, but taking my pants off still feels like I'm peeling off a layer of skin.

I change as quickly as possible in the small space, my feet kicking the edges of the tent. Eventually, I'm able to get all my sweaty clothes off and put on clean comfy clothes for sleeping. The bandana falls off as I'm changing, and I put it to the side so I can wear it again in the morning. I leave my hair braided—it's the best I can do to maintain the mess I'll need to detangle in the morning.

"Okay, I'm done," I say, unzipping the tent door.

"I'm learning so much about you on this trip," Caleb says,

climbing in next to me. The space is crowded when he crawls in, making me question if the tent actually is made for two people.

He zips the door closed and lies down, already relaxing into his sleeping bag.

"Like what?" I ask, still sitting up and feeling unsettled.

"Well, like how you like to sleep in pj's on a backpacking trip."

"What else am I supposed to sleep in?"

He shrugs. "I don't know. But backpackers tend to not carry extra clothes."

"Well, good thing I'm not a backpacker," I say, moving to unzip the sleeping bag, which is looking less welcoming as time goes on. Beside me, Caleb shifts, this time taking his shirt off. "Whoa!" I shout, surprising myself with my volume.

"Don't worry, I'm not getting naked." He shrugs the shirt off and tosses it to his feet.

I try to keep my eyes anywhere besides his bare chest. But I keep catching glimpses of him, even out of the corner of my eye, and I can't help but let my imagination go wild.

"I just can't sleep with a shirt on. Too constricting."

He shimmies deeper into his sleeping bag, covering himself so I'm forced to snap back to attention. He turns to grab the headlamp, which is lying on top of my sleeping bag. I panic when I see him grab the light, and I reach out, my hand covering his.

"Wait," I say. The words come out rushed, a blush burns to the surface of my skin.

Caleb looks at me, eyes wide, waiting for me to say more.

"Can we keep it on a little longer?" I ask, trying to make the words sound casual.

He looks at me, eyebrows lifted. "Do you need anything before I turn the light off?"

I look around the tent quickly, trying to find an excuse for needing the light, but nothing comes to mind.

"I don't like the dark," I admit, hoping I can laugh it off as a joke even if it may be true.

Caleb lets out a small chuckle, then stops himself, his face serious again.

"Come on, lay down." He pats my sleeping bag, and I unzip it, peeling the top layer away until I can tuck my feet in. It's tight quarters as I shift and scoot myself into the bag, and I only feel clumsier as I move, trying not to lean too much toward Caleb. Finally, I lie down, shifting until I'm on my side. Marly told me to bring one of her dad's blow-up backpacking pillows, but it doesn't feel like nearly enough cushion for my head.

The sleeping pad helps soften the ground, but lying down now, it's clear just how uncomfortable this night will be. The ground is too hard, even with the padding, but at least I'm warm. In the past few hours, the heat from the day cooled off so much it was making me almost want to break a sweatshirt out. Thankfully, the sleeping bag provides plenty of warmth.

Caleb watches me as I settle into my spot, his hand on the light.

"I mean it," I whisper to Caleb, my eyes glued to the light—my last bit of comfort tonight.

"I'm just turning it to a lower setting," he says in a hushed tone. I hear a soft click from the headlamp, and the light remains on, but it's softer now.

"You sleep like this every night?" I ask, my hip pressing into the ground even with the sleeping pad fully blown up.

"When you walk far enough, even the ground feels comfortable."

I frown, adjusting myself, but I find no configuration where my body settles into place.

"Apparently, I didn't walk far enough," I mumble, shifting onto my side so I'm facing Caleb again. He smiles at me softly, only a couple of inches between our faces. From an outsider's point of view, this could qualify as a romantic moment. To remain sane, I try to imagine how tomorrow I might look back on this and think of how sweet sleeping in the tent was, but for right now, it's hard to think of romance when we both smell like we haven't showered in a couple days.

Caleb leans forward to unzip the covers for the mesh windows, allowing cool air to flow in and out of the tent. I'm tempted to ask him to close them again so I don't have to see the darkness outside, but I'm afraid of how hot and smelly it may get in here otherwise.

"So, if you're scared of the dark, what made you come on this backpacking trip? We don't typically walk around with night-lights."

"I'm not scared of the dark," I say, pulling the sleeping bag toward my chin.

"So, I can . . . ?" He holds the light up, but I snatch it out of his hand before he can turn it off.

He laughs as I clutch it close to my chest.

"I won't turn it off," he says.

"You're not allowed to make fun of me. You sleep out here every night. You're telling me you weren't even a little freaked-out the first couple nights?"

His face softens. "Not that I'll ever admit publicly."

I give him the light back, and he places it between us. We sit in silence, but I can hear soft murmurs from the other hikers as they settle in around us for the night. Leaves rustle occasionally, and my heart speeds up in response, thinking an animal is outside our tent.

I frown, my eyes on the light.

"What's wrong?" Caleb says quietly.

I don't respond at first, listening to the forest around us.

"It's so quiet," I say, hearing how still the air is. "When there's a sound outside, it feels so much louder."

Caleb reaches his hand out, brushing it over mine where it pokes out through the sleeping bag.

"Why don't you close your eyes and relax?"

"I don't want to fall asleep yet," I say. My body is still wired and full of energy—not because I have energy, but because I'm afraid at any moment I'm going to have to bolt out of this sleeping bag and make a run for it.

"Just relax. I'll keep talking to you."

I let out a sigh and close my eyes. His hand continues to rest on mine, and I try to focus on that.

"Talk about what?" I say, my eyes still closed.

"I don't know. What do you want to talk about?"

"I don't know." I try to relax into the sleeping pad. Keeping my eyes closed helps. It makes it easier to pretend we're just talking to each other when I don't want to think about where we are. "What's been your favorite part of the trail so far?"

His hand shifts away, and I almost open my eyes to see where he's gone, but then he comes closer, and his hand rests on the top of my arm. I want to open my eyes to look at him, but I'm afraid if I do, I'll break the moment.

"The people," he murmurs, running his hand up and down my arm like he's trying to coax my body into relaxing. "Everyone here has a different story to tell. We're all out here for a reason, you know? No one's here because it's fun—though it is some days. We're all here to challenge ourselves. We can all bond over that at the end of the day, no matter how different we are from one another outside trail life."

"But you said you started hiking so you could come up with a game plan for when you get home," I say.

"I wouldn't call it a plan. I've never been a planner, but I am a searcher, so I guess I'm searching for the next thing."

"And you think you'll find it out here?"

"I found you."

He says the words so gently that I open my eyes, as if that will confirm whether or not he means it, but the light is out. We're sitting in the darkness, but my eyes have adjusted enough to allow me to see Caleb's face, which is only a few inches from my own.

"You turned off the light," I say, trying to look to where it might have been, but Caleb has moved forward to take up the space where the light was resting.

"I did."

I lift my head a little, looking around. Through the mesh window of the tent, I can see trees in the forest, the moonlight shining on them just enough to create a dim outline. I lay my head back down, but my heart rate has taken off again.

"Lori, try to relax," he says gently.

How stupid to be afraid of the dark. In all the years of my life, I've accomplished so much, but sleeping in the pitch dark is not one of those things.

"Have I ever told you I'm not much of an outdoorsy person?" I say in a breathy, nervous voice.

"I've gotten the impression." He adjusts and pulls himself closer. "Come here." Caleb puts his arm out, and I move until there isn't any space between us besides our sleeping bags. I bury myself in the silky nylon fabric, hiding my face in his chest. One of his arms moves under my head, replacing my pillow, while the other reaches over my torso, pulling me to him.

I'm rigid next to him, but the contact allows my body to relax. He lifts his arm from my side and moves to brush hair out of my face. I urge my muscles to relax one by one.

"So, backpacking isn't a very good date idea, then?" he says softly.

My laugh is muffled against the sleeping bag. "Maybe if you met someone who doesn't mind sleeping on the ground."

"And somehow you're still here."

"Because I wanted to spend the day with you," I say, brave with my words in the darkness.

"We could have just gone hiking for the day. Or waited until I was a little farther along and needed another rest day." He runs his hand up and down my back in a soothing pattern.

"The farther north you get, the more I start to wonder if I'll ever see you again."

Caleb is quiet for a moment, his hand going still. "Do you want me to see you again?"

"Of course," I say, surprised by my own eagerness. "But I have a job and classes, and I need to continue my yoga certification so I can get a job at a studio. I have this plan, and . . ." I trail off, a little overwhelmed by it all.

"You're busy," Caleb says.

As overwhelming as today has been, one of the best parts has been not needing to focus on anything except the one task at hand. I've never gone this long without worrying and trying to plan out my life. Today I just got to live. I put one foot in front of the other until I couldn't walk any farther, and for some reason, I feel like I've accomplished more today than I have in weeks.

"I don't want to be this busy," I admit.

"What about taking something off your plate?"

I cringe just thinking of trying to give something up. It goes against my nature to let go of a task I've committed to. I've always been the person to take more things on, not stop when things start to get hard.

"I can't. I told a bunch of people I would cover their shifts so they could go on vacation. And then I have a summer class I'm trying to finish so I can graduate early. And then—"

"Wait, graduate early?" Caleb says.

"Yeah, I want to graduate in three years."

"Why?"

"Why not?" The question confuses me. College has always seemed like a necessary evil. It's the thing you do before you start your career, and I want to get to the career part already.

"So you can enjoy your life."

"I know, but I have this plan . . ." My voice trails off, and my mind starts to reel—not because of my plans, but because of the thing that made my plans go awry. The first year of college was hard, but I still can't pinpoint if it was because of losing two parental figures in my life, watching my best friend suffer, or trying to survive even the most minimal amount of college work while everything was slipping out of my grasp. "And things haven't been going well."

"Maybe just focus on the things you can look forward to."

"Like what?"

"What are your plans for summer?"

I'm a little confused by the question. "I told you. Summer classes. Lot of shifts working at Angela's, and if I'm lucky, I might start teaching yoga classes at a studio if I can get someone to hire me."

"No, I meant fun things, like going to the beach or going on a vacation."

"Nothing planned yet," I say, though I know that even if I wanted to, I don't have time to go on vacation. This backpacking trip is probably the closest I'll get—which is a depressing thought. I never have more than one or two days off at a time, and I use those days to catch up with things I've fallen behind on. Even being here today, I know I'll have that much more chaos waiting for me when I get back. My apartment has been a mess for weeks, and I planned on using today to do a deep clean on everything—seeing Caleb just means cleaning my apartment will have to wait that much longer.

"Nothing?"

I'm suddenly self-conscious of my work schedule, wondering if perhaps I should have carved out more time for myself.

"Just this, I guess."

"Hmm."

"What?" I ask, trying to shift so I can see his face, but his arms are wrapped around me, and I can't move.

"I didn't think you'd consider backpacking as something fun."

I definitely don't. I haven't slept yet, and I'm already regretting how much my back is going to hurt in the morning.

"It's okay," I say, realizing that with Caleb here, it's tolerable. With his arms wrapped around me, I feel safe, even if the mysteries of the woods are on the other side of the tent.

"Just okay?"

"Ask me again in the morning," I say, shuffling closer.

Caleb laughs, and his body relaxes as sleep starts to pull us under. Around us, the forest stays awake, leaves rustling on branches when the occasional breeze comes through. Eventually the woods go silent, and all I can hear is Caleb's soft rhythmic breathing as he sinks into a deep sleep.

CHAPTER 20

It's probably my worst night of sleep. Once we stop talking, Caleb falls asleep almost instantly. I stay close to him, the contact of his body making the night bearable. I fall in and out of sleep, but it feels like the night will never end. It's not that it's quiet; it's that the woods are void of sound. Sometimes I think it can't possibly be that quiet, but then Caleb breathes loud enough to break the spell.

There are a few moments in the night when I start to panic as I lay in the darkness, but then I shift closer to Caleb, and his arm tightens around me, and I'm able to relax again.

Sometimes the silence of the forest is broken, and I'll hear a twig snap or leaves rustle, and my heart rate spikes, my mind tricking me into thinking there's a large animal on the other side of the tent. But no matter how hard I listen, there's never another sound, and eventually I calm down.

I must fall into a somewhat-restful sleep because I wake up to light shining into the tent. I have no idea what time it is, but what I do know is that I have to go to the bathroom—badly.

I pull myself out of Caleb arms, and he stirs, rolling onto his back. I unzip my sleeping bag, but in the silence of the morning, the sound is deafening. I unzip the tent next and reach for my shoes.

"Where you going?" Caleb asks, his voice groggy.

"Bathroom," I say, crouching down halfway out of the tent to slip my shoes on. My feet scream in protest as I tie the laces.

"Do you want me to walk you?"

"No, I've got it."

The air is colder once I step out of the tent. I didn't realize how warm we got last night, cocooning ourselves around each other, but now that I've peeled myself away, the air is chilly.

The morning feels fresh, and even though I barely slept last night, it's like my body has been dosed with a shot of caffeine.

I go by the cooking area, where our food was stored in bear boxes for the night. The boxes are undisturbed, and a woman is already sitting, cooking her breakfast with a tiny stove. She smiles as I walk by.

I take the turn to find the privy, and when I get there, there's a man waiting despite there being two privies.

"Mornin'," he says when I step into line behind him.

"Do you know what time it is?" I ask, curious.

"Five. Somewhere around there." The man shrugs as a woman steps out of one of the privies, and then he goes in. The woman passes me, already dressed in her hiking clothes. Suddenly, I'm self-conscious of my sweatpants, like I'm underdressed even for a camping trip.

Another man gets out of the other privy, and I go in, holding my breath as I try to go to the bathroom as quickly as possible. When I step out, there's already someone else waiting.

As I walk back, I come across a few hikers who are already packed up and walking with their bags. They give me a quick wave as they pass, continuing northward to the hiking trail Caleb and I did yesterday. It's shocking how many people are not only awake but seem to have been awake for a while even though it's so early.

I pass the intersection of the trail that leads to the pond and take a few steps that way, finally noticing the colors in the sky. The trees glow a soft orange, but over by the pond, the sky and water are a collage of colors as the sun rises and peeks through the trees. I take a few more steps, and that's when I see it. The moose is massive, standing next to a tree on the other side of the pond. He's standing at the edge of the water, drinking as the morning light shines through the trees behind him. My breath catches when I see the moose, and I have no idea what to do.

I'm a little stunned to see such a large animal out in the open. Having lived in New Hampshire my entire life, I've seen moose before, but it's always been from a safe distance and usually when I'm sitting in a car or building. This time the only thing between me and the moose is a small body of water.

I take a few steps backward, trying to be as quiet as possible, too afraid to turn my back to the moose. It's not until I've put enough distance between us that I can barely see the moose that I turn to run back toward the tent.

I try to slow my pace into a fast walk as I pass the cooking area, where three hikers are making breakfast now.

When I get back to the tent, I unzip it quickly, crawling in as if the thin shelter will do much to protect me from a massive moose.

"Everything okay?" Caleb sits up as soon as I get into the tent, noticing my jitteriness.

"Moose," I say, looking around, wondering if we should be packing up the tent. What's the protocol for moose in the woods?

"Really?" he says, pushing his sleeping bag away and crawling out of the tent.

"Yeah, over by the pond."

"Come on," he says, grabbing my hand and pulling me back to where I came from.

"What are you doing?"

"Let's go see it."

"Caleb, no. They're dangerous." I try to pull in the other direction to get him to stop, but he's too strong to even notice.

"What part of the pond is he on? Is he close to where we were sitting last night?" He finally slows down.

"No, the other side of the water. Directly across."

He smiles at my answer. "Perfect."

We walk by the cooking area again, and Caleb slows down to talk to the other hikers.

"Lori spotted a moose at the pond if you guys want to check it out."

All three hikers perk up, dropping their things and moving to get up immediately. I might as well have told them I spotted a pile of cash in the woods for how quickly they get up. They follow Caleb to the pond, and this time I feel even more foolish for being afraid of the moose as everyone flocks over to watch. I try to stand back, but Caleb takes my hand and pulls me closer.

The moose is huge—a large bull for sure—bigger than any I've ever seen, but this is also the closest I've ever been to a moose. The water creates a gap between us and the moose, but even from this distance, I can make out the fine texture of his fur perfectly.

Everyone is quiet as they lock eyes on the moose, pointing and smiling as they watch. Two of the hikers from the cooking area pull their phones out to take a picture, which only makes me wonder where in the world I left my phone. It's probably in a pocket of my backpack with a dead battery.

"Good eye," a woman says to me after she takes a photo.

We all stand a short distance from the water, observing the moose, who doesn't bother to look up at us. The moose's antlers are wide and look like they should leave the animal lopsided and heavy, but he moves his head down to the water in smooth, slow motions.

Eventually he lifts his head from the water, he looks directly at us. My body is tense, preparing to run.

"You're okay," Caleb whispers softly into my ear. He's standing behind me, moving his hands up and down my arms, telling me to relax.

The moose stares at us for what feels like a lifetime before he breaks his gaze and turns, moving back into the trees before he disappears in the opposite direction. I relax when he's out of sight.

"That was so cool!" a guy standing next to Caleb says,

tucking his phone back into his pocket. "I've been hiking for four months, and this is the first moose spotting."

"Same!" the woman who was taking photos says.

"Thanks for telling us," says the third hiker, an older man with cropped hair.

"How did you spot it?" the man next to Caleb asks, turning to me. He looks vaguely familiar. Maybe he was one of the guys at the privy.

"I was on my way back from the bathroom."

"I must have just missed him, then. You've definitely got an eye for it."

"I'm Flow, by the way," the woman says, giving me a wave.

"Trail Trash," the guy I ran into at the privy says.

"Bugs." The older man waves.

"Lori," I say, feeling like I'm introducing myself wrong.

"No trail name yet?" Trail Trash says, looking toward Caleb, who still has his hands on my shoulders. He drops one of his hands, opting to wrap an arm around my waist instead.

"She's been on trail for less than twenty-four hours. I'll be dropping her off at her car today."

Getting back to my car sounds like a dream come true.

"I don't need a trail name," I say. As we stand there, all I notice is how everyone is already dressed and ready to take on the day except for me; I'm standing in the woods in sweatpants and feeling more and more out of place by the moment.

"Sure you do! We've all got one!" Trail Trash takes a tiny step forward, like he's gearing up to give a big speech. "I'm Trail Trash because I pick up trash I find along the way. Flow is one of the easiest hikers to partner up with; she just goes with the flow. And Bugs has all the bugs flock to him. Great company to keep because all the mosquitoes and black flies bite him instead of you."

Bugs rolls his eyes.

"And you already know why I'm Chip," Caleb says.

"You don't need a name if you don't want one," Flow says, perhaps understanding how much all of this is out of my element.

"Do I pick my name?" I ask.

Trail Trash shrugs. "The name picks you."

I glance around like I'll see my trail name written on a tree somewhere.

"I haven't met a Moose yet," Bugs says.

"Oh! Moose would be fun!" Flow says, eyes going wide.

"How about it?" Caleb asks.

All eyes turn to me, waiting for approval.

"Moose?" All I can think is how Moose is a boy name and a name for a pet, though I suppose compared to all the other trail names out there, it isn't the worst in the world.

"You'll forever be known as the girl who's the good luck charm when it comes to finding moose," Bugs says.

"You'll be everyone's favorite hiking partner." Flow smiles.

"Sure, I guess." I shrug.

"Well, she'll be Moose in my brain now." Bugs turns to me, giving a kind smile, as if I've just been invited into an exclusive club.

"Moose it is." Caleb smiles.

"We have to get going if we want to beat the heat today. We'll catch up with you guys later. It was good meeting you, Moose!" Trail Trash waves before he and everyone else starts to walk away. The group sparks up a conversation as they make their way back to the cooking area, their voices murmuring and mixing together as they leave.

"You don't have to use your trail name," Caleb reassures me when everyone is out of sight.

"Moose," I say, making a face. "Makes me sound like I'm a tough guy."

Caleb smiles. "You're tough, just not a dude."

I frown, looking back out over the water where I saw the moose.

"What?" Caleb asks.

"I've spent the past twenty-four hours scared out of my mind and ready to make a run for it."

"Could've fooled me." He says the words so seriously that I think he's being sarcastic. "I mean it. If you've been ready to run, you haven't shown it. I know this isn't your thing, but you've been doing great. And you're going to make hiking seem very boring again when you leave today."

I smile despite how defeated I feel. "What if I told you hiking *is* boring?" I tease.

He grins, putting a hand on my back and leading me back to the tent.

"You and I both know hiking is anything but boring."

CHAPTER 21

We take our time cooking breakfast. I change into the clean pair of clothes Marly told me not to pack, while Caleb puts on the same smelly shirt from yesterday. Even with his theory that more clothes means more weight to carry in a backpack, I can't see the logic behind having to wear the same shirt and pants over and over again.

Breakfast today is oatmeal, and my bowl of water is already heated and stirred into my oats while Caleb begins to boil his own meal.

"So, what's the plan for today?" I ask, blowing on the oatmeal so it won't burn my mouth.

"Walk with you back to the car and then turn around and keep walking until I can't walk any farther."

Steam starts coming from the little pot he's using to cook, and he switches the fire under the pot off. He pours a couple packets of oatmeal into the pot before mixing it all together.

"Did I make you fall behind?" I ask.

He takes a big bite of oatmeal before responding. "What do

you mean?"

"You didn't make any progress with me yesterday because you have to re-hike everything we already did. I wasn't sure what your schedule was to finish."

"Schedule?" he asks, eyebrows raised as if offended by the word. "There's no such thing as schedules out here."

"You know what I mean."

He takes another bite, seeming perplexed. "Some people hike with a goal in mind. They want to hike fifteen miles a day. Take one day off a week. Hike five miles one day and then ten miles the next day so they can finish by a certain date. So, some people have schedules. I don't."

"How will you know if you're going to finish on time?"

He shrugs. "People like to finish by September so they don't have to run into snow or cold weather. I'd like to do that, but at the end of the day, I'm going to finish when I finish."

Even though I'm not a thru-hiker myself, the thought of not knowing when or if I'll finish the Appalachian Trail feels wrong. My life has been nothing but structure and schedules, so the thought of not having a clear goal or deadline leaves a pit of worry in my stomach.

He takes another bite of oatmeal, seeming unbothered by how ludicrous all this seems to me.

"You don't have a job waiting for you when you get back?"

He glances up, seeming put off by my words for the first time. "College dropout, remember?"

And that's when it's clear to me just how different we are. While I run like clockwork, he lives life moment by moment, figuring things out when issues arise. I'm juggling a job, college, and trying to become a yoga instructor, while he's walking in the woods with no idea when he's going to return to reality. It almost makes me angry, the thought that he's out here in the woods, avoiding the responsibilities of life.

A heavy cloud of doubt rests on my shoulders. Reality crashes down around me, and the past couple weeks getting to know Caleb feel like a dream I've just woken up from.

When we finish eating, we rinse out our food bowls and pack up the tent. I take my time folding my sleeping bag and stuffing it back into my backpack, but Caleb dismantles the tent quickly, without needing to put in much effort. Within a couple minutes, we're all packed up and ready to go. I sling the backpack on, the straps feeling heavier than yesterday, my calves and thighs already sore.

Caleb leads the way back to the trail that will take me to my car, and it's like a miracle that I've made it this far. I have no idea how many miles we've covered together, but it's definitely more than the four miles I told Caleb I would hike with him.

"So, do you want me to text you the next time I need a rest day?" Caleb asks. We're walking side by side since the trail is wide enough, but in this moment, I wish I could hide my face from him, because I don't have an answer.

I want to say yes, but if the backpacking trip taught me anything, it's that we're living on two completely different planets. While I crave stability and structure, Caleb thrives in chaos that I can't even begin to comprehend.

"I don't know," I say, the words sounding more tired than I

mean them to be.

Caleb slows, turning to me as we walk.

"What do you mean?"

"It's just a lot, Caleb," I admit, more defeated than ever. I'm not sure if it's because I'm mentally or physically tired, but I don't want to do this anymore. "For the next month, or however long, you're going to be walking farther and farther north until one day, you'll be home again. And I don't know what you plan on doing with your life after that, but I'll be in New Hampshire, working. And I can't drop everything for you." I try to say the words gently, but no matter how softly I say the words, they still mean the same thing: we don't work together.

"It can work if we want it to," Caleb says so quietly that I'm not sure if I was supposed to hear him.

"What am I supposed to do? The trail is the easy part. You're living in la-la land, walking in the woods. What happens when you return to reality?"

My words come off harsher than I intended, but I'm too tired to try to fix it. For the short period I've known Caleb, I've never seen him irritated, but I can tell my words have gotten under his skin. He doesn't say anything. Instead, he picks up the pace, walking a few strides ahead of me.

For a while, we walk together, our feet moving forward even if the conversation has stalled. I know I should say something, should apologize, but my body and mind want nothing more than to be home.

"You like me, right?" he asks me suddenly, coming to a stop. "I mean, I know the past twenty-four hours sum up just about everything you hate, but you still came, so you must like me."

"I told you, I don't hate hiking," I whisper.

"So, did you come for me or the exhilarating hike?"

"For you," I finally say.

Never in a million years would I have gone backpacking with anyone else—not even Marly. Of all the guys I've dated, Caleb is the only one I'm comfortable around. I can't explain why or how, but when I'm with Caleb, I feel like I'm home. From a stranger's perspective, we don't work. We don't have the same hobbies, lifestyles, or even views on goals, but for some reason, we work. Despite all the chaos in my life, he makes me happy, and that means something, even if I don't know what.

Caleb steps in front of me, his eyes pleading. "Then give us a chance. Let's see if this is a thing worth fighting for." He grips my hand lightly, tugging me forward.

I want to tell him yes, but right now, just the thought of it makes me exhausted. Relationships are supposed to be easy, comforting, and I guess it feels that way when I'm with Caleb, but even then, it's like we're being pulled in opposite directions.

"Caleb—"

"Give me a chance." His face is soft, begging me to see reason, but he's the one living in a fairy-tale land.

I want to let go of his hand just so I can wrap myself around him and never let go. But I'm scared. I'm scared that the life I've been fighting to hold on to is slipping away from my grasp again, because Caleb isn't the guy I'm meant to be with. I've always seen myself with someone with goals just as big as mine. And not to say hiking the Appalachian Trail isn't a large goal, but what happens after that? How does Caleb fit into my life then?

"I don't know what to say," I finally admit.

"Then let's see what happens."

My lip twitches, the fear bubbling to the surface.

"Next time I need a break, we'll see each other. We'll take it day by day. We'll live in the moment."

Caleb makes it sound so simple that I start to believe him.

"Okay," I whisper.

We walk hand in hand for the rest of the hike, though my future is more unsure than ever. It's during the walk back to the car that I start to realize what Caleb meant by having too much time to yourself on the trail. In our silence, I run through about twenty scenarios in my head of how Caleb and I work, all of them ending with me heartbroken. There are versions of the story where Caleb never texts me again. Or he gets back to Maine and dumps me. Or I move to Maine and my dreams fall apart. The longer I spiral in my thoughts, the worse my story ends.

After what feels like an hour, we round a corner, and a parking lot opens up, my car sitting exactly where I left it.

"Finally," I say, mostly to myself. I shrug the backpack off as soon as I'm beside my car, letting it fall with a soft thud. I kick my shoes off next, standing in the gravel parking lot in just my socks, no longer caring about anything besides giving my feet some air so they can stop rubbing the sides of my shoes.

I'm digging in the backpack, searching for my keys, and can feel Caleb's gaze on me. When I stand up, keys in hand, he's standing an arm's length away.

"You did really great out there." His smile is small, almost sad. "I know hiking and camping aren't your thing, but you handled it like a champ."

"Thanks," I say softly.

In the parking lot, I'm more lost than ever. We've agreed to see each other, but those are just words. It doesn't mean anything, and I don't know if I want it to mean anything. Maybe we'd be better off saying our goodbyes and going our separate ways.

"Do you need anything from town?" I ask. My car keys are clutched in my hand, and even though I spent all night thinking about how happy I'd be to see my car again, a small part of me is afraid that if I get in this car, I won't see Caleb again.

"No, I should probably get to walking." He hesitates, but I close the distance between us, moving to wrap my arms around him.

The hug is awkward since he's still wearing his backpack. I have to reach my arms up and over his shoulders, standing on my toes so I can get as close to him as possible. His arms move to circle around my waist, and I'm reminded again of how much he feels like home, which makes saying goodbye even harder.

"I'll see you soon," he says softly as he shifts to kiss my temple.

"Good luck," I whisper.

He pulls away just enough for me to see his smile before he kisses me. It fills me with hope that maybe we can work against the odds and fight for each other. The kiss leaves me breathless and dizzy, and when Caleb finally pulls away, my heart aches at the thought of leaving him.

"Just a couple days," he promises.

I nod, the emotions bubbling under the surface. I don't want to allow myself to believe the words. I can't. Not when our lives are running in different directions.

Caleb is the one who breaks the bond, taking a step back and letting our arms drop to our sides. He turns away. We aren't ready to say goodbye, but we're embracing the finality of this moment.

I turn back to my car, not allowing myself to watch him as he disappears into the woods. I throw the backpack into the trunk of my car, along with my shoes, which smell worse than they ever have. There's an old pair of sneakers in my trunk, and I slip them on despite the blisters on the sides of my feet. When I'm finally in the front seat of the car, I look back at the trail, but Caleb is long gone.

CHAPTER 22

I maintain my dignity until I get back to my apartment. For the entire car ride, I keep a straight face and focus on the long drive home. I'm perfectly focused on the highway, only thinking of the directions I need to take to get home. The mask starts to slip as soon as I pull into my apartment complex parking lot. My breathing gets heavier, but I don't dare slip up while I'm still in public.

I make my way up the stairs and down the hall to my door, unlocking it and slipping in before anyone can notice. The tears come in silent stretches down my face, like I'm still in shock, unable to believe it all.

We didn't say goodbye, didn't want it to be goodbye, so why does it feel that way?

§

When I wake up the next morning, my eyes are puffy and tired, but I shower, give myself a lackluster pep talk, and head out the door to work my shift at Angela's. At the restaurant, I walk through the day in a haze, no longer sure if I'm upset because I miss Caleb or because I'm still sleep-deprived from backpacking.

The following day, I don't have to work until the dinner rush, so I decide to give myself something to focus on. I open my laptop at my desk, ready to jump back into my online class. I have to sit through prerecorded lectures, and even though it should be the easiest part of my day, I find myself zoning out. No matter how hard I try to listen to the lecture, my mind keeps wandering to Caleb.

Caleb sends occasional texts to update me on where he is, but the names and locations are lost on me. I reply to each message to cheer him on, but we never have a conversation since I only hear from him about once a day.

My mind wanders off, and I have to replay parts of the lecture I'm watching, hoping one of these times my brain will be able to retain the information. After an hour of failing to focus, I push the laptop away and pull my phone out, dialing Marly's number. The phone rings a couple times before she finally picks up.

"Hey!" she answers, her voice chipper.

"Hey," I say, low and monotone.

"What's wrong?"

I put the phone on speaker and place it on my desk, wiping my hands down my face. How can I still feel tired no matter how much sleep I get?

"I went camping." I laugh in a sarcastic tone.

"Oh! How did it go? I thought you must have chickened out

or something since I never heard from you."

"It went about as well as it possibly could have," I say.

"So, you liked it?" she says, surprise in her voice.

My face goes flat. "It was tolerable, I guess."

Marly laughs softly on the other line. "Okay, so what's wrong? You went backpacking. It was tolerable. You survived. Now what?"

"I don't think it will work," I say, exacerbating the words.

"Details, Lori."

I take a deep breath and say everything as quickly as I can. "When we were talking, I found out he's a college dropout and the only reason he's hiking is because he doesn't know what to do going forward. The more we talked, the more I started to realize that we're just *very* different people. He doesn't know when he's going to finish the Appalachian Trail or what he's going to do when he gets home. He doesn't want to go back to college. He seems totally against college. He doesn't have a job lined up when he gets home either."

Marly laughs softly.

"What?" I say.

"Caleb really is just the guy version of me."

I blink a couple times before the words are able to process fully. "What?"

"Lori, I dropped out of college too."

"He didn't drop out. He failed all his classes."

"I probably would have failed all my classes eventually if I hadn't dropped out," Marly says, unbothered.

"But that's different. Your parents died."

"You don't need a tragic story to have a good reason to stop doing something you hate. I went to college because it felt like I was supposed to—my parents wanted me to. It wasn't until later I realized I didn't need the degree for my career."

I groan, hiding my face in my hands to muffle the sound. "I really am dating the male version of you."

"Hey now, don't sound so upset about that. I'm a catch," she says, laughing.

I drop my hands, more confused than ever. "Why does it bother me so much that he doesn't like college?"

"Is having a college degree a requirement for dating?"

I pause, feeling like I've been cornered. "It sounds stupid if you ask it that way."

"Answer the question," she pushes.

I let myself consider it. "Not really. I guess if he had a good career . . ."

"So, it's not the college part that bothers you; it's the stability."

"You make me sound archaic," I mumble.

"Wanting someone stable isn't a bad thing," she says gently.

"I don't think it's that. It's just, how can I connect with someone who doesn't have the same view on life and goals as I do?"

Marly sounds like she's trying to suppress a giggle again. "I don't know. You've been doing it so far. Being the same isn't the recipe for romance. Sometimes it's just about making each other better people. Every relationship has a push and pull. Caleb's pushed you out of your comfort zone, and I'd like to think it's made you a better person. More carefree, maybe?"

I let out an exasperated sigh. "It's made me more unfocused,"

I say, staring at my laptop and textbook, which have been shoved to the side.

"You were hyper-focused before, too busy working to play. Now you're just focused."

I run my hand through my hair. "It doesn't feel that way."

Marly pauses for a second, the line silent. "How old is he?"

"I think he's our age, maybe a little older."

"Then so what if he doesn't have a game plan? Most people our age don't have a game plan. Admit it. Most people go to college to figure out what they want to do with their life. Heck, most students still take a couple years after they graduate to figure things out."

"But how can he figure things out when he's not even in college in the first place? Instead, he's living in an alternate reality where he lives in the woods and doesn't have to deal with problems in the real world."

"Ah! There's the problem," Marly says suddenly.

"What?" I say, confused.

"You think what he's doing is taking a vacation. It's not hard work. He's avoiding his issues instead of facing them head-on."

I can almost picture Marly smiling to herself because she's solved the puzzle.

"When you were backpacking, was any of that easy?"

I don't have to think about the question too hard. My legs are still sore. "No."

"Backpacking isn't vacation. Backpacking is testing your body and your mind. Caleb may not look like he's figuring his life out, but trust me, he is. There're no distractions out there.

When you're staying up late watching Netflix, he's thinking about if he wants to go back to college. When you're driving to work with the music blasting, he's trying to figure out what job he wants to do for the rest of his life. While you're sleeping in your bed—"

"Okay," I interrupt her. "I get it."

"I'm just saying, he's working on it. Not everyone has a five-year plan."

"You remember that?" I say, a little embarrassed.

"Of course I remember your five-year plan. You talked about it every day in high school."

"Okay, fine. But what about the fact that he lives in Maine? I don't want to move there. My life is here. I know it wasn't specified in my five-year plan, but the yoga studio I own one day is supposed to be in New Hampshire."

"Who's to say Caleb won't be the one to move?"

"I just don't think he will," I admit.

"Why not?"

I stare at my phone, the screen glowing with Marly's name at the top.

"Because if he was considering moving here, wouldn't he have said something?"

"Maybe he's thought about it but didn't want to mention it and freak you out."

"Why would I freak out?" I say.

Marly laughs to herself, likely reminiscing on my strong ability to overreact.

"Call him," she insists.

"No," I say out of reflex.

"Why not?" Marly says, starting to sound frustrated.

"Because . . ." I drag out the word, knowing I don't have a good reason. "I think it would be easier for both of us to just forget about each other."

Marly lets out a sigh. "You know, for someone who loves watching rom-coms and Hallmark movies so much, I would've thought you'd be fighting tooth and nail for this guy."

"Trust me, this backpacking trip was not a Hallmark movie. It was too smelly for that." I cringe thinking about how awful I smelled when I finally got home. I took the longest shower of my life, and then I felt like I needed to put my clothes in the washer twice.

"Well, most of the movies tend to have horses, and we both know they don't smell like roses, so who knows. They could totally make your love story into a Hallmark movie."

I roll my eyes. "Oh, please. No one would want to see how gross I was hiking around all day while trying not to have a mental breakdown."

Marly laughs, and I know we'll be talking for the next hour as I fill her in on all the details. "Now this I have to hear more about."

CHAPTER 23

despite Marly's insistence, I don't call Caleb. He continues to send updates once a day, but I try to focus on my summer class, which is finally finishing up. The class was only a month long, but it felt like it stretched just as long as a regular semester. After I submit my final paper, I only have a week to relax before my next summer class starts.

I shift my focus to the 500-hour yoga certification, but it doesn't take long for me to realize the fee to take the class is way out of my budget. I'll need to work more shifts at Angela's in order to cover the cost, but I won't be able to afford it for at least another month or two. By that point, my fall semester will have started, and I won't have time to take the certification.

If I had any idea what I was doing, I would just open my own yoga studio and start teaching classes, but I don't have the slightest clue how to open my own studio. I'm two years into college and have taken more business courses than I can count, but none of them have taught me a thing about leasing a building, tracking expenses, or paying taxes. Caleb's reminder that "classes don't teach you anything about owning a business; owning a business will teach you about owning a business" rings in my ear.

In my head, owning my own studio has always been a clear part of my future. I can picture how students will be able to walk into the building, and the lobby will be decorated with a small water fountain, and they'll have to walk by an indoor koi pond to get to the front desk to check into class. There'll be a spot to sit and take off shoes and hang up jackets. Then students go into the next room over, which will be huge and open, with yoga mats stored off to the side in large baskets. I'll have a closet filled to the brim with props like yoga blocks, blankets, and yoga straps. I'll set up a sound system so the music will be surround sound. I might even get a mic pack for myself so I never have to raise my voice.

It all started as a Pinterest board a couple years ago. I have the color scheme and a few furniture items picked out for the studio already. The vision is clear; I just have no way to execute it. Since I've always intended to work at another yoga studio first, I figure I'll learn how to build my own business by watching how someone else made theirs. But someone needs to hire me first.

I spend time between working shifts driving around New Hampshire, finding studios where I can drop off my résumé and speak to the owner. The owner is usually teaching a class or not there, so I'm always stuck talking to a receptionist who looks like they may just throw away my résumé the second I walk out the door.

To put it simply, I'm starting to feel hopeless.

Meanwhile, being a waitress is still going strong, even if I hate every second of it. I work almost every day and have worked ten days in a row since my backpacking trip.

Caleb lingers in my mind, but I keep working, using that as an excuse to attempt to remove him from my thoughts. Should I call and see if he wants to meet up? No, I don't have any days off anytime soon. When he wants to see me, he'll let me know. Until then, all I get to know is the name of the shelter he's sleeping at in the woods.

Today I'm working a double shift, filling in for someone who called in sick. Normally I'd hate working a double, but lately when I'm at home, I'm too distracted waiting on another text from Caleb to do anything productive.

All this, and my head has started to feel a little too crowded to get my work done correctly. I already knew I was a mediocre waiter at best, but lately all I've been doing is forgetting orders left and right.

I'm standing at the entrance to the kitchen, looking at the notepad where I wrote down table seven's order. I only have three meals written out, but there were four people at the table. Did I zone out?

I think back, trying to retrace my steps in my mind to see whose meal I'm missing.

There was a steak dinner. Chicken parm. Caprese salad. What was the last one?

Mac and cheese bake!

I write it down quickly and run into the kitchen to drop off the slip.

"Table two," Mary says, reminding me of a table I haven't tended to in a while.

"Sorry," I say, more frazzled than usual.

I rush to the table, checking that none of my other tables need me as I walk by, so I don't have a chance to glance at the new table before I pull my notepad out.

"Hi, I'm Lori. I'll be your server for the evening. Can I—"

I freeze when I notice that the person sitting in the booth is Caleb, wearing the same flannel jacket he had on the first night I ran into him at Angela's.

"Hi," he says softly, trying to hold back a smile.

"What are you doing here?" I try to do the math in my head, as if I haven't been meticulously counting already. Ten days. It's definitely been ten days. But there's no way he already finished hiking the Appalachian Trail. And he just texted me last night to tell me what shelter he was sleeping at. I have no idea where it is, but I assumed he was still hiking north.

I try to quell any excitement, afraid to get my hopes up.

"I ran into one of my buddies, Dusty. He was making a trip home for a wedding, so he let me ride with him."

I try to process what this means, but I can't. I'm standing at the end of the table, gripping my notepad, and I have no idea what to say.

Caleb's smile starts to fade when I don't respond right away. I have to remind myself to breathe before I can reply.

"Why didn't you tell me you were coming?" I say.

"I wanted to surprise you," he says earnestly, but I can see his enthusiasm fade. "Was that a bad idea?"

"No!" I respond quickly. I look around. The restaurant is busier than ever tonight. As happy as I am to see Caleb, now is not the best time to catch up. "I'm glad you're here, but it's super busy tonight. Can we talk after my shift?"

He works to compose his face. "Yeah, of course."

I smile and try to put on my best work face. "Do you want anything to drink?"

"Pepsi, please."

"Coming right up."

I turn to walk away, but Caleb speaks up behind me. "What time does your shift end?"

"In about two hours," I say, glancing over my shoulder with a smile before walking away, utter panic making me want to sprint across the room.

I take a moment to compose myself, running into the break room. My face flushes, a smile creeping in, but I try to focus.

I pull my phone out and type a message to Marly.

!!!! Caleb's here. At Angela's!!!!

I hit send and tuck the phone into my back pocket so I'll get her response when it comes in.

When I step out of the break room, I practically collide with Allison, who's grinning from ear to ear.

"I was just looking for you!" she says, all smiles.

"What?" I say, the words coming out sharp.

If Allison notices my tone, she's unbothered. "That guy you were flirting with is back!"

I laugh nervously. "I know."

"What's wrong?" she asks, finally picking up on my tone.

"Nothing," I say, brushing past her to deal with my other tables, though now I wonder how frantic I must look.

I do my best to keep my eyes away from Caleb. Lucky for me, it's a busy night, so it's easier to ignore Caleb without making it look obvious. Eventually, I make my way to the kitchen to grab his Pepsi before Mary yells at me for letting a table wait too long—but I figure Caleb won't mind.

With a deep breath, I walk back to table two. I try to quell my enthusiasm, but Caleb's smile when he sees me walk over only makes my stomach flip.

"Do you know what you want to order?" I ask, trying to stay focused. I'm afraid if I go off-topic, I'll get wrapped up in a conversation and forget all the other tables exist.

"What do you recommend?" Caleb asks, grinning at me with a sheepish smile.

I roll my eyes. "The chef salad is my favorite, but something tells me you'd like the lobster ravioli a little more."

He raises his eyebrow, intrigued. "Sounds good to me."

"Okay, then." I smile, my eyes settling on his face for too long. If Allison is watching, I'm sure she's swooning. I'm about to walk away, but curiosity strikes. "How long are you here?"

"Dusty and I head back tomorrow morning."

I can feel myself deflate. So, tonight is all we have, then.

My phone buzzes in my pocket, and I pull it out, glancing at the text from Marly.

OMG! is all it says, but any of the excitement I felt earlier is gone now.

"I'll be back with your food in a little bit," I say, giving Caleb the best smile I can muster before I turn back to my other tables.

For the next two hours, each time I glance at Caleb, my focus shifts, and I start to mess up orders again—nothing major to get me in trouble, but enough that my tips seem a little lower than usual.

Out of the corner of my eye, I see Allison visit Caleb's table, refilling his drink, which I didn't realize was empty.

"What are you doing?" I ask when she tries to skirt by.

"Helping." She smiles.

"With his order, or getting information?" I eye Caleb as I talk, and his eyes are on his phone.

Allison shrugs. "Both."

I glare at her, and she giggles.

"If I find out anything juicy, you'll be the first to know. So far, he's been annoyingly close-lipped."

"You're such a gossip." I laugh, rolling my eyes.

She gives me a wink before returning to work.

Eventually, Caleb leaves. When I go over to clean up his table, there's a note on the receipt he signed.

Meet me outside.

When the last couple minutes of my shift finally wrap up, I make my way to the break room, grabbing my stuff before heading out the door, wondering why I have a pit in my stomach. Even with his note at the table, I start to wonder if he really did wait for me.

"Have you been set free?" a familiar voice says when I step out of Angela's. I turn to see Caleb sitting on a bench that's normally reserved for those waiting to be seated at their tables on a busy night. Now the dinner rush is over, and it's just Caleb out here in the darkness.

"I thought you'd text me when you wanted to take a day off so I could drive up and visit you," I say.

He shrugs. "Figured it was my turn to make the journey."

Whatever willpower I was using to keep us apart breaks in that moment.

I move to sit beside him on the bench. The air is hot and muggy tonight. It's cooled down as the sun has retreated, but the air is still heavy. I'm sure if we were in a tent, we'd be miserable and sweaty. Or at least I would.

"So, what brings you into town?" I say, leaning onto the back of the bench. I gaze up at the night sky, hoping to see stars, but the lights from town are too bright to let the sky shine. I frown, thinking of how different the view was when we were backpacking. Is it possible I miss it?

"Like I said, Dusty had a wedding to go to, so I thought I'd hitchhike with him and go for a ride."

"How was the wedding?" I ask.

He gives me a face, confused. "What do you mean?"

"The wedding you guys went to?"

"Oh," he says, understanding. "I didn't go. Dusty did. He's at it right now. I just came for a ride."

"Came all this way for lobster ravioli?"

"I wanted to see you again," he says, his voice firm and unwavering. He's never been shy about his feelings for me. If anything, I've always been the one pushing him away. But he somehow seems surer, like it's the thing he's most certain of.

I have no response. I know what I want to do, which is to tell Caleb that I've been thinking of him ever since he walked away from my car. But while my heart says *Caleb*, my brain says *focus*, and those two things don't get along very well.

"I've been hiking more and more every day. I thought, the faster I finish, the faster I may be able to see you again. But then I realized, the farther I go, the farther away I get from you. When I ran into Dusty again, he told me he was coming to New Hampshire for a wedding, so I asked if I could come with him."

My face starts to burn up. He missed me that much? It doesn't seem right or logical for him to stop his trek to come find me, but maybe it doesn't have to.

"You came all this way just to see me for one night?" I ask, but I can hear Marly's voice in my head, begging me to ask better questions. I *should* ask him if he'd ever consider moving to New Hampshire after the trail. But I can't. How can I ask him to uproot his life when it's not something I'm willing to do?

"I really like you," he says simply. "I admire how focused and driven you are, and how no matter how uncomfortable you were backpacking, you kept moving forward because you're the type of person who refuses to give up. I love how you practice yoga, even though you seem like the most stressed-out person I've ever met."

I let out a sad laugh.

"But mostly, I like how I feel around you," he continues. "The past couple months have been lonely, and I thought that's what I needed on the trail. I thought the only way to figure out what I want to do with my life was to be alone and wallow in everything I've done wrong. I've been on trail for four months, but I learn the most about myself when I'm with you."

I can't get myself to speak. I watch Caleb, and I see him talk as I hear the words, but they almost don't make sense. I can't believe it.

"I don't know how you feel about me. I know with me being on trail, it's nearly impossible to have any sort of contact. After backpacking together, I don't know if you think I'm annoying, or weird, or just plain crazy for hiking the Appalachian Trail."

"You might be crazy," I say, and he smiles.

"For months, I've been hiking north, telling myself I was hiking home. But now I'm not sure anymore."

I stare at him, confused, but he just smiles.

"Home can be a person."

My head starts to spin with a sort of euphoria. How many times have I watched romance movies, swooning over the scenes where guys confess their love? I've pictured it for myself many times, but never like this, and never with a guy like Caleb. But somehow, that only makes it better.

"Just tell me if you want me to go away," he says, his voice low, like he's afraid I may tell him I never want to see him again. His words shock me enough to break me out of my frozen spell.

"Of course I don't want you to go away," I say.

CHAPTER 24

"Allison was trying to investigate for you," Caleb says as I unlock my apartment door.

I'm already cringing as I open the door for Caleb, and he walks in. "I tried to rein her in, but she can't be tamed."

"She was asking me what brings me into town again, how long I'll be here, if I was visiting anyone. Those types of things." He grins, a little smug.

"I'm not sure if she was investigating for me or for herself, because she never updated me with your answers." I shake my head, locking the door and hanging my keys on the rack by the entrance.

Caleb makes his way across the apartment and into my living room, settling in with an arm slouched over the top of the couch.

"I gave her vague answers." He shrugs.

I sit next to him, keeping a few inches of separation between us, but his arm stretches so far across the couch that his fingers graze the top of my shoulder.

"Probably for the best. She's a bit of a gossip."

"So, if she saw us leaving together . . . ?" He leaves the question hanging.

"Every single one of my coworkers—and perhaps even a few customers—will know by tomorrow morning."

He grins, shaking his head in amusement.

"So . . ." I say, wondering how to start this conversation. "Can I ask a less casual question?"

Caleb stiffens beside me and adjusts his seating to sit up straighter. "Just jumping straight into it, huh?"

I give an awkward smile. "Not my fault you'll be leaving tomorrow morning, so might as well cut to the chase."

He gives a breathy laugh. "Okay, go for it."

"Can you explain the college thing in more detail? Like the whys and the hows?"

He touches a hand to his face, rubbing his chin before relaxing into the couch again. "Okay." He pauses to take a deep breath. "When I was in high school, teachers, my guidance counselor, and my parents made college out to be necessary. You either go and be successful, or you don't and you're homeless. I never did well in school, so I tried to explore other avenues, but everyone was always shoving college down my throat like it was the be-all and end-all. So, I went, and I hated it. In a lot of ways, it felt more like high school, and in other ways, it felt way worse. I wasn't good at any of it. For the first year, I just barely passed, and by the second year, I was outright failing. And I was trying. I was studying, but I'm just not good with that sort of thing, so eventually, I just dropped out."

"What was your plan B?" I ask.

He shrugs. "I didn't have a plan A, so there wasn't really a plan B."

"What did you want to do with your college degree?" I ask, a little stunned.

"Nothing. No one ever gave me the choice, so I never got the choice of what I wanted to do with it. People made it out that you go to college and get the degree, and then the rest falls into place. I was having such a hard time with the first step that I never got far enough to think about what would happen after college."

"You didn't have any idea of what you wanted to do?" I try to make the words light to avoid hurting his feelings.

"I was still a kid—or I still am, I guess. How am I supposed to know what I want to do with the rest of my life? Did you know what you wanted to do in high school?"

"Yes," I say quickly.

He raises an eyebrow. "You're telling me it's still the same thing today?"

I nod, and when it seems like he doesn't believe me, I elaborate. "I wanted to graduate in three years, become a yoga instructor, teach at a local studio, and eventually open my own studio one day."

Caleb stares at me, and I can't tell if he believes me or not.

"What?" I ask.

"You've had that planned out since high school?"

I nod.

"And you're on track? Still set up for success and ready to take on the world?"

I pause, trying to ignore just how much my plan is falling apart.

"No, actually." My body deflates. "My best friend's parents died our first semester of college. We were roommates in the dorms, but she dropped out of college. I stayed enrolled, but I cut back on most of my classes and moved out of the dorm. We got an apartment together so I could make sure she was okay. They weren't my parents, but I still loved them. And it felt like I lost my best friend too."

There's a long pause before Caleb speaks. "I'm sorry."

"It's fine. She's better now. Me too. It's just . . ." I think of that first year, how it felt like I was trying to pull my best friend out of a black hole. "She moved to Colorado, and she's happy now—and I'm so happy for her. But I'm just here dealing with the aftermath of it all."

"What do you mean?"

I start to choke up. I haven't told Marly any of this. I've barely admitted it to myself. Whenever the thoughts pop up in my mind, I push them away, ashamed of myself for feeling the way I do.

"*Aftermath* isn't the right word." I start to backtrack.

"Then what's a better word?" Caleb says, and I start to break open, like there's a piece of myself I've been holding back, and it has finally been let free.

I laugh in a sad, quiet way, afraid if I do anything else, I'll cry. "After the accident, it felt like the world was on pause. I stopped everything. I needed to make sure Marly was okay, and when she finally was, I could focus on myself again. But by then

206

I'd already fallen so far behind that it didn't feel like there was anything left to fight for."

"That's not true," Caleb says gently.

I shake my head. "In order to graduate in three years, I had to take extra classes each semester, but that first year I had to drop a lot of classes. Now I'm just taking as many classes as they'll allow, which is why while everyone else is enjoying their summer break, I'm writing essays and reading college textbooks."

"Then just graduate in four years. That's what most people do anyway."

"That's not—" I pause, realizing how ridiculous it all sounds. Why bother stressing myself out trying to graduate in three years when it so obviously isn't working?

"Plans change." Caleb shrugs. "I should know."

I let out a nervous laugh. "I don't think I could handle any more change in my life."

Caleb picks up on the deeper meaning behind my words and shifts, turning his body to face mine. His knee comes up to rest on the couch as he leans to his side, his leg grazing my thigh. His arm stays stretched out, his thumb moving slowly over my shoulder.

"Do you wish your friend still lived here?"

"No," I shake my head quickly. "She's happy and of course I miss her, but it's not just that. I miss the life we'd been planning since freshman year of high school. We were supposed to live in the dorms together, go to college parties, get drunk and talk about all the guys we thought were cute. But now she's off doing her thing and thriving, and I'm here." I put my arms out to motion to the apartment.

"If you wanted the college experience, why didn't you move back into the dorms? Sounds like you've got all the stress of college without any of the fun benefits," he says with a soft laugh.

I let out a deep sigh, hearing the same question I've been asking myself for so long. "Because I constantly feel behind. I don't want to live in the dorms because I don't want to lose my focus. I still want to be able to graduate in three years, and I think living in the dorms will distract me."

"Because it's the last part of your plan for college that you're trying to hold on to?"

This time it's me who looks at him with confusion. "What do you mean?"

He shrugs. "You wanted to live in the dorms, but now you're in an apartment. You wanted to go to the same college as your best friend, but she dropped out. You wanted to at least have an apartment with your best friend, but she moved out of state. Now all you've got left is graduating in three years."

I lean forward, covering my face with my hands. "Is it bad to just want one thing to stay the same?"

His hand comes to rest on my back, rubbing slow circles up and down my spine.

"There're other parts of your plan that will work out; they just haven't happened yet."

I drop my hands and sit up. His hand moves from my back to my shoulder, pulling me a bit closer to him.

"Like what?" I ask.

"Owning your own yoga studio."

I let out a groan. "Yeah, well, I'm probably going to need to give up on that idea since no one will hire me as an instructor."

"I doubt that."

I raise my eyebrows. "Ask the thirty studios I've contacted so far."

He gives me a reassuring smile. "Well, the good news is you only need to find one willing to hire you."

I don't say anything, feeling that familiar pit of despair I experience every time I check my email or phone to see that none of the yoga studios have reached out to me yet.

"When did you officially become an instructor?" Caleb asks.

"At the beginning of June. But I only have the 200-hour certification, so I think I may have a better chance if I get the 500-hour certification. But I can't afford the next certification yet, so I've been working extra shifts when I can."

Caleb lets my words settle before catching my eyes again, his tone serious. "Can I give you a healthy dose of reality?"

I find myself wanting to lean away, but I remind myself to take a deep breath. "Sure."

"It's been a little over two months. I know you said you feel like you're constantly trying to catch up, but what if you don't need to catch up? What if you just wait until you stumble across someone looking to hire a yoga instructor and you take the regular amount of classes required by students? And you work enough shifts to pay your bills and worry about the 500-hour certification later?"

I'm about to open my mouth in protest, but Caleb stops me.

"We are on this planet for a finite amount of time. You don't want to waste it getting stressed out and putting so much on your plate that you forget to stop and smell the roses."

"How philosophical of you," I say.

He shrugs. "Trail life gives you a lot of time to think."

"And to smell the flowers?"

He gives me a wide grin. "Now you're getting it."

I smile, leaning my head against the couch, brushing my temple along his arm. When I glance up at Caleb, I find myself stunned. Never in my life would I have gone for this type of guy. The mental image of the guy I *thought* I wanted to go out with makes me laugh, because now I can't picture myself with anyone but Caleb. Where I'm high-strung and stressed, Caleb is laid-back. Where I'm book-smart, he's street-smart. We work in opposite ways to balance each other out.

"I'm not always this uptight," I say, lifting my head again.

He moves his hand until his fingers are cupping my cheek. "Yeah?"

"Well, sometimes. But it's one of the quirky personality traits that I hear makes me so appealing."

The corner of his mouth turns up, and we both hover closer, making the distance between us disappear until our lips meet. It's not like any of our other kisses; instead, I feel free. It's like I've been holding myself inside a box all these years, and for the first time I've been opened up to fly free.

His hand moves, shifting from my cheek to the back of my neck, pulling me closer. His other hand comes to my waist, and everywhere he touches me is ignited, brought to life.

When I pull away, it's only so I can look at him to be sure this is all real. His arms move to my waist, holding me close. I let my hand fall to his cheek, running my fingers over the stubble of his beard.

"You are not the guy I've been looking for all these years."

He grins in a way that makes my stomach flip. "That's because you've been looking for the wrong thing."

CHAPTER 25

for tonight, I've given myself permission to live in a dreamland where Caleb isn't going to leave in the morning. Instead, I'm going to "live in the moment," as Caleb would put it, and enjoy this moment rather than worry about tomorrow.

"Are you going to make me watch a chick flick?" he asks when I grab the remote and start scrolling through Netflix.

"No," I say, pulling up a movie that's been on my watch list for at least a month. I play the trailer to see if Caleb's interested, but as soon as it ends, he gives me a smirk.

"That's a chick flick."

"No, it's not. It has some action sequences with cars and stuff."

"Those are the parts they throw into the movie so boyfriends can tolerate sitting down for two hours."

"Oh, I see." I nod, mocking him. "Well, guess it's a good thing you haven't sealed the deal on the boyfriend thing, or you would be screwed." I stop scrolling and turn back to Caleb, who's giving me a knowing look. "What?"

"Are you looking for a boyfriend?" he asks with the type of smirk that makes me want to close the small space between us and kiss him.

"I'm not *looking* for a boyfriend," I say, trying to stay casual.

"You're a strong independent woman?" he says, eyebrow cocked.

"Exactly." I turn back to the TV and return to my search for a non-chick flick movie that also won't bore me to death.

"Well, when you're ready to start looking, let me know. Is there an application to fill out?"

"There might be." I grin.

"Oh, great." He chuckles.

I wait for him to say more, to deliver the punch line, but he doesn't. I turn to him, making a face.

"Caleb," I say. He's sitting on the couch, arms behind his head as he leans back in the most cliché way possible.

"What?" he says, grinning.

I roll my eyes and turn back to the TV, but I'm not seeing the movies anymore. I'm just hitting a button, my mind running wild.

"You aren't ready to be a boyfriend anyway," I say jokingly, though I'm still a little bitter that he wouldn't get to the point and ask me.

That gets his attention. His calm, cool, collected exterior shifts, and he sits up.

"What do you mean?" he asks, suddenly serious.

I smile, attempting to bring the banter back. "You disappear into the woods." I laugh.

"It's still an option," he says.

Suddenly, our joking is put aside, and it feels like we're having a much more serious conversation.

I put the remote down and turn to face Caleb. The corners of his lips are turned down, and he has a far-off gaze.

"Us being together is an option," I say, "but I don't see the point of making things official when we don't have any idea *how* we'll be together after you finish the trail."

"I plan on seeing you," he says so quickly his commitment almost blindsides me.

"How are we going to do that?" I say, smiling, but the words are desperate. "You don't know where you'll end up a month from now, so how can we plan a future together?"

"I want to."

I have to look down. I want to smile and cry all at once. "But you need to figure yourself out first."

When I look back up, Caleb's frowning. Worst of all, I want to ignore every word I said. I don't want Caleb to figure his life out first. I want him to follow me here, to New Hampshire, but it's too selfish to ask for that. He needs to figure out his own dreams first.

"So, in order to get you to be my girlfriend, I have to get *my* life together?"

I laugh a little. "Not your whole life. Just the next couple weeks, maybe.

He lets out a heavy sigh and sinks into the couch. "A few weeks?" He lets himself think. "I'll be finishing the trail. If I can, I'll see you every couple of days when I do resupplies, and then you'll be there at the finish line."

"And where's the finish line again?" I ask, feeding into his fantasy.

"The summit of Mount Katahdin."

I stifle a laugh. "I can meet you at the bottom, after you're done."

"I'm not going to get another mountain out of you?" He grins.

I shake my head. "You're lucky you got a backpacking trip out of me."

"Okay, no summit. So, does that plan work? For the next couple weeks at least?"

"I can't see you every couple days," I admit. His face falters, but it's so slight, I almost miss it. "Between work, class, and the yoga thing, I don't have time to drive back and forth every couple of days."

He thinks about it for a moment and sighs. "I guess that's true." This time he picks up the remote and starts scrolling through the movie selection.

"Do you have any idea what you want to do when you get back to Maine?" I ask, and I can feel the question of moving to New Hampshire on the tip of my tongue.

"No," he says quietly, like he isn't willing to admit defeat.

I try to form the words, to ask him to stay here, but I can't. "Will you go see your parents?" I say instead.

"Probably. Let them know I'm alive, but nothing more than that."

I wait for him to say more, but he doesn't open up. "You don't get along with your parents?"

He hesitates at first, then gives up. "My dad was pissed when I told him I was leaving to hike the Appalachian Trail. He thinks it's a waste of time. The only thing he'd be happy to see from me is college. He and my mom went to college, so they think it's the only way to get by. When I flunked, they were more embarrassed by me than concerned for my future. They think I'm not 'living up to my potential.' " He puts air quotes around the words and rolls his eyes. "But that's not who I am. Or who I want to be. School and I don't mix well."

I have to suppress my gut reaction, which is to agree with his dad. "Have you told him that?"

He shakes his head. "He doesn't listen."

"It's just because he cares," I say, only because I know that's why I want to push Caleb toward the same thing. "If you tell him what you want to do and why, maybe he'll understand."

"How am I supposed to figure out what I want to do when I feel like I'm not good at anything?" His voice rises, and I can tell I've struck a chord.

"That's not true," I say, tugging on his hand so he'll look at me. "You can't tell me you're not good at anything when you've survived out in the wilderness for months."

"That's not going to get me a job."

I shift on the couch, bringing myself closer until my thigh overlaps with Caleb's. He lets his arm rest on the back of the couch, lingering over my shoulder.

"Don't focus on the job," I say, hoping he'll hear the seriousness in my voice. "When you get back out there on the trail, don't think about jobs, or school, or any of that. Think about what makes you happy, and the rest will fall into place from there."

"Easier said than done." Caleb frowns, looking down, and it's the first time I've seen his optimistic exterior crack.

"That's what I did," I say softly. "Yoga makes me happy, and opening my own studio is what I've been fighting for. I'm working to make all the puzzle pieces fit together. It's not going as planned, but it will happen—that much I'm sure of." The words feel true as I say them.

Caleb's face brightens, and he looks up at me. With a soft smile, he leans his head back until he's practically looking at the ceiling and closes his eyes. A few seconds pass before I break the silence.

"Do you think you'll miss hiking when you finish the trail?" I ask.

"Hiking?" He laughs a little. "I won't miss the hiking part, that's for sure. But the other parts I will. Like the community. Everyone you meet feels like a friend, no matter how long you've known them. You start to see the kindness in the world again when you're out there. People give you food and water, they drive you into town without accepting gas money. People want to help you because they understand what you're doing is hard and want nothing more than to see you accomplish your goals.

"I think it has a lot to do with the fact that life is simpler on trail. You're not worried about politics or checking social media. You have two tasks every day: walk and survive. You wake up, make your meal, clean up camp, and then just start walking. Living with the basics is where the magic happens. And when you do that, you can appreciate things more. A bar of candy feels like a godsend even though you can buy one whenever you want at a gas station. And a roof over your head is a luxury." He stops himself, getting caught up in the moment. "I don't know. It makes me wish everyone went on a backpacking trip at least once in their lives so when they return back to society, they have a better appreciation for everything."

"You almost make me want to join you out there," I say, watching the way his eyes are still glazed over in wonder.

"Yeah?" he says, turning to me, curious.

"*Almost*," I say with a grin. "The memory is still too fresh from last time."

"Give it time. I'll get you back out there."

We both laugh, and eventually we settle on a movie. It's a rom-com, and Caleb doesn't voice any protest when I turn it on, even if this one lacks the action scenes that the first movie I suggested had.

Throughout the movie, I think of bringing up the boyfriend conversation again, worry prickling at the back of my neck. Here we are again, spending a night together when I know he's leaving in the morning. And come morning, what happens? Will it be a long-distance relationship? Will we text every day and then eventually talk less and less frequently until one day it stops completely?

The questions swirl around in my head throughout the entire movie, but I push the worries aside, determined to enjoy this moment. We're watching the movie on the couch, and I'm cuddled up across his chest, a blanket pulled up and over the both of us.

We stay up all night watching movies, which goes against everything in my core. I've always been a stickler for a healthy sleep pattern, but knowing Caleb has to leave in the morning makes sleep seem like a waste of time.

I keep my eyes peeled open, begging myself to enjoy this moment, because in the morning, reality will come crashing down again.

"You sure you don't want to go to bed so you can sleep? You have to hike tomorrow," I say as we pick out the next movie.

"I'll sleep on the car ride if I need to," he says, pulling me closer to his chest, both of us understanding the limited time ahead of us.

CHAPTER 26

We fall asleep on the couch at some point. I'm not sure when it happened, but when I open my eyes next, light filters in through the window behind the couch, making the morning too bright and cheery. I try to sit up, being careful not to jostle Caleb too much as I move, but then an alarm starts screeching loudly, making us jump.

Caleb's arm shoots up from under the blanket, reaching for his phone on the side table next to him. He finally turns the alarm off, still blinking his eyes awake.

"Good morning," I say, feeling like I barely got any sleep at all. I glance at his phone screen and see that it's six a.m. "Why do you have an alarm for six a.m.?"

Caleb starts to shift, so I move to the corner of the couch, pulling the blanket with me.

"I told Dusty I'd be ready for six thirty." He starts typing, probably texting Dusty.

"I didn't know you were leaving that early," I say, realizing we only have half an hour together, and I've wasted so much time.

"Is it okay if I give him your address to pick me up? His friend is driving us back to the trail."

"Sure," I say, then rattle off my address so Dusty knows where to go.

Caleb grabs his backpack from where he left it at the entrance to my apartment and digs a few things out before disappearing into the bathroom. I stay rooted in place, trying to piece together everything I want to say before he leaves.

"Do you mind if I shower?" he says, coming out of the bathroom and putting something in his bag before grabbing another item.

"Uh, sure. There're spare towels in the cabinet above the toilet."

He disappears, and my heart sinks at the thought of him leaving again. I want to tell him that I'll be his girlfriend, that at the end of all this, we'll figure something out. He'll decide what he wants to do after the trail ends, and I'll be there beside him. But I have no idea how to say those words with such little time left. I want to backtrack on the conversation we had last night, where I said he wasn't ready to be my boyfriend, but it feels impossible to undo.

I hear the shower turn on, and I start pacing the apartment, letting my mind worry in circles. I keep glancing at the clock, watching the time tick away as six thirty approaches. Finally, the shower turns off, and I jump back a little when the bathroom opens.

"You okay?" Caleb says, his eyes wandering over me. I haven't done a thing besides pace the room since he got in the shower, and I start to wonder if the pacing is making me more frantic.

"How much longer do you think you'll be on the trail?" I ask.

He makes his way back to his backpack slowly, while I stir in panic silently, barely able to contain myself.

"Two weeks, give or take." He starts to riffle through his bag again, putting things away. He's changed into the hiking clothes I'm used to seeing now.

"What happens with us in two weeks?" I say, trying to keep my words bold.

He freezes, letting go of his bag, leaving a pocket open as he stands. "What do you want to happen?"

My lips waver. I want to tell him that he should come back to New Hampshire and figure out his life here, but I can't get myself to say the words. It's too much to ask him to come here, especially when we've still only known each other for such a short period of time.

I bite my lip, wondering how to go about this.

"I want *something* to happen."

"Something?" he says, eyebrow raised with a grin.

"I want you to focus on you," I say, gesturing toward him. "But once you figure all that out . . ."

He smiles. "You want me to focus on you?"

My face heats up and I go red. "Not if you don't want to."

He lets out a low laugh, watching me. "I might want to."

My stomach does a little flip, and I try to refocus. "But in the meantime . . ."

His grin widens, and he shifts on his feet. "I would like to keep seeing you every couple days—if you can fit me into your busy schedule."

I can feel myself deflate. My next summer class starts in two days, which means all my free time will be taken up by studying. I'm about to tell Caleb that I won't be able to see him until he finishes the trail when a text comes in on his phone. I feel a tiny bit of frustration at the text message, wishing I could have gotten my words out first.

"I have to go. Dusty is outside," Caleb says, his eyes on his phone. He throws the backpack on and reaches his hand out. "Walk me out?"

I smile, giving up on the conversation, and take his palm. I realize I'm still in my clothes from yesterday and have no idea if I have as much of a bed head as I normally do when I wake up. If I look like a slob, Caleb pays no mind, gripping my hand tightly as we make our way outside.

I'm not sure where we're going until a car with its window rolled down pulls up in front of us.

"That's Dusty." He points to the car.

"Come on, Chip. We ain't got all day!" The man sticks his head out the window, and I vaguely recognize him from the first night I met Caleb at Angela's, but his beard and hair are longer and more untamed than ever.

Caleb goes to the back of the car and pops the trunk open, tossing his bag beside another huge backpack, which I assume belongs to Dusty.

"All right," Caleb says, closing the trunk and turning to me.

He wraps me in a hug before I can think to respond in any other way. The instant his arms are around me, I melt into his body. I grip him, begging myself to embrace this moment since I won't see him again for the next two weeks.

"Good luck," I say, shifting to kiss him. This kiss is short and sweet.

Caleb pulls away too soon, keeping his eyes trained on me.

"I'll see you soon," he says, the words final.

"Two weeks."

"Maybe sooner if you want to visit." He grins.

My face falters, knowing that isn't an option, but I try to force the smile on.

"Maybe," I catch myself saying, because I can't bear making him disappointed.

He kisses me quickly again before walking toward the back seat of the car.

"I'm looking forward to it," he says, pulling the car door open.

He gets in, and I take a few steps back, watching as Caleb and Dusty make their way back to Maine, forever moving northward.

CHapteR 27

Somehow, five days pass without me pulling my hair out by the roots. The new summer class is Shakespeare, and I took it because it was the only remotely familiar class I could take that would fit my world literature requirement for my degree. I thought I'd be able to get off easy by watching some of the plays rather than reading, but even then, the storylines of the plays go over my head. I give up on watching the play remakes and go back to my textbook to dissect them line by line, trying to understand the Old English.

The only bright spot in my day is getting a daily text from Caleb. He tries to send photos he takes during his hike, but he doesn't usually have enough of a signal. For the most part all I get is an update on where he's sleeping for the night. Occasionally, he'll mention a town that he passed through, which is the best I can do to pinpoint his location. Caratunk is the latest town, and when I find it on the map, I'm disheartened to see how much farther he still has to go.

He's back, Caleb texts, waking me up. I don't get it at first, but an hour later a photo comes in of a chipmunk standing on its hind legs, staring the camera down.

Living up to your name? I type out, smiling. His signal must be spotty because I don't hear from him again until the next day.

I keep seeing them everywhere. I think I'm being stalked.

Another text is waiting for me when I finish working my shift at Angela's, but it's just a photo. It's another chipmunk, and he's sitting on Caleb's backpack.

You feeding them or something? I type.

Silence. Again.

Texting is starting to feel impossible and pointless since it takes Caleb at least twenty-four hours to respond. I keep reminding myself he doesn't have cell phone signal, or that maybe he keeps his phone off to save battery life, but when all I can do is think about him, it drives me up the wall to not even be able to text him.

It's the next day, and I check my phone, waiting for Caleb's next text to come in, but it never does. My message is still unanswered even after twenty-four hours.

I'm trying to tame my curls into a braid before work when my phone starts ringing. My fingers are knotted in the hair at the nape of my neck, but I reach across the room and answer the call without looking, my eyes trained on my hair. I put the phone on speaker before going back to working with my hair.

"Hello?" I say. I unknot my hair, smoothing it to form a tight braid going down my back.

"Lori?" I recognize the voice on the other end of the line right away.

"Caleb, how's it going?" I ask, my voice lifting.

"I was going to text, but I figured it would be easier to call. I'll be hiking to a trailhead today. I need to go into town and pick up more supplies, then I'll have the rest of the day to hang out before heading back on trail in the morning. I wanted to know if you wanted to join me. I know you're busy, so if you can't, I get it."

It takes me a minute to realize what he's asking. He wants me to pick him up in Maine? Today?

"Where are you?" I ask, even though I already know I can't make the trip. I pick up my phone to look at the time. I have to leave for work in fifteen minutes.

But what if I could see Caleb today? I can already feel my will starting to crumble.

"I'm still at camp. I haven't left yet. I wanted to make a plan before I started walking. But the spot I need to be picked up at is in Blanchard."

The town name means nothing to me.

"You don't have to if it's too far," Caleb continues when I don't answer.

I watch the clock on my phone turn over, warning me that I need to leave soon. "No," I say, my eyes wandering around the room, searching for a way out. "It's fine." But it's not fine.

"Really?" Caleb says, and that's when I realize he never expected me to drop everything to come pick him up. He was fully prepared for me to say no, and I should have, but I didn't.

"Yeah, um . . ." I keep looking at the clock. My boss is going to kill me. Even if my boss doesn't kill me, I can already feel myself regretting calling in sick. "I'll leave in a few minutes. Just text me where to go."

"Perfect," he says, and I can practically picture the smile on his face. "I can't wait to see you. I'll text you where to go."

"Okay," I say, my voice full of dread, but Caleb doesn't notice, hanging up the phone and leaving me to deal with the chaos I've just created.

I've never called in sick. I mean, maybe once when I had the flu, but I was running a fever. I've always been the person my boss calls when she needs someone to fill in a shift last minute. I'm the backup plan, so who's the backup plan when I need someone to cover for me?

"Shit," I mutter, pacing the room. I'm already dressed for work, but I go into my room, changing into jeans and a blouse that I bought a couple days ago when I went shopping for an outfit to wear when I saw Caleb again.

I type out a text to my boss.

So sorry to cancel last minute. Just threw up.

I cringe at the quick excuse, but it's good enough. I hit send on the message, feeling nauseous as I do it; maybe I'm getting sympathy pain for myself. I start running around the apartment, searching for my keys and purse, guilty knowing I'm not going to work when I should be.

Once I'm in my car, I'm about to put the keys into the ignition when I half jump out of my seat from my phone ringing. I groan when I see Mary's name pop up.

With a deep breath, I answer the call.

"Hello?" I say in my best under-the-weather voice.

"Hey, I just wanted to make sure you're okay. You never call out," Mary says. She's always been a decent manager, but hearing how concerned she is only makes me like her more, which makes faking my illness even harder.

"Yeah, I'll be fine. It's probably just food poisoning." I regret the words as soon as I say them, realizing I ate some of the dishes at Angela's during my shift last night.

"It wasn't something from here, was it?" If Mary was concerned before, she's even more concerned now, especially since she knows I usually eat something off the menu during my breaks.

"No, no." The words come out quickly, and I'm pretty sure it's becoming obvious that I'm lying. "I picked up takeout on my drive home from work." I recoil at my own story. Who buys takeout when they've just eaten a giant plate of pasta at the end of their shift?

"Oh." If she's suspicious, she's choosing to believe me. "Well, I just wanted to make sure you're okay. Hope you feel better."

"Thanks," I say, hanging up the phone before she has the chance to ask any other questions. My head falls back into the seat, and I let myself stay there for a moment, festering in my idiocy.

I just hope I have a job waiting for me when I get back.

Another text comes in, and I'm afraid to see if it's Mary again, calling me out on my bullshit, but it's the GPS coordinates from Caleb.

I copy the numbers into my phone and start the GPS, trying not to wince when I see the drive is four hours long. I put the car into drive, reminding myself that for the next twenty-four hours, I'm going to go with the flow. I'm going to be the type of girl who can date a guy like Caleb. But for the first four hours at least, I'll be a nervous wreck, questioning what I've done.

§

The drive is awful. I get stuck in traffic twice, and the four-hour drive turns into almost five hours. Top it off with the fact that it starts raining, and it feels like the trip is doomed to end badly. When I finally get to where Caleb told me to go, it's just a spot on the side of the road where the trail intersects. The only relief is that I can see Caleb waiting for me. I almost don't recognize him because his bright orange backpack is covered in a weird gray tarp. But it's Caleb standing in the rain, his hair soaked down.

"Can I hitch a ride?" he asks as I get out of the car. The rain is a steady downpour, and it only takes a couple seconds for me to be just as soaked as Caleb looks.

I reach into my back seat, where I usually leave an umbrella. I fish it out, pushing it open, the pink fabric opening above my head. "I don't typically pick up hitchhikers, but you look cute enough."

We both smile, and he closes the distance between us, wrapping me in his arms and lifting me off the ground. I fumble with the umbrella as he kisses me quickly, both of us laughing. I bury my face in Caleb's shoulder, then instantly regret it.

"Oh my god," I say, pulling away a little bit.

"What?" he says, his arms still around my waist.

"You smell awful," I say, unable to help myself.

He shakes his head, still laughing. "I thought you grew immune to my scent when you went backpacking."

"Caleb, no one can grow immune to that. I just stopped saying anything because I couldn't figure out if it was you or me I was smelling."

"I didn't want to tell you." He fakes a guilty expression, and I push him away, but it only makes his grin widen.

"Get in the car. You smell more like a wet dog with each second."

Once we're driving, Caleb directs me into town, searching for a grocery store where he can pack up on food again. We're going down the snack aisle, where he's selected the biggest jar of peanut butter he can find.

"So, what's the plan for the day?" I ask, eyeing the odd variety of food in the cart. There're plenty of supplies for PB&J sandwiches, but he also picked up candy, ramen, and just about every Little Debbie snack I had as a kid growing up.

"I tried to book a hostel while I was waiting for you to pick me up, but they were full, so I just went with a cheap hotel. It's getting to be the end of the journey anyway, so might as well splurge."

"Nothing like a tiny room with questionable sanitation."

Caleb laughs. "All that matters is that I can shower."

He pushes the cart and continues onward into the grocery store, his eyes scanning everything until he reaches the granola bars. He takes a handful of flavors and puts them into the cart.

"Do you mind if I stay with you tonight?" I ask.

He pauses, raising an eyebrow.

"Not in that way," I say, shoving his arm a little until he stops making a face at me. "The ride here was four hours, and I don't want to drive back tonight."

I did the math the entire drive up. If we get up early in the morning like Caleb always does, then once I drop him off, I can drive straight home, shower, and have just a few minutes of peace to myself before my next shift at Angela's starts. And if I look flustered when I walk through the door? Well, I can just blame that on food poisoning.

"The room only has one bed," he says, more as a challenge than an excuse to make me not want to stay.

"I'm a good cuddler." I shrug.

He laughs, taking the cart again and leading us toward the checkout. "You're more than welcome to stay, but no funny business."

In the next hour, we're checked into the hotel. Caleb dumps the contents of his bag onto the floor, putting a few spare clothing items to the side to be washed. Meanwhile, I dump everything from the grocery store onto the bed, eyeing it, trying to figure out how it will all fit into his backpack.

"I'm going to shower and get into clean clothes. Can you take everything out of the boxes?" He takes one of the boxes of granola bars and rips it open, dumping all the bars out.

"All of them?" I ask, examining seems like an excessive amount of food.

"Yup. And I'll be back in a bit."

With that, he disappears into the bathroom, the only

reminder of his presence the sound of the shower running.

I work my way through all the boxes, bags, and excessive packaging. When I'm finished, the pile of food looks a little more manageable. I reach over to Caleb's backpack, pulling out the food bag he used when we were backpacking.

The food bag is long and thin. It reminds me a lot of the sorting cubes I use when I pack a suitcase, except this doesn't have a zipper; it just folds down and clips into place to seal shut. The bag is mostly empty, but I unbuckle and unroll it, dumping out its contents. Inside are a few bars, chips, and trail mix, but the rest is just wrappers. I organize it quickly, throwing wrappers into the trash to make room for the new food. It takes a little coaxing, but after lots of shoving and squeezing, I'm able to clip the bag closed again.

"Did you put the food away?" Caleb asks, stepping out of the bathroom wearing only a pair of shorts. His hair is still damp, and it looks like he ran a towel through it, leaving it pointing out in every direction.

"I think I got it all," I say, handing the bag to him.

He tosses it from hand to hand and then puts it on the bed.

"It's perfect." He smiles, making me feel like putting the food away was the best thing I could have done all day. "Do you want to go out to eat? Get a proper date in?"

I smile. "I'd love that."

Caleb grabs the same flannel shirt I've become accustomed to seeing him wear and slips it on. We leave the hotel, dropping Caleb's dirty laundry off at the front desk so it can be cleaned and ready for him by morning.

I drive us to a nearby Italian restaurant, knowing Caleb's a sucker for meals that include giant platefuls of pasta.

"So, any luck coming up with a plan?" I ask when we're halfway through our meals.

"Plan?" he asks.

"Yeah, about what you're going to do when you finish the Appalachian Trail. You've only got a little over a week left."

He nods. "Right. That."

"You've thought about it, right?" I try to keep the words as casual as possible, but I realize how pushy I'm being, and I don't like it.

"A little," he says, returning to his food and taking another bite.

I wait, hoping he'll continue and say more, but he doesn't. I try to let it go, to be that laid-back girl who was having fun earlier in the day, but she's gone now, replaced with the ever-uptight Lori.

"Do you want to talk about it?" I ask, because I know I want to.

He doesn't answer at first, midbite, but he shakes his head, so I know the conversation isn't going to go anywhere.

"Not right now."

My face falters, and the subject shifts. Caleb starts talking about how the excitement on the trail is amped-up with the finish line so close, but I start to fade away from the conversation, my mind wandering back to what Caleb's plan may be and what he may come up with.

When we get back to the hotel later that night, I still feel like I'm in a fog as Caleb packs all his gear up and tucks his backpack into a corner of the room, ready for the morning. We were even able to pick up his clothes early; they were ready for us when we got back from eating.

"Do you want to see if there are any movies?" Caleb says, grabbing the remote and turning on the TV. The volume is high as a reality TV show plays through the room, and he wrestles with the remote to lower it.

"You don't want to head to bed early?" I ask, eyeing the clock.

He shrugs. "I was thinking of taking a break tomorrow. I've been doing a lot of miles lately, and it feels like my body needs a rest. We can even hang out tomorrow if you'd like."

"I can't," I say, my words final. Caleb's face drops the smallest bit. "I have to work tomorrow. As is, I called in sick today so I could come here. I didn't have the day off."

He sits back, a little stunned. "You called in sick? Why didn't you tell me? I assumed if you were coming, you had the day off."

"I know, but I wanted to see you. And I didn't tell you because I didn't want you to feel bad. But I've been trying to be so . . ." I struggle to find the right word. "Rigid all the time. I'm always that girl who sits in the corner, planning her life away, making to-do lists, and filling every ounce of free time with tasks. I'm the type of girl who shows up early for work, not the one who calls in sick."

Caleb watches me, his eyes narrow, mouth open the smallest bit like he's about to say something, but he doesn't.

"I'm sorry," I say, because I don't know what else to say.

He shakes his head. "I never asked you to change. I didn't want you to change."

"I know, but—"

"Lori, I like you for *you*. Is it annoying that you work practically every day? Yeah, but I also admire you for it. You're doing the thing I should be doing, which is getting my life together and getting a job."

I start to waver under his attention. It feels so opposite. I've been trying to live up to the carefree, go-with-the-flow Caleb, but somehow he's looking up to me.

"I don't want to be that person anymore," I admit.

"So, be whoever you want to be." He takes my hand and pulls me to him. "Be the thing that makes you happy."

I close my eyes as my emotions prickle to the surface. When I reach up, I kiss him, realizing we're two halves of a whole, gravitating toward each other like magnets. I just don't understand how we're supposed to work together.

CHapteR 28

i wake up to the blaring alarm. Caleb is faster to get out of bed, turning it off before I have my eyes open. I let out a deep groan, burying my face deeper in the pillow.

"You're the one who wants to go to work today," Caleb says, reminding me that he was ready to take the day off to spend it with me. I'm almost tempted to call in sick again, but I know one more phone call from Mary and she'll probably call me out on my lie.

We get ready in silence, wandering around the room to gather our things.

Our relationship is at a crossroads. We both know things will change once Caleb finishes the Appalachian Trail, and we want to be together, but we don't know what that will look like or how it will happen. The question Marly wanted me to ask bubbles to the surface again: Would Caleb be willing to move to New Hampshire? The longer I think about the question, the more I start to dread his answer.

I drive Caleb back to where I found him yesterday, and I

don't know if it's because we're both tired, but we don't say a word to each other until I pull off to the side of the road.

"Can you tell me what's wrong?" Caleb says suddenly, and it takes me a moment to comprehend what he's saying.

"What's wrong?" I ask, dazed.

"You've barely spoken to me all morning. Even after we got back from dinner last night, you seemed off."

I stare at him, wide-eyed. It takes me another moment to build up the courage to say the words. "Would you consider moving to New Hampshire?" I ask.

He doesn't respond right away, and I'm not sure if that's a good or bad thing. He looks away, his eyes roaming over everything, never looking at me. I'm about to say something when he finally speaks.

"It's an option," he says, his words level, like he's trying to say what he thinks is right, not what he wants to do. "But when I started the trail, I always intended to go back to Maine. I was going to see if I could get my old job back—I worked at a hardware store in high school. Figured some sort of job was better than no job. That and I already know the manager there likes me."

I can feel my face flush. This is it, the reason I didn't want to ask.

"But moving to New Hampshire?" I ask, my voice not sounding like my own.

"It has its benefits." He gives me a sheepish grin.

"Then can I be honest?" I say, waiting until I'm sure he's listening. "I really like you, but I don't want to do the long-distance relationship. Maybe temporarily, like right now, but not knowing when I'll see you next is too hard. I need to put myself first this time, and that means I can't drive back and forth from Maine ."

I didn't plan on telling Caleb any of this, but I know in my gut it's what he needs to know, and it's what I need to admit to myself as well. Maybe it will play a role in the decision he makes, or maybe it won't. Either way, I need to make it clear what I need.

Caleb doesn't question me. He just nods his head in a slow solemn way.

"Okay," he says, voice gruff, looking down. "I'm not against moving to New Hampshire—and I'd be lying if I didn't admit it's been a thought in the back of my mind since I met you—but it's not what I pictured. I've been walking for months, trying to imagine how I'll rebuild my life in Maine. Now it's hard to think of how to do it in New Hampshire."

"You'd get a fresh start," I offer.

He glances over. "A fresh start would be nice," he says, but the words lack enthusiasm.

"But you want to go home," I say, because if I'm going to get my heart broken, I might as well get it over with.

"Going home would be the safe bet," he says gently, but it feels like the energy is being drained out of me. "You wouldn't want to move to Maine, would you?"

I shake my head. "My college is here. And hopefully my yoga studio."

He smiles, seeming unsurprised by my answer. "Didn't think it would hurt to ask."

"But you'll consider coming here?" I ask again.

"I'll have a couple long days in the woods to think about it," he says jokingly, but I can't get myself to perk up at the words. I force a smile, hoping beyond everything that he'll want to come back to New Hampshire.

We get out of the car, and I move to the trunk, watching as he slings his backpack over his shoulder.

"How far are you going today?" I ask as he takes a few steps toward the path. I follow close behind until we both linger at the entrance to the trail. Caleb turns, and when we lock eyes again, it feels like a part of me is breaking. What if he decides to stay in Maine?

Caleb wraps me in a hug, but it's too serious for the moment. I was supposed to be dropping him off, just like I always do. Why does this feel so much like a goodbye?

"As far as my legs will take me," Caleb mutters, my head resting against his chest. When he releases me, he gives me a faint smile before disappearing into the woods.

§

The next couple days go by in a blur. The texts that come in from Caleb are sparce and seem to space out more and more in frequency. Hearing from him less makes me anxious, and I wonder if he's decided to stay in Maine. Maybe slowly cutting me off is his way of breaking things off. When I do hear from him, it only sparks up my emotions again.

I get home from a twelve-hour shift at Angela's, and an email comes in over my phone, notifying me that my grade for my latest paper on Shakespeare has been posted. I click the link in my email, walking to my mailbox while it loads. I'm expecting my usual bills and junk mail, but instead, there's a handwritten envelope with no return address. I rip it open, but then my phone loads, and I see my grade.

D+

Everything around me freezes. If this was my first bad grade in the class, I'd brush it off, but this is the second D I've gotten on one of my papers.

I've been trying more for this class than I have for any other class, but no matter how much effort I give, nothing clicks for me. With all the hours I've been working, I usually end up doing homework late into the night when my brain is foggy.

I'm fighting back tears and wondering how I'm going to pass this class when I finish opening the envelope and see Caleb's signature at the bottom of the letter.

Since the trail is almost done, I've been trying to figure out the biggest thing I've learned, but I keep getting stumped. I want to say I've learned to be self-sufficient or how to walk twenty miles in one day, but that's not the biggest thing. The biggest thing I've learned is how to be driven. And I didn't learn that by walking every damn day. I learned that by meeting you.

Trail life was getting hard by the time I reached New Hampshire. I was too tired of it all to keep going. I was getting ready to give up and go home. I was going to crash on someone's couch until I figured out what to do with my life, but then you showed up. You were the perfect spark of motivation I needed. I think at first I kept hiking because I was trying to impress you, but the more we talked, the more I learned just how driven you are.

When I summit Mount Katahdin, know that you're the reason I got to that point, because I was ready to call it quits.

Caleb

I reread the note two more times, my thoughts coming in a flurry of emotions. Fresh tears spring to the surface.

A text comes in from my phone, and I fumble with it, convincing myself that it's Caleb. There's another wave of emotion when it's Marly's name on the screen instead.

Video chat? is all the text says.

I almost forgot today is our scheduled weekly video chat check-in.

Currently on an emotional roller coaster, I text.

All the more reason to video chat.

I let out an unsteady huff of air and make my way back to my apartment, plugging my laptop in before calling Marly. She picks up right away, her face serious.

"What's wrong?" she asks before I can say anything.

"I got a D+ on my paper." I laugh in a sad, hysterical way.

"Then why are you smiling?"

I hold up the note. "Caleb sent me a letter."

Her eyes widen. Marly's been keeping close tabs on the Caleb situation. She's been Team Caleb since the moment I was willing to go backpacking just to spend time with him, but her enthusiasm for him only grew after learning he came to visit me while I was at work.

"What does it say?"

I read her the letter, and by the time I finish, she's grinning from ear to ear.

"Lori," she says, completely giddy.

I shake my head, tears prickling to the surface, which only makes me more upset.

"What's wrong?" Marly says, confused. "Isn't the note a good thing?"

"Of course, but—" Why am I crying over this?

I blink, and the tears I was holding back stream down my cheeks. My bottom lip starts to quiver, and I want to say something, anything, but I'm afraid if I do, I might burst open.

"Is this just about the bad grade? Lori, it's just one paper. You can make up for it later."

"I can't handle anything else," I whisper, because it's the closest thing to the truth. "I can't focus on getting my grade up with Caleb around."

"You don't want to be with him?" Marly says, more confused than ever.

"No, I do." I blink, urging the tears away, and try to refocus on Marly.

She doesn't respond right away. She just watches me, waiting for the tears to stop before she speaks up. "Can you be honest with me?" she asks.

"I am being honest," I say, reminding myself to breathe and keep calm. I push back the pit of worry that's been building the past couple months, becoming more and more impossible to ignore.

"Then answer yes or no. Is this about your five-year

plan? Are you worried adding Caleb into the mix will screw things up?"

I almost want to laugh because hearing Marly say it forces me to realize how ridiculous the whole thing is.

Caleb is exactly what I want. This note should make me over-the-moon happy.

"No," I say, but it's clear she doesn't believe me.

She sits in silence for a moment longer. "Do you feel like you've fallen behind on everything you want to accomplish because my parents died?"

I'm shocked by her bluntness. Marly's never the one to bring up that subject. "It's not like that."

"Answer please," Marly pushes.

My lip quivers, and I think back to that first year and how many classes I had to drop. My grades were terrible, and I missed more assignments than I can count. I spent months planning our dorm room only to move out within the month. It felt like things were being ripped away from me one after another, and I kept telling myself it would all be okay in the end. But here I am, nearing the end of my three years of college, and graduation still feels just as far away.

"Yes," I whisper.

Her face drops when she hears me, and I want to take back my words.

"It's not your fault. I chose to drop out of classes. I let my grades drop. I made the decision to move out of the dorm."

"If I'd stayed in the dorm, would you have moved out?" she asks.

I don't say anything, but we both know my answer.

"I didn't want everything to affect you too," she says, letting out a deep breath.

"Everyone who loved your parents was affected, Marly," I say, watching as her face goes pale before shifting to a shade of pink. It's a look I became familiar with that first year after her parents' deaths, whenever she was trying to hold herself together so she wouldn't cry.

"I'm sorry," she says.

How many times have I heard *I'm sorry for your loss*? For months, that was all I ever heard, but the words were never directed at me. Each time it was said, it was said to Marly, or her aunt, or her grandparents. It was only ever said to her family, but never to me. I never thought I needed to hear the words because I wasn't family. In my gut, I knew what I'd lost. I grieved what I'd lost. But it's not until now that it feels like I'm acknowledged for that loss.

I wipe my hands across my face, tears spilling down my cheeks. Not for the first time, I wish Marly wasn't in another state and that we could have our usual girls' night where we talk, laugh, cry, and watch some trashy reality TV show that we can make fun of together.

"Well, this isn't the direction I thought the conversation was going." I laugh when I'm finally out of tears.

"Figured it was my turn to make you cry," Marly says.

"If you wanted to make me cry, I would've preferred we just watch a sad movie, but I guess this works too."

"Maybe we stream a movie together after we're done talking."

"You mean this conversation isn't over?"

"We haven't talked about Caleb."

The air feels heavier. "What about Caleb?" I ask, my eyes lingering on the note.

"Do you want to be with him?"

I hesitate, and she changes her question.

"Failing college classes and long hours at work aside, do you want to be with Caleb?"

I cringe at the mention of failing my class, but my answer is obvious. "Yes."

"College and your ridiculously overloaded work schedule are temporary. Leaving Caleb behind isn't. And if he makes you happy, I don't think that's something you should let go of."

I let out a heavy sigh. "So, how do I survive in the meantime?"

Marly smiles. "You just have to learn to embrace the chaos."

My need to control the chaos wavers, and I let myself mull over the possibilities. For the first time, I consider changing everything.

CHAPTER 29

t he next morning, I'm staring at the paper pinned to my corkboard. In big bold letters is *FIVE-YEAR PLAN*, and underneath is each year and a list of things I'm supposed to accomplish. The things I've accomplished are crossed off, but most of the items on the list are still left unchecked.

I pull the paper off the board and flip it over to reveal the back side. When I first made my plan, I thought it would be easy to accomplish everything. On paper it looked feasible, but once reality set in, I had to be more specific with my goals. I used the back of the paper to figure out *how* I was going to accomplish these goals.

While the front of the paper is written in my most perfect handwriting, the back side is nothing but chicken scratch. The thing I struggled to figure out the most was how to graduate college in three years given I'd spent the first year of college getting only twenty-one credits when the original plan was to finish the first year with thirty credits.

The paper is riddled with notes from me trying to problem-solve the issue of having too few credits and not enough semesters left to accomplish my goals. That's when I started to take summer classes into account as well, signing up for additional credits whenever possible.

I grab a marker from my desk and flip back to the front page and look at the goal of graduating in three years. Without letting myself think about it too much, I cross off *three* and replace it with *four*, so now the goal reads *graduate in four years*.

It feels like a weight has been lifted, just knowing I'll allow myself an extra year to graduate. Then I have to laugh at myself, because it's not an extra year—it's the usual amount of time it takes someone to graduate college. I turn to my laptop, logging into my student portal to view my class schedule for next semester. I have seven classes on my page, and I look them over quickly and select three of the classes, unenrolling myself.

I open up my email, contacting my advisor to explain the shift of plans. I begged her to sign off on my extreme plans to graduate in three years. If anything, I'm sure she'll be relieved for me. I sign off the email by mentioning my struggle in the Shakespeare class and the possibility of dropping out of that class as well. At this point, it's better to quit and not worry about bringing my grades up than spend the rest of my summer stressing out about failing a class.

There's a tiny nagging hint of regret when I send the email, but I let myself focus on the feeling of relief instead, the freedom of knowing I'll actually have time for myself, which I'm starting to think is the thing I need most.

A text chimes in, and when I check my phone, it's Caleb's

name on the screen.

I should be finishing on the 19th if you still want to be there.

I smile when I read the message, but when I pull up my work calendar, my schedule is already full. I'm covering for Allison that day so she can go on a family vacation.

After dropping so many classes and taking so much off my plate, why does this one shift at work feel like the biggest roadblock yet?

I'm scheduled to work, but I'll find someone to cover, I reply, knowing it's time I do what I want instead of working every moment possible.

§

I'm adamant about not missing Caleb's finish to his hike, but every one of my coworkers gives me a hard time. Each person I text gives me vague answers without providing a legitimate excuse, and it's even more infuriating given the number of times I've covered shifts for them without question.

Any luck? Caleb texts the next day.

No.

It only takes a minute or so for Caleb to respond. *It's fine.*

I wait for another message to come through, but nothing ever does. In a fit of frustration, I dial Allison's number.

"Hello?" she says.

"Hey, Allison, you know how I'm covering your shift on the nineteenth?"

She hesitates. "Yeah?"

"I have a date with that cute guy I met a couple weeks ago," I say, knowing exactly what she needs to hear to buy into the trap.

"Really? That's great!"

"I need you to take your shift back," I say quickly.

Silence again. "Can't you go out with him on a different day?"

"I can't. He's an AT thru-hiker, and that's the day he's going to finish the trail, so it's kind of important."

"I can't take the shift back, Lori. I have a flight booked already."

I deflate. Why did I ever agree to take on so many shifts for people?

"But what if you see him earlier?"

"What do you mean?" I ask.

"You're on the schedule to work tomorrow, right?"

"Yes?" I say, not seeing the point.

"Well, I can work your shift tomorrow so you can drive up and see him and celebrate."

I run the idea over in my mind. It's not the best option, but it's something. And I could surprise Caleb, which might make up for me not being able to be there when he finishes.

"That would be great," I tell Allison.

Now I just have to figure out where to find Caleb along the trail without him knowing.

CHAPTER 30

i spend all night stalking Caleb's Instagram account, trying to figure out where he is on the trail. The last couple nights he's been vaguer about his location, probably because he realized the shelter names don't mean much to me in terms of location, so I've resorted to internet stalking.

He doesn't share much information online, but he's tagged in a photo posted by someone under the username @ trailhungry85. Trailhungry85 has more information on his profile and even tagged his location less than twenty-four hours ago. With that, I'm able to pull up a map of the Appalachian Trail and do some guesswork to try to figure out where Caleb may be, comparing it to the last town I know he passed through. Knowing how far Caleb hikes in a day and when he plans on finishing, I think he'll be on Greenville Road in Monson, Maine. I look it up on the map, and it seems obvious enough, but it's still a shot in the dark.

All I can do is cross my fingers that Caleb will be there.

The next morning, I wake up at four a.m. to leave, trying to get to the trail parking lot as early as possible, having no idea when Caleb may appear. It's another long day of driving. I get in the car long before the sun rises and watch the sky lighten as the miles go by.

Finally, when I can't drive for a moment longer, I pull into a parking lot, where there seems to be quite the crowd parked to hike and explore the area. Rolling the windows down, I prepare to wait.

Minutes turn to hours as I sit in the car, watching the entrance to the trail, examining each person as they come and go. I perk up every time I see a new person, but I lose hope just as quickly when I realize it's not Caleb.

A van parked close to the trail entrance has set up a pop-up canopy and a few foldout chairs. In between scanning each hiker who comes through, I watch the man as he pulls out a grill and starts cooking burgers and hot dogs, handing them out to hikers.

At first, I assume the man must know all the hikers, but as more people come and go, all of them stopping for food and drinks, it seems impossible that he knows every single person.

Maybe there's an event going on?

I squirm in my seat, trying to lean forward to see if there's a sign, but I don't see anything. Hiker after hiker, people talk to the man, shaking his hand and grabbing food before sitting down in one of the foldout chairs under the canopy.

I make an excuse to get out of my car, eager to stretch my legs. I pace closer to the canopy, glancing over to see better, but it still remains a mystery to me. I head back to the car.

At some point, I blink awake, and I'm covered in sweat.

I lucked out when I first arrived, my car sitting in the shady portion of the parking lot, but now I'm sitting in the sun.

I push the car door open and step out, wishing there were more relief from the heat; instead, I'm just greeted with more humidity.

"Damn summer heat," I mutter to myself.

I glance up. The van is still parked, but the canopy is packed up, and the man is putting his things away and getting ready to leave. I search the parking lot, hoping to see Caleb by some miracle, but he isn't here.

"Excuse me," I say, crossing toward the van. The man looks up after shoving one of the folded chairs into the back. "Did you run into anyone today by the name of Caleb?"

"Caleb?" the man says, looking confused. The guy is probably four times my size, easily a foot taller than me, and on the heavier side.

"His trail name is Chip," I add, hoping that may be more useful.

The man's face lights up. "Chipmunk Chip?" He smiles. "Yeah, he was here yesterday. I've run into him a couple times."

I smile, relief flooding through me. "Oh, good. Where did you see him?"

The man cocks an eyebrow. "Here." He nods, closing the back door to his van.

The words don't process for a second, and I'm left standing there, staring back at this stranger, struggling to find words.

"You mean . . ." I glance over to the trail, where Caleb must have been yesterday. "He's already gone." My hope is dashed as

I say the words. I tuck my phone away, taking a few steps back, my eyes still on the trail in disbelief. "Okay, I'll meet him at the next spot." I pull out my phone to look at the map of the trail, but I don't have enough bars to get anything to load.

"The next spot?" the man asks, his tone curious.

"Yeah," I say, trying to compose myself and hide my disappointment. "I was trying to surprise him."

The man's face turns down. "I'm sorry, kid. There won't be another point to meet up with him for a couple days. He just entered the Hundred-Mile Wilderness."

The more the man talks, the more confused I get. "Hundred-Mile Wilderness?"

"Yeah. It's the longest section of the AT without roads or places to resupply. You know, wilderness." He shrugs.

I can feel myself shrink, getting smaller as I hear the words. "How long does that usually take?" I'm hoping he can't hear the emotion laced on the edge of my words.

"It can take anywhere from six to ten days."

I nod, trying to make sense of it all. "I'm guessing there's no cell phone reception either?" I ask, now regretting not texting Caleb in the first place. I could have saved myself the drive, but I don't even care about that. I just wanted to see him and wish him luck before his big finish.

"Sorry," the man says, and then there's a moment of awkward silence. "I'm Burger Bob, by the way."

I laugh to myself at the name. I almost want to tell him I'm Moose—my trail name—but I don't feel like I've earned the title, despite what Caleb may think. "Lori," I say.

"Chip didn't tell you where he'd be?" he asks, curious.

I shake my head. "It was supposed to be a surprise."

He nods with a low grunt. "Well, if you wait at Abol Bridge the next couple days, he should show up there eventually."

I give a weak smile, not bothering to tell him I have no idea where Abol Bridge is.

"So, are you a part of the Appalachian Trail?" I ask, watching as he packs the last of his things into the van.

He laughs at the question. "You could say that, sure." He leans against the side of the van, turning to face me. "I hiked the AT a couple years ago. I ran into trail angels along the way, and I promised myself that if I finished, I'd make it my mission to feed every hungry hiker I could find, just like I'd been fed so many times before."

Caleb mentioned trail angels before, but I never imagined it was on this large of a scale. "You feed all those hikers yourself?"

He shrugs. "I cook the food, but I get donations too. I pay for a lot of it as well, but I can't take all the credit."

"Wow," I say, sucking in a breath.

"We arrive too late?" another voice shouts.

I turn and see two new hikers wander out from the trail, their backpacks large and heavy looking.

"Out of food for the day, but I can give you a ride into town if you need to resupply," Bob says, waving to the new hikers like they're old friends.

"That'd be great!" the hiker says. The man is tall and skinny, making the bag look much too heavy to be carried around on his back. His shorts are bright orange, and he's wearing a loose-fitting tank top in desperate need of a wash.

A woman walks a couple paces behind him, her hair cropped short and pointing out in all directions. They both look like they need a long hot shower.

"I hope you find Chip," Bob says, turning back to me. He gives me a wave, and I nod, taking small steps back as Bob and the hikers converse over where they need to go.

It's an entirely other world out here. I always assumed the people who hiked did it for the good views, or they had a sick and twisted idea about what workouts should be. Watching how Bob meets and feeds so many hikers makes me wonder what else drives people out into the woods. Maybe it's not the views or the calories burned, but the people along the way.

When I get back to my car, I'm more lost than ever. I had one chance to find Caleb—one day off from work—and I arrived too late. Just a day late. What a joke.

Sitting in the parking lot, I watch Bob drive off in his van with the other hikers. I know Caleb isn't going to magically appear, but I have no idea what to do next. I came here without a plan.

Going home isn't an option. Going home would mean everything about today was a waste, and there's no way I came this far only to not see Caleb.

I set the GPS on my phone for the nearest and cheapest hotel I can find, not letting myself overthink anything anymore. From this point on, I have zero plans and zero expectations.

That fact becomes painfully clear when I pull into the parking lot of a Holiday Inn and realize I don't have anything to stay the night—not a change of clothes, toothbrush, or even pajamas.

I stare at the entrance to the building for a long time, wondering again if I should go home with as much dignity as I can salvage.

If the roles were reversed and Caleb were sitting in the car, trying to decide if he should put his life on pause for the next few days to chase down a girl, I'd like to think he'd do it.

The engine is still purring, reminding me I have a decision to make: stay here and make a plan B, or go home and give up on seeing Caleb.

With a deep breath, I step out of the car and toward the entrance of the hotel.

the woman at the front desk looks at me strangely when I check in, asking if I need help carrying my bags since I walked in empty-handed.

No, miss, I don't need help carrying my bags because I don't have any.

I want to see Caleb. I know that's going to be a part of my plan. What I don't know is how I'm going to make that happen. I can't just wait around all week for him to show up, but after driving so far and sitting out in the parking lot all day, I'm in no mood to drive home tonight.

I'm sitting in my hotel room, trying to do the math in my head. I have to work on the nineteenth, which is still seven days away. And according to the internet, when Caleb gets out of the Hundred-Mile Wilderness, he'll just have a day or two left of his hike before he completes the trail. Can I bank on him possibly finishing early? If he finishes early, I could go home tomorrow, work a couple days, and then come back, see Caleb, and go back to work the nineteenth. I could text him to find out when he thinks he'll be out of the Hundred-Mile Wilderness, but if there's no cell phone reception, what's the point?

The only thing I can do is wait for Caleb at Abol Bridge and hope for the best. This is all assuming I can find someone to cover my shifts.

I grab my phone and dial Allison's number, crossing my fingers that she'll be willing to take on a few more of my shifts since I'll be covering for her vacation.

"Lori?" she says, sounding excited. "How did it go?"

I cringe, thinking of how today was supposed to go. "He's not here."

"Oh," she says, voice deflated.

"I talked to someone who saw him yesterday. Apparently, I won't get the chance to run into him again for a few more days."

"I'm sorry."

I hesitate, wondering if I'm asking for too much. "When do you leave for vacation?"

"The eighteenth."

I silently swear. "So, you wouldn't be able to cover my shift on the eighteenth, then?"

"No, sorry."

"What about the seventeenth?"

She laughs a little. "You really like him, huh?"

"Just answer, please."

She lets out a playful sigh. "Yes, I can cover your shift on the seventeenth. If and only if you fill me in on all the juicy details when I get back from vacation."

There's a moment of relief. "Thank you! I will."

"I'd say you owe me, but technically I owed you in the first place." She laughs.

"I just wish I could find someone to work the nineteenth."

"Call out sick. Angela's will live to see another day even if you aren't there."

"I can't. It will look too suspicious. I already fake called out sick last week."

"You are way too concerned." Allison laughs again.

"It's not funny," I say, starting to whine.

"It's just one day of work, Lori. Who cares? It's not like they'll fire you over missing one day. You're working more hours than anyone else. They'd need to hire two people to replace you."

"I don't even like this job," I say, burying my face in my hand. "I'm supposed to be working in a yoga studio teaching classes, not waiting tables."

"Then why aren't you?" Allison says.

We aren't the closest coworkers in the world. Allison and I exchange stories here and there, but we don't usually dive too deep into each other's lives. She knows I'm working on becoming a yoga instructor because I mention it all the time, but she doesn't know just how badly I want this—or just how far behind I am at making this goal a reality.

"Because . . ." I start. Because no one will hire me? Because I need to keep working a job I can't stand to save up money to get another certification that may or may not help me get my first gig as an instructor? "No one will hire me to teach yoga classes."

"Are you certified?"

"For 200-hours, but not 500-hours. I'm trying to save up

money to take the next course." I'm rattling things off, but what does it matter? Allison probably doesn't know the difference between the certifications.

"Oh! Well, that's perfect."

"What do you mean?"

"My mom goes to a yoga studio a couple towns over. She said they've started changing her class schedules because one of the instructors quit. You should go apply there."

I blink a couple times before I can form a response. "What's the name of the studio?"

"Uh . . ." She pauses. "I don't know, but I can text my mom and get back to you."

I smile, trying not to get excited yet. For all I know, it's a studio I've already applied to and been rejected by.

"That would be perfect," I say.

"Okay, I'll text her now. Good luck with tracking Caleb down!"

"Thanks," I say, ending the call with a soft click.

My head is spinning. I wonder if what Allison said is too good to be true. Is it possible there's a yoga studio I missed? Or maybe the instructor just quit recently? Maybe I haven't been looking as diligently as I should be.

A couple minutes later, I get a text from Allison.

The place is called Reed Studios.

I don't recognize the name. I google the studio, and the result comes up right away. It's not one of the yoga studios I've called yet, and it's in a town just half an hour away from my apartment.

A Facebook page pops up on the search, and I click on it, hoping they'll have a few pictures of the studio, but the first post I find is a large graphic that reads "Help wanted."

We're looking to hire an instructor to teach Vinyasa and All-Levels Yoga. Knowledge in alignment and anatomy required. At least one year teaching experience preferred. Call the front desk to apply.

I stare at the post for a long time, my eyes scanning over the part where one year of teaching is preferred. Do I even stand a chance?

Maybe.

I dial the number and hold my breath.

CHAPTER 32

"Hi, this is Cassie from Reed Studios. How may I help you?" The woman answers the phone after only a couple rings, not allowing me enough time to think about what I'm supposed to say.

"Hi." My voice catches, and I remind myself to keep it together. "I saw that you're looking to hire a new yoga instructor, and I wanted to apply."

"Oh!" Cassie says, her voice shifting. "What's your name?"

"Lori Hayes."

"And have you taught yoga classes in the past?"

My confidence wavers. "Not officially, but I have my 200-hour certification, so I've done the practice classes, and I've been teaching classes to friends." To say the yoga I did with Caleb was a class is a stretch, but I need Cassie to give me a chance.

"Do you think you'd be able to come in tonight for an interview?"

I'm sitting in the hotel room, mentally kicking myself for not just driving home.

I brush a hand over my face. "I'm actually out of town today, but I can come in tomorrow morning."

Cassie doesn't say anything for a few seconds, and I start to think I blew it. Me driving all the way to Maine to see Caleb is going to be the thing that prevents me from getting a job as a yoga instructor.

"Let me talk to my boss. I'm going to put you on hold for a second."

The line goes silent, and I scold myself while I wait for Cassie to come back. I start pacing the hotel room. Could I get to the studio tonight if I leave right this second? It doesn't take long for me to come up with an answer: no.

"Hi, Lori, this is Ellen," another voice says, and my attention shoots up.

"Hi," I say, frazzled all over again.

"I'm the owner of Reed Studios. Cassie was telling me you're interested in the instructor position. Do you have time to do a quick interview over the phone?"

I perk up immediately. "Yes, of course."

Ellen starts by telling me about the studio, how long they've been around, and what types of classes they offer. She explains that the position is only part-time, but that as long as student feedback is good, I can start taking on more classes over time. We go over the schedule, making sure I'm available to teach their morning classes, which is perfect because all the classes I have left in my course schedule for next semester are in the afternoon. Ellen moves on to asking me about what type of training I've had, my experience teaching, and my personal connection with yoga.

"What made you get into yoga in the first place?" she asks.

"It keeps me grounded," I say, the words rolling off my tongue. I've always known my *why*. It's what's kept me sane during the hardest parts of my life. "I tend to put too much on my plate and get stressed out easily, but doing yoga is like a light switch. I can just turn off all the noise and hustle and bustle of life. When I'm doing yoga, it's the only time I'm able to hear my thoughts clearly."

"I know the feeling," Ellen says with a soft chuckle that makes me feel like I passed a test. "When do you think you'll be able to come in and teach a practice class so I can get a feel for your style?"

I struggle to come up with an answer, my eyes roaming over the empty hotel room.

"When would work best for you?" I say, because all of a sudden, I can't think straight.

"How about tomorrow at ten a.m.?"

I let out a huff of air. For once, this is perfect.

"Sounds good. I'll be there," I say, knowing I'll have plenty of time before my shift at Angela's in the afternoon.

"Perfect. It was great talking to you, Lori."

"You too," I say.

The line clicks, and the room goes quiet again. My mind swirls around, a sense of euphoria lighting me up. I grab the hotel-branded notepad and pen off the desk in the corner of the room and start writing notes for what I want to do for my yoga class.

§

It's my second day in a row waking up at four in the morning. How exciting.

Despite the ungodly hour, it's surprisingly easy to get out of bed and check out of the hotel before the sun rises. I don't bother much with getting ready for the day since my plan is to get back to my apartment, shower, and then put on my best yoga-instructor-you-should-hire outfit.

My energy starts to fade on the drive home, but once I'm back in my apartment and take a shower, there's a renewed pep in my step. I've just finished picking out my favorite yoga outfit when I hear my laptop going off, so I sprint to the other end of my apartment, where I left it on the kitchen counter. Marley's photo pops up, requesting a video call.

"Shoot," I say, grabbing my laptop and bringing it with me to my room. I texted Marly last night telling her I had an exciting update, but she was too busy to call. It appears now is the time she's free to chat.

"Hello!" I say once Marly's face pops up on the screen. I dart away from my computer and start digging in my closet to find the new pair of sneakers I bought. "So, I can't chat long. Job interview."

My back is to the screen, but I can still hear Marly. "Oh! That's the news? Congratulations! What job?"

"Yoga instructor!" I say, turning quickly to smile at the camera.

Marly's face lights up. "Really? That's great!"

"I know! Anyway, I'm running late, so wish me luck!"

"Running late? Since when?"

I find the shoes and slip them on before walking back to my laptop. I grin in a guilty sort of way, keeping my eyes off the screen so I don't see Marly's reaction as I talk.

"Since I drove to Maine last night to see Caleb and then had to wake up at four a.m. today so I could get back to my apartment, shower, change, and leave" — I check my phone — "*now* to get to the studio on time."

I start walking again, taking the computer with me out to the kitchen, where I left my keys.

"You saw Caleb?" she says, perhaps more excited than when I told her I have a job interview.

"No," I say, cringing a little. "Long story. I'll fill you in later. But I gotta go."

"Good luck!" Marly says, giving me a quick wave before I end the video chat. I grab my yoga mat from where I left it rolled up in the living room and tuck it under my arm.

I run out the door and start my car again, pulling out of the parking lot and doing as much positive thinking as I can.

By the time I pull up to Reed Studios, I've fully immersed myself in the idea of being able to work there. I spent all night planning the perfect mock yoga class for today in hopes that I can impress Ellen.

The studio is in an old mill building. The tall brick walls would make it hard to guess there's a yoga studio here if it weren't for the sign at the front door. The building is so big that it's not just the yoga studio inside. According to the signs outside the building, there's also a coffee shop, bookstore, and clothing boutique.

A thrill of excitement goes through me as I think of just how perfect this will be if I get the job.

When I enter the building, there's a large hallway with a few signs directing me where to go. The front door to the coffee shop is directly to my left, and I can see the logo for Reed Studios decorating the glass door at the far end of the hallway.

I take one final deep breath as I make my way to the door, pulling it open with as much confidence and purpose as I can muster.

When I step in, I'm transported from the old mill building into a yoga sanctuary. Piano music plays softly in the background, with the sound of flowing water coming from a tiny artificial waterfall in the corner of the room. The entrance to the studio is small, with just enough space for a front desk, but no one's at it.

Off to the right is a hallway with a coatrack and cubbies for everyone to store their shoes. The hall is filled with dozens of shoes, and a few gym bags peek out from the cubbies. There must be a class going on.

"Oh!" a woman says, walking out from another hallway off to my left. She walks behind the desk and smiles. "Sorry, I was organizing a few things back there. How may I help you?"

I smile, clutching my yoga mat, which is sticking out of my bag. "My name's Lori Hayes. I talked to Ellen yesterday about the yoga instructor position."

The woman's eyes light up. "Lori! Yes, that was me you spoke to. Sorry, sometimes we get latecomers to yoga classes. I thought you were a student." She smiles and grabs a clipboard from the desk. "Feel free to put your shoes over there." She points to the hall, and I kick off my shoes to put them with the others.

When I turn back to Ellen, she moves away, heading back down the hallway she came from. "Follow me," she says.

The entire studio is painted a soft lavender color, and there's a light smell of incense that only grows stronger as we walk. We pass a closed door, and I can hear the soft murmur of the yoga class on the other side.

Ellen leads me to an open room across the hall and steps in, turning on a light.

"We've already spoken about all the important things over the phone, so now I just want to see how you teach. Every instructor is different, so I'm not looking to see if you teach the right or wrong way; I'm looking to see if you fit in this studio. We have a certain expectation for classes, and today I want to see if you can meet them."

Ellen walks to a corner of the room and grabs a yoga mat from a basket before laying it out on the floor.

"What style of yoga do you like?" I ask, unrolling my mat across from hers.

"Doesn't matter to me. I just want to see what comes naturally to you."

I can feel the doubt creep in as I sit down on the mat, centering myself.

So, this isn't about meeting standards. I either naturally fit the role, or I don't.

"Sounds great." I smile even though my confidence is already starting to waver.

"The floor is yours," she says. "Let's pretend we're doing

a half-hour yoga class. I'm looking for an all-levels yoga class that will work for beginners and modifications for those who are more advanced."

Ellen gives me free rein. I prepared for this, and I run through the class I composed for myself last night. We move through the poses slowly, and I provide modifications for each one to make it easier and harder, just like she asked. I guide us through breath work, focusing on long exhales.

I enter a state of bliss as I teach, forgetting this is a practice class and that my job as an instructor is riding on it. I glance over at Ellen every now and then to make sure her form is good, but otherwise I'm completely in my own world, letting my body move and flow with my breath and each pose.

After finally finishing the class with a Savasana, I instruct Ellen to come to a seated position, and it feels like I've just bared my soul to the world. With a final slow breath, I let the feeling of bliss course through my veins.

Until I see the time.

My demo class was only supposed to be half an hour, but it ended up becoming a full forty-five minutes.

I pray that Ellen doesn't notice, but she stretches her arms and looks over her shoulder to see the clock.

"Sorry," I say, cringing at my own mistake. "Got a little caught up in things."

She smiles but doesn't say anything as she shifts to kneel so she can roll up her yoga mat. She asks a few more questions, and I answer them on autopilot, not even registering exactly what she's saying, just obsessing over the fact that I went over my time by fifteen minutes.

"All right, well, I have to head back to the front desk," she says. I roll my mat up quickly, a pit forming in my stomach as I follow her out of the room. "We have another class that people will start arriving for in the next couple of minutes."

"What's the class?" I ask, trying to hide my unease.

"Power yoga." Ellen smiles and leads me through the main hallway and back to the front desk. "You're welcome to join if you'd like."

The pit in my stomach grows deeper. I know I should stay, that it may help me become more familiar with the studio and the other instructors, but most of all I want to take my things and scoot out the door before Ellen can tell me I didn't get the job.

"I actually have to get going, but maybe another time," I say, knowing if I don't get the job, I'll never show my face at this yoga studio again—or go to the bookstore, coffee shop, or boutique. It's a lose-lose all around.

"Well, I have a few other girls I'm meeting with about the position, but I'll call you in a couple days to let you know."

I fake a smile, putting my shoes back on and grabbing my gym bag and yoga mat. "Sounds great."

I'm screwed.

CHAPTER 33

have to leave for work in an hour, but instead of getting dressed, I'm lying down staring at the water stain on my ceiling. I should be getting changed out of my yoga clothes and into my work clothes, but it feels easier to sit and sulk for a while.

I dial Marly's number.

"How did it go?" she says as soon as she picks up.

I groan, covering my face with my hand even though she can't see me. "So good, but so bad."

"Why do you say that?"

"I taught the class great. I think it was great. But I went over my time limit by fifteen minutes. Not only that, but she said she's looking for someone who fits the style of the studio, so I either fit it, or I don't."

"I'm sure you did great."

I frown. "You've never even seen me teach yoga."

"I've seen you do yoga," she amends.

"Anyone can do yoga."

"I can't," Marly says, and I have to laugh this time. "Is that all you're tripping up on right now? The fact that you went over by fifteen minutes?"

"I guess so," I say. "That and the fact that she mentioned she'll be meeting with a few other girls to interview for the position, so not only do I have to fit in with the studio, but I have to be the best option."

"How long until you know?" Marly says.

"She just said it would be a couple of days."

"Hmm," she says. "In the meantime, you can always find more studios to apply to."

I frown, not mentioning to Marly that I've already reached out to dozens of yoga studios and this is the first one that's actually looking to hire someone.

"Can we talk about something else?" I say, eager to move on to something that might be more positive.

"Okay, how about you tell me what happened with Caleb?"

"Oh," I say. Is it possible to move on to an even more uncomfortable conversation? "Do you want the long version or the short version?"

"Long version," Marly says.

I take a deep breath. "Well, I decided to give up on my epic five-year plan."

"What—"

I cut Marly off before she can finish. "I'm not giving up on the plans; I'm giving up on the timeline. Instead of worrying about making sure it all happens in five years, I decided I'm just going to make sure it happens . . . eventually." I pause to think about it and then correct myself. "Ten years max, not five. I'm tired of taking the maximum amount of credits and working every shift I can fit into my schedule. I want to be able to look back years from now and say I enjoyed my time in college."

"And you're not right now?"

I let out a shaky breath. "No," I admit.

Marly is quiet.

"And it's not because of college," I amend. "It's because of me. I've been so focused on checking things off my to-do list that I forgot to do the fun parts."

"Like all those wild parties?"

I laugh. The parties were never my thing, but I've skipped out on way too many campus events in the past year. I always imagined college to be half about the work and half about the social experiences. It's mostly been all work so far, and I can't remember the last campus event I attended.

"More like having a social life," I admit.

"Is this where Caleb comes in?"

"I guess so." I smile, thinking of the first couple days we spent together. Somehow, the camping trip was the most fun I've had all summer. Caleb has to really be something to make me look back on sleeping in the woods fondly.

"So, you went to go see him . . ." Marly eggs me on.

"He texted me saying he'd finish the hike on the nineteenth, but I can't find anyone to cover my shift that day. I tried to surprise him by driving up yesterday, but I did the math wrong, and he'd already come and gone by the time I got there."

"I'm sorry, Lori."

"That's when I decided, screw it, I'm going to find him." I

can hear Marly laugh softly. "I'm having people cover my shifts at work so I can go back to Maine in a couple days, sit at the intersection of the trail, and wait for him."

Marly lets out a single laugh. "Wow," she says, failing to hide any sort of doubt. "When you have your sights set on someone, you really zero in."

"Am I being stupid?" I ask, knowing Marly will give me an honest answer.

"You're being . . ." She pauses, trying to find the right word. "Unpredictable."

I make a face. "What does that mean?"

"You're not the type to ask people to cover your shifts so you can go chase down a guy. You're the responsible one."

"Not that responsible. I still haven't found someone to cover my shift for the eighteenth," I argue.

"You're just proving my point." Marly laughs.

I let out a groan. "Are you in support of me going to Maine or not?"

"Full support," she says, and I know she's smiling. "I'm just saying, I notice a change."

"Is that bad?"

"It's a very good thing. He helps you remember to live a little."

§

The next couple days are painfully slow. I go to work, counting down the time until I can go back to Maine. I talk to every single person I work with, asking—no, *begging*—them to cover my shift on the eighteenth, but I don't have any luck. Apparently, the eighteenth and nineteenth are popular days for vacations, birthday parties, and family reunions.

I don't let that put a damper on my plans though. Instead, I try to focus on Caleb finishing early, so that when I drive up on the seventeenth and wait at Abol Bridge, he'll be there.

On the seventeenth, I drag myself out of bed at four in the morning, which is starting to feel a little too familiar at this point. My body buzzes with eager energy on the drive up. The drive this time is longer than ever, taking over four and a half hours, which only feels longer as my eagerness grows.

When I finally get to Abol Bridge, it's nothing more than a long cement-and-steel bridge that a road crosses over. I pull my car off to the side and get out and walk around, trying to spot signs on the hiking trail.

I've been there for about an hour when I start to see hikers come through. They emerge from off in the distance, walking along the road that goes over the bridge. The first backpacker to come through is a woman who looks too tiny to carry such a massive backpack, but she walks forward, eyes bright and eager.

One by one, hikers show up, crossing the bridge. They all look worn, like they need to lie down for a bit, but no one ever stops to rest. A few see me and give me a kind wave, but they all continue forward toward their journey.

None of them are Caleb.

Today is my only chance to see him. If Bob is correct about when he ran into him, it means Caleb's been in the Hundred-Mile Wilderness for six days. It's possible to see Caleb today, but as more unknown hikers pass by, my hope starts to dwindle.

What if he needs seven days to complete the Hundred-Mile Wilderness?

I walk up and down the bridge, walking about half a mile down the path before turning around and making my way back toward the car. I spend my entire day this way, tacking on the miles, only getting a tiny glimpse of the amount of effort thru-hikers make each day.

When the sun begins to set and turns the sky bright pinks and oranges, I make my way back to the car, sitting until the color drains from the sky.

Caleb isn't here. And though I can't confirm it, I'm sure if he were going to emerge from the woods today, he would have by now. He likes to set up camp when there's still daylight.

I start up my car and drive to the hotel I booked for the night, knowing that tomorrow I need to wake up and return home, Caleb or no Caleb.

I'd hoped to find him and that we could spend the night together before I had to say goodbye again. The hotel was supposed to give me a few extra hours with Caleb—hours I don't get.

Now the hotel is just a place to crash after driving so far and standing out in the sun for nothing.

Back at the hotel, I'm washing my face, trying to imagine going to work when I know Caleb will cross that bridge any day. I'm so lost in thought that I almost miss the beep my phone keeps making, notifying me that I have a voicemail.

When I finally check my phone, the voicemail is from Reed Studios.

CHAPTER 34

"What the hell?" I mutter to myself, pacing the hotel room, kicking one of the pillows that I knocked to the floor.

My anger at the inanimate object is probably irrational, but I've been waiting days for this call, and it went straight to voicemail?

I give up on investigating the issue and hit play.

"Hi, Lori, this is Ellen from Reed Studios. I'm calling because I wanted to go over things again to make sure you're still free to teach classes the days we discussed when we spoke over the phone earlier this week. We'd love to add you to our team. I think you'll be the perfect fit. Just give me a call back at this number when you get the chance."

I can barely believe the words when I hear them. I got the job? How did I miss this?

I look back at my missed calls and see the one from Reed Studios, which somehow came around noon. My phone didn't even ring, but I know the cell reception was spotty. It never occurred to me that Reed Studios was going to call me back the only time I didn't have cell phone reception.

Without thinking, I dial the number to call Ellen back, but no one answers. I'm not surprised; it's almost ten at night.

I drop my phone and start pacing the room, my mind wandering all over the place.

I got the job. If I got the job, then I don't have to be a waiter anymore. If I don't have to be a waiter, then . . .

No. I can't just not show up for my shift tomorrow. I already know there's no one available to cover my shift.

So, why am I still considering it?

I dial Marly's number, desperate for someone else to give an opinion, to make the hard decision for me, but she doesn't answer. I start to dial my manager's number, wondering if I should call and put in my two weeks—or better yet, tell her I won't be back at all.

A tiny sliver of doubt builds. If I call, maybe I'll jinx everything. What if I talk to Ellen and find out something's changed? Could she have changed her mind in the time it took me to call back?

My phone rings, and my heart jumps, but it's Marly, not Ellen.

"Hey!" I say, a little flustered, still trying to process everything.

"Sorry, I was at the store. Did you see Caleb today?"

"No, but I got the job!" I say, unable to contain myself.

"The job?" she says, not catching on at first. "You mean *the* job? At the yoga studio?"

"That's the one!"

"That's amazing! Congratulations! You need to celebrate. Ugh, I wish I was there. I need to fly back and visit soon."

I have to control my excitement. "Thank you, but that's not what I need to talk about."

"Okay?" Marly says, a little confused.

"I didn't run into Caleb yet, but I'm supposed to go back to work tomorrow."

"At Angela's?"

"Yeah."

She doesn't hesitate. "So quit. You've already got a job lined up and waiting for you."

"But shouldn't I do the two-week notice?" I'm an entire state away, and I'm more than tempted to just disappear and never step foot in Angela's again.

"I've quit a job without a two-week notice," Marly says, a little hesitant. "And I believe you were the one who encouraged me to do it."

I feel my face go red, thinking about how last summer she was the one who was states away on a road trip and needed to unexpectedly quit a job she hated. "It's easier to give someone bad advice when it's not your life," I mumble.

"Hey!" Marly says. "It wasn't bad advice. I think we can both agree it was life-changing."

"True," I admit.

"My vote is that you quit Angela's."

"It's easier to give someone bad advice when it's not your life," I repeat, and we both laugh.

We chat for at least another hour, but while I love talking to

Marly and hearing the latest about where she's been traveling to for photography, I know the real reason I'm keeping her on the phone is to avoid calling my manager.

Part of me wants to just ignore the issue and not show up tomorrow, maybe pretend I forgot I had to work or got my days mixed up. It seems like a believable lie, but the idea of deserting them when I know there's no one to cover my shift leaves a pit of guilt in my gut.

It's almost eleven by the time I get off the phone with Marly and muster the courage to call Mary. I hope calling her this late at night means she won't answer.

I pace the room, working to concoct a story of half-truths as my excuse for not being able to work anymore. I'm hoping Mary won't pick up so I can leave a voicemail and won't have to face any questions she may have.

I dial her number, and the phone begins to ring. I count them as they go by.

One.

Maybe I'll be lucky since it's so late.

Two.

Or she'll be tired and grumpy.

Three.

Can she force me to go to work?

Four.

Maybe she won't answer.

Five.

I hold my breath, waiting for another sound.

"Hi! You've reached Mary. Leave a message, and I'll get

back to you."

I gasp for air at the relief of knowing I won't have to talk to her.

"Hi, Mary, it's Lori. I wanted to let you know I won't be able to make it in for my shift tomorrow." I pause, wavering. "Between my classes and everything else, I'm just a little too overwhelmed, and I won't be able to work at Angela's anymore. And because of circumstances . . ." I pause, knowing everything I'm saying is sounding worse the more I talk. "I can't come in to finish my remaining scheduled shifts. Sorry."

I don't hang up right away, wondering if I should say anything else. I hesitate too much, regretting my words and wondering if I should've just sucked it up and gone into work tomorrow. When I finally click the end button on the call, the sense of unease finally goes away and is replaced with a new sense of freedom.

§

Today is the eighteenth, one day before Caleb said he would summit Mount Katahdin to finish his hike. He's been in the Hundred-Mile Wilderness for a full week, so today should be the day he crosses Abol Bridge, but . . . I'm doubtful. Not because I don't think he'd be able to cover the distance in a week, but because it feels like each time I make a plan to see Caleb, something pulls us apart again.

Maybe Mary will call me back, demanding I come in for my shift.

After leaving a voicemail for Mary, I called Ellen again, this time leaving her a voicemail to tell her I wanted the job, but even then, it feels too good to be true. What if Ellen calls me back and it goes straight to voicemail because I'll be at the bridge all day? Will she get sick of playing phone tag and give up on me?

I give Ellen another call, but she still doesn't answer, so I hang up, hoping for the best. I look up the hours for Reed Studios, and their first class today doesn't start until eleven a.m. I'll be out at the bridge by then, waiting for Caleb, and I can't risk leaving just to get cell reception. Given my luck, he'll walk by right when I leave.

Knowing I at least left a voicemail for Ellen, I leave for Abol Bridge.

I get there even earlier than yesterday, parking on the side of the road just as the sun begins to rise, eager to catch every hiker in case one of them is Caleb.

Today is an especially humid day, and the temperature climbs higher and higher. I twist my hair into a tight French braid while I wait, eager to get it out of my face. I'm wrapping a hair tie around the end when I see him. He's so far away that I think I must be imagining things at first, but his bright orange backpack is clear as day.

That's when I panic, because in all the waiting I've done to see him, I've never once thought of what I'll actually say. I assumed it would just come to me, but all that's coming to mind now is a long string of curse words because I'm so unprepared.

I'm standing by my car, and I take a step toward Caleb before I stop myself and turn back to the car like I forgot something.

I take a deep breath, wiping a layer of sweat off my forehead.

When I imagined our reunion, it was a little less sweaty than this.

I turn back, keeping my eyes glued to the ground as I walk full speed ahead. I don't dare look up until a car drives by, giving me a humid rush of air, throwing me out of my trance.

When I look up, Caleb's already looking at me, the bridge an empty landscape between us. A smile starts to form at the corners of his lips.

"Lori?" he says.

When I hear my name, I can't contain myself any longer. I close the gap between us, running across the bridge and toward him. He isn't prepared for me when I run into his arms, but he grips me a second later and starts laughing.

"What are you doing here?" he asks.

I pull away just enough to look at him. There are deep circles under his eyes, like he hasn't gotten enough sleep, his skin is covered in a thin layer of dirt, and the smell . . . I won't say anything to him, but it's a very distinct backpacking smell I've become all too familiar with.

But I'm grinning wider than ever.

"Surprise," I say softly.

He's smiling, but he won't stop looking me up and down, as if he doesn't believe I'm actually standing in front of him.

"You came early? How did you know where to find me?"

"Burger Bob," I say.

He looks impressed. "You talked to him?"

I shrug. "I talked to him the day after you started hiking the

Hundred-Mile Wilderness. I was going to surprise you then, but I was too late, so Bob told me where to go to run into you before you hiked Mount Katahdin."

He shakes his head in disbelief. "You tried to surprise me earlier?"

"I wanted to talk to you."

He raises an eyebrow, holding back a laugh. "You could have texted me."

"I wanted to say it in person."

We untangle ourselves, but Caleb holds my hand, pulling me forward as we walk slowly down the bridge.

"I'm all ears," Caleb says.

I bite my lip, realizing I don't know what to say. "I'm done being stressed out and overwhelmed all the time."

Caleb makes a face like he doesn't believe me.

"I quit my job," I say, admitting it out loud for the first time. "And I dropped about half my college credits for next semester. I'm also not going to worry about getting the 500-hour yoga certification."

"What?" Caleb says. He pulls us both to a stop, looking over at me in concern. "Why?"

"Because I'm tired," I say, exasperated. "I'm so tired of working and studying twenty-four seven. For the last two years, I've been trying to get my life back on track because of things that happened that were completely out of my control. Then I met you, and even though I never want to hike the Appalachian Trail, I can't help but be a little jealous. Not of the backpacking, but of how you just . . . *live*. And that's what I want to do. I want to live. This summer, the things that've made me happiest have been all the times I've spent with you—even the long, sweaty, sleepless backpacking trip we went on."

He grins. "So, if I said you had to go on another backpacking trip with me, you would?"

My face drops, but I compose myself. "Would you consider an air mattress?"

Caleb laughs, and I wonder if I'm forgiven. He starts walking toward my car, and I follow suit, keeping pace with him.

"Where are you going?"

"Katahdin Stream Campground," he says, words coated in enthusiasm.

"You weren't serious about the backpacking thing, were you?"

He gives me a sly grin. "I've been walking through the wilderness for seven days. It'd be nice to have some company."

My face goes flat. "You're joking."

"You can bring an air mattress if you can find one. Bring it to the campground."

"I don't have an air mattress. I don't even have a sleeping bag. I've been staying at a hotel."

"I'm sure we can figure something out." He smiles, clearly enjoying my discomfort.

"You're serious?"

Caleb laughs but doesn't respond to my question. "I've been thinking about a lot of things in the past week, and I've finally figured out what I want to do after this."

I perk up. "What?"

"I'll tell you tomorrow."

I frown. "Come on, you can't do that."

"Tomorrow's the day!" he says, tone chipper. "Maybe I'll make a big speech at the finish line. Will you be joining me for the finale?"

I stop in my tracks. When Caleb notices, he stops and turns.

"I can't hike with you again."

"Why not? You don't have to work at Angela's anymore, right?"

"Right, but—" But I have no excuse. I already quit. "You want me to hike up another mountain?"

He smiles, amused by my response. He turns slightly and points to a massive mountain off in the distance. Mount Katahdin pokes through the sky, looming over the trees. Yesterday it was too cloudy to see in the distance, but today the mass of land is clear and prominent. It's hard to imagine getting to the top.

"That's the finish line," Caleb murmurs, almost reverently.

"That's crazy," I say. I must look like a cartoon with how my jaw literally drops.

"You don't have to go with me. But I'm just saying, I have this epic speech prepared, and I'm not sure if it's as impactful at sea level."

I roll my eyes, laughing a little. "You really want me to be there?"

He doesn't pause to think about it. "Yes."

I shake my head, but I already know what's going to happen. By some logic that I'm clearly lacking, I agree to go.

CHAPTER 35

I left Caleb so he could finish his hiking for the day and so I could drive into town to run a few quick errands. Caleb only has a couple miles to go, so odds are he'll be waiting for me by the time I finish driving around. He plans on sleeping at the campground tonight, and luckily for me, I don't have any supplies to camp with him. I'm just going to sit at the campfire until it's time for me to retreat back to the hotel.

Caleb sent me into town on one errand in particular: to buy food for tonight and tomorrow. By this point, I'm familiar with his high-calorie diet while hiking, so the trip to the grocery store is as simple as cramming as much food into my cart as possible.

I also wanted to come back into town to get cell phone reception so I could talk to Ellen and make sure I didn't just make the biggest mistake of my life by quitting my job before knowing without a doubt I have another job lined up.

While I'm in the grocery store, I wait for a missed call or voicemail to pop up, but nothing does, only leaving a nervous pit in my stomach. There's a voicemail from Mary, but it's just her letting me know that she got my message and that they'll miss me. I'm glad I missed that call at least.

I make my way back to the hotel to grab some of my things, and I suck up my pride and dial Ellen's number. It rings a couple times before I finally hear the click of someone picking up.

"Hi, this is Ellen at Reed Studios. How may I help you?"

I let out a sigh of relief. "This is Lori. I'm calling back about the job offer." I muster as much confidence as possible as I speak, sure that if I act like I have the job, the rest will fall into place.

"Lori! So good to hear from you. I had it on my list to give you another call. Yes, so the job is yours if you want it. And just as a reminder, I have you down for a Sunday morning all-levels yoga class, a Wednesday morning gentle yoga, and then Friday morning for another all-levels yoga. Does that still work with your schedule?"

"Yes, that's perfect."

"Great! Then I just need you to come in when you get the chance to fill out some paperwork. When's the soonest you'll be able to stop by? I'd also love to get a photo so we can add you to the website as an instructor."

I hesitate. "I'm in Maine right now, but I'll be home in two days." There's a pinch in my gut, thinking of how I just saw Caleb again and now I have to leave already, but I can't let this go. We'll work something out later.

"Great! Stop in anytime. I'll be here sorting through some stuff while the instructors are teaching."

"Thank you so much," I say, a smile coming across my lips.

"Of course. See you Sunday."

There's another soft click, and the call ends.

I'm a mix of utter joy and a bundle of nerves as I stand in the hotel room, but when I look over to the clock, I rush out the door, realizing it took me a little longer than I thought to go grocery shopping.

I take off in my car, but as I get closer to the campground, I realize I have no idea how to find Caleb once I'm there. Do I just drive around until he pops up? I don't even get the chance to pull into the entrance of the campground before I see Caleb standing, his backpack at his feet. He sees me when I pull up, putting his thumb out like he's trying to hitchhike. I come to a stop, rolling my window down.

"Can I get a ride?" he asks, giving me a grin.

I roll my eyes and lean out the window. "Where am I supposed to go?"

He shrugs. "The campground's full tonight, so I have to find somewhere else to stay." He frowns, clearly disappointed.

"Would a hotel work?"

He chews the side of his lip. "That doesn't seem like a very epic way to spend my final night on trail."

"As opposed to sleeping in the woods somewhere?"

He shrugs. "It's what I'm used to."

I shake my head. "Get in." He hesitates, so I give him my best smile. "I'll make it special."

Whether he believes me or not, he picks his bag up and tosses it into my back seat before joining me in the front.

"Where to?" he asks, buckling up.

I make a U-turn and head back into town. "First things

first—you need a shower."

He gives himself a sniff and cringes. "The Hundred-Mile Wilderness is not for the faint of heart."

When we get back to the hotel, I usher him into the bathroom as soon as we're through the door.

"In a rush?" he asks as I help him pull his backpack off.

"No, you just smell awful." I walk into the bathroom and grab a fresh towel and throw it at him. "Now go shower."

He digs in his bag for some of his things before disappearing into the bathroom. I rush around the room, trying to clean up some of the mess I made last night. I'm sure Caleb doesn't notice the way my clothes are thrown across the floor or how my suitcase looks like a bomb went off, but I do.

When I'm positive he's in the shower, I make my way to his backpack and go digging, trying to find the tiny camping stove he uses. I rummage through his bag, finding all sorts of supplies and tools that I have no idea how to use, but I grab everything I saw him use for the camping stove and stuff it into the grocery bag from my errands earlier.

A few minutes later, Caleb steps out of the shower.

"Are you hungry for dinner yet?" he asks, moving toward his bag, and I wonder if he'll notice that I went through it.

"It's part of the surprise I have planned for you."

He cocks his head, then pulls a shirt from his bag and slips it on. He's back in the flannel I've come to know and love. "Surprise?"

"You said you wanted your last night on trail to be special." I walk toward the door and open it, holding the grocery bag.

"So, let's go." I step into the hall and wait for him to follow. He smiles, eyeing me up and down.

"Lead the way," he says, coming to grab my hand as we walk back to my car.

I don't have much of a plan, but it's something. When I was driving around town today, I got lost and stumbled onto a scenic outlook that I'm positive Caleb would love. It isn't much, but it's something.

The drive to get there doesn't take long. The road curves, and a small spot on the side of the road clears, giving a perfect view of Mount Katahdin. I pull my car off and park. The break in the patch of woods is so small that I'm sure most people drive by it every day without much notice.

"I assume you aren't surprising me with a walk in the woods," Caleb says when I park.

I laugh at the thought of subjecting myself to that again. "No. Dinner with a view." I hold up my grocery bag.

We don't walk far. We're only a couple feet away from the road when we find a fallen log to sit on. Mount Katahdin looms tall in front of us, and it's highlighted by a massive lake that sits at the foot of the mountain. The water is perfectly calm, reflecting the silhouette of Mount Katahdin at our feet. The sun's already beginning to set as the day comes to a finish, making the clouds glow in shades of pink and purple.

"It's nothing fancy," I say, opening the grocery bag and taking out the ramen noodles I bought earlier. "But I figured you don't want fancy until you cross the finish line."

Caleb smiles. "There's nothing I've been craving more."

I pull out his little camping stove, and his eyebrows rise in surprise.

"When did you get that?"

"While you were in the shower."

"Little thief." He laughs.

I start making our dinner, watching as the water heats to a boil and our noodles cook.

"Thank you for coming," Caleb says, voice suddenly serious.

"Of course."

"I was going to call you when I finished the trail." He leans forward to turn off the gas before the water has the chance to boil over.

"I was going to track you down either way," I say, and it stuns me how easily the words roll off my tongue.

Caleb settles in, leaning back as he takes in the view.

Watching the clouds shift to different shades of orange and pink, I can see the appeal. I've always appreciated nature in photographs, but sitting surrounded by nothing but expansive views, it's impossible to deny how much better it all is in person.

"I can't believe it ends tomorrow," Caleb says. There's a shift in his voice, and when I look over, the corners of his lips are turned down.

"You going to miss it?"

He shakes his head. "Not all of it." He moves to wind his arm around me, pulling me close. "I'm going to miss the people though."

I flush, thinking about how I'm one of those people, but I hope I'm not someone he says goodbye to after the trail.

I force a smile. "Some of the people might stick around."

He glances over, but his face is serious. "I'm not going back to college."

I start to waver, knowing it's not the same choice I would make. But his answer doesn't shock me. This is Caleb. He wasn't made for college. He was made for something different. Something better for him.

"Okay," I say.

"If I tell you my plans for after the hike now, will you still come to the top of Mount Katahdin with me tomorrow?"

The tone of the night shifts, and I can feel the tension building, but I will it away. I want Caleb to tell me, whether I agree with his decision or not. All I hope is that I'll be part of his plans.

"I'm not a fast hiker," I say, laughing in a nervous way.

"I'm not in a rush," he tells me, which only makes me want to shake the information out of him.

"What are your plans, Caleb?"

He smiles, seeming to enjoy teasing me with just bits of information. "Does New Hampshire have any tech schools?"

"Yeah, there're a couple. I know there's one close by, but I forget what it's called." I say the words so quickly I don't make the connection at first, but once I do, it all clicks into place. "You want to go to tech school?"

"I think so." He shrugs. "I've always been a hands-on guy, not a book guy. Working at the hardware store taught me that much at least. I figure I'd probably be better off learning how to build a house or plumb a toilet. Tech schools will let me do that, so once I finish this hike, I'm going to apply."

"You know, before all this, I would have thought hearing you talk about plumbing would be gross, but right about now, I'm really happy for modern-day plumbing." I laugh, leaning into him.

"The unsung heroes," he says, hugging me closer to him.

"Wait," I say, catching something else he said. "You were asking about tech schools in New Hampshire?"

He grins in response.

"Not Maine?"

"Not Maine," he confirms.

I don't have a response at first. I have to fight the giant grin forming across my face, which is only mirrored in Caleb's response.

"Really?" I say when I can finally compose myself.

He shrugs. "I've got nothing waiting for me in Maine, but New Hampshire's got a pretty good draw. I was waiting for a cell phone signal to start looking into apartments and—"

I kiss him, totally and completely overcome by excitement. Caleb falls back a little, needing to catch himself before I knock him off the log we're sitting on.

"If I'd known you'd be this excited, I would have told you right away." He laughs.

"Of course I'm excited. I'm sick of saying goodbye to you." And that's when it really hits me: I won't have to end this trip with goodbye, because we'll be walking away together.

Caleb wraps his arm around me, kissing my temple. We sit in silence for a moment, watching as the colors fade until the darkness of the night starts to creep in.

"Oh!" I say, sitting up. "I have good news."

Caleb shifts to see me better and smiles with me, the energy contagious. "What?

"I got a new job."

He looks confused at first, but then I can practically see him piece everything together.

"As a yoga instructor?"

I nod.

"That's amazing." He pulls me into a hug, and when his arms wrap around me, a part of myself starts to break free, and a surge of utter joy lifts me up. When I pull away, there are tears going down my cheeks, and I'm not sure who's more shocked, me or Caleb.

"What's wrong?"

I wipe my cheeks dry while Caleb's hand runs up and down my arm. I laugh, practically giddy. "Nothing."

Caleb shakes his head and kisses me, making my head spin and practically lift off into another world of wonder.

I'm only left to question how it is that I pushed him away for so long, unaware that he was the person I needed in my life to free me from the impossible standards I'd created for myself.

My head is still spinning as I grip his forearms, holding myself as close to him as I possibly can.

Caleb lets out a low chuckle, and I turn to him, his gaze trained on Mount Katahdin.

"What?" I ask.

"I can't believe I get to finish the trail tomorrow." He glances over at me, awe painted over his smile. "You sure you want to come along?"

Mount Katahdin's strong profile gets lost in the sky as the horizon darkens. My confidence wavers, and I ignore the nervous twinge in my stomach.

"Of course," I tell him.

CHAPTER 36

Caleb goes to bed almost as soon as we get back from watching the sunset, exhausted from a long day of hiking. I take a shower when he's asleep, but I can't get myself to relax enough to go to bed. Instead, I start googling Mount Katahdin, trying to see what I've roped myself into this time.

The results aren't great. Almost every website I find warns of how rocky, steep, and hard the hike is. According to Google, *Katahdin* means "greatest mountain," but it doesn't sound like it's going to be a great experience.

I make the mistake of looking at photos, trying to put my mind at ease. Instead, I accidently stumble onto a YouTube video of someone hiking Knife Edge, one of the trails to reach Mount Katahdin, and my stomach drops.

In the video, it looks like the camera is attached to the hiker somehow, because he uses both hands to climb up what I assume is supposed to be the trail but looks more like a steep pile of boulders. I skip forward in the video, and the trail only gets worse, the hike turning into something closer to rock climbing and balancing on a stone balance beam.

I exit the page before I have the chance to psych myself out more, but the images are burned into my brain. This time, I know I'm in over my head.

§

When I wake up in the morning, it's because Caleb is walking around, making noise. He's already up, moving around the room and packing his things. He pulls the curtains open, revealing the sun just starting to lighten the sky. I pull the blanket over my head and groan.

Caleb grips the sheet and pulls it away. He's just inches from me, a huge grin across his face. I wish I had the same level of enthusiasm.

"Time to get up," he says. He kisses my temple before walking away, and the casual gesture is enough to stir me awake.

"What time is it?"

He starts stuffing his bag. "Six fifteen."

I pull myself out of bed and make my way to my suitcase, thankful I packed a few extra things even though I didn't plan on staying this long. I change in the bathroom, and by the time I come back out, Caleb is packed and ready to go.

I grab the last of my things and throw them into the suitcase, eyeing Caleb's backpack, which is about the same size as my suitcase. It's almost laughable knowing he's lived out of his backpack for months and I packed just as much stuff to spend one night.

Caleb starts to pick up his backpack.

"Let me try," I say, reaching for it.

"I've got it." Caleb slings his backpack over his shoulder and then grabs my suitcase. Now he's just showing off.

"I want to see how heavy it is. I can handle a walk to the car." I take the backpack from him, but it falls to the ground with a soft thud, heavier than expected.

Caleb smirks as I pull the bag up, and I have to use all the momentum I can to swing it up and onto my back. I'm not sure if it's heavy or if I'm just that weak.

"You good?" Caleb smiles, taking a few steps away.

I have to work to keep composure on my face as I follow Caleb into the hall. The first few steps feel a little unsteady with the added weight.

"Perfect," I say.

By the time we reach my car, it feels like if I don't open the trunk fast enough, I'm going to get permanent damage to my back. Once the trunk is ajar, I release the bag, letting it fall. The relief is instant, and I massage the muscles on my shoulders.

"You want to hike up the mountain with the bag, Ms. Muscles?" Caleb laughs as he lifts my suitcase and puts it into the trunk next to his backpack.

"The distance from the hotel room to the car was far enough," I say, trying to ignore the smug grin on his face.

Caleb is practically radiating energy as he sits in the car, but no matter how excited he is, I only get more and more anxious the closer we get.

When we pull into Baxter State Park, it's already swarming

with cars and hikers. Thankfully, we're able to find one of the last parking spots.

"Good thing we didn't sleep in," Caleb says, swinging the door open and getting out.

I meet him outside as he opens the trunk and pulls his backpack out.

"Do you need that? Won't we only be hiking for a couple hours?" I say.

He swings it back over his shoulders. "I still need food and water. I could empty it out, I guess, but it feels more ceremonial to have the bag with me."

"Do I need a bag?" I ask, suddenly nervous. After our backpacking trip, I feel empty-handed.

"I've got enough food and water for both of us."

"What about shoes?" I ask, looking at the hiking boots Caleb's wearing. They're coated in mud, and when I look down at my sneakers, I realize just how unprepared I am. I packed sneakers and workout clothes, knowing that tracking down Caleb might involve a little bit of walking, but I didn't expect a full-blown mountain.

Caleb looks down at my sneakers. "They're not as good as boots, but people hike in sneakers all the time."

"You sure?" I ask.

"Of course," he says, starting to turn away, his eyes following a group of hikers as they make their way across the parking lot. "I think the trail starts this way."

He takes a few steps away from the car, eager to finish what he started, but I can't manage to get myself to move away from the car. The videos and photos I saw last night before going to bed keep coming up in my mind.

"You coming?" Caleb says when he notices I'm not following.

I force a smile, leaving my car behind as we make our way toward the trail.

Caleb's strides are longer than mine. We haven't even reached the start of the trail, and I'm already starting to lag behind. We walk through a sea of hikers in the parking lot, and they all look stronger and ten times more prepared for this hike than I am.

"Caleb," I say softly, my eyes lingering on a hiker who looks like he's putting on the type of harness used for rock climbing. I start to feel dizzy.

Caleb's still a few steps ahead, so he doesn't hear me. I continue forward, trying not to watch the way the man clips more gear than I have names for onto his harness. We reach a sign that marks the beginning of the trail, and Caleb turns when he finally notices my panic.

"Lori?" he asks, the excitement draining from his face. "What's wrong?"

My eyes follow a hiker who walks past us and up the trail. "I don't think I can do this."

"Why? What happened?"

"Caleb, this trail is super steep. I looked it up online. Not to mention you walk along this scary-looking ledge."

He looks confused for a moment before something clicks. "Oh! Knife Edge?"

"I can't do that, Caleb," I whisper.

"We're not doing that trail."

I watch him, waiting to see if he's lying. "What do you mean?"

"There're a couple different trails to get to the top. We're taking one of the easier ones."

"Easier?"

He shrugs. "As easy as scaling a mountain will ever be." When I don't respond right away, he places his hands on my shoulders, forcing me to look at him. "You can handle this, Lori. This hike today is just like the last one we did together, except this time you don't need to carry a backpack. I've got the heavy bag and everything we need to stay safe. You're going to be fine."

I look down, and he moves his hand to lift my chin.

"Just follow the trail," he says gently.

"I'm not a hiker," I remind him.

His face falters, and he tries to hide it with a fake smile. "I can go alone and meet you back at the car," he says. He drops his hands and turns to look at the start of the trail. I know he isn't doing it to egg me on and that he really means it, but I can't let him finish the trail alone.

"I'm going," I say.

"You don't have to."

"No." I walk past him and take the lead. "I'm going to watch you finish this."

The trail starts off with a steady incline. For the first mile and a half, I almost laugh at myself for thinking it would be too hard for me. At the two-mile mark, I start to officially regret my decision.

"How much farther to the top?" I say, leaning on a boulder. We're deep into the trees now, and the parking lot feels like a lifetime away.

"The honest answer or the answer that will keep you moving forward?"

I turn around, looking at Caleb like he's utterly insane. "That's not encouraging."

He lets out a soft chuckle and keeps walking until he's standing next to me again.

"You're doing great. Just keep it slow and steady."

I let out a huff of air. I'm going to have to start doing cardio again if I plan on keeping up with Caleb.

"You lead." I point forward.

"You sure?"

"If I lead, I'm going to keep stopping every two steps."

"Come on," he says, grabbing my hand and walking forward. We continue hand in hand for only a couple more steps before we have to break the bond to make it through the trail without tripping.

Caleb leads, but he never lingers too far toward the front. He stops every couple steps, turning to watch me, never pushing me to go faster than I'm comfortable with. I contemplate turning around and heading back to the car a couple times, but I don't want to turn around alone, and I don't want to force Caleb to turn around as well.

Up is the only option.

The trail manages to get even steeper, and multiple groups

of hikers pass us, giving us a quick greeting before they leave us behind.

There's a tiny moment of anger when I realize just how much harder this trail is than the last one I did with Caleb. If I thought that trail was steep, then this trail is a straight-up incline. There are no moments where my legs can rest for a couple strides. We're always going up.

My legs feel like they're being torn in half with every move I make, and my clothes cling to me like a second skin, sweat coating every inch of me. My hair is pulled back in a tight French braid again, but I'm sweating so much that my hair is pulled down to my scalp from the moisture.

"Come on, Moose. You've got this," Caleb says.

I almost don't respond because I have no idea who Caleb is talking to, but then it clicks. He's talking to me.

"Maybe I'd go faster if a moose started chasing me," I say, laughing quietly to myself. Everything in my body hurts—not just my legs, but my hips, arms, and abs.

I keep my eyes down, watching where I step and gripping rocks as I pull myself up. It's not technically rock climbing since I don't need to be harnessed in, but I had no idea how much of an arm workout I'd get in just trying to hoist myself up this trail.

"Whatever motivates you to keep going."

I look up at Caleb, and he looks back at me, beaming with pride. He doesn't care how long it takes me or how slow I go. He's just here to cheer me on. I'm not even entirely sure he cares about reaching the summit anymore.

A renewed sense of energy kicks in as I push forward. Caleb

lets me catch up, but he always stays a few paces ahead, giving me a pep talk whenever I start to slow down.

We keep up the pace until we finally reach a break in the trees, and a view opens up around us. It looks like an entirely different world. If I thought the view we got during the backpacking trip was good, this is ten times better. Mount Katahdin is massive, and being at the summit is like standing at the top of the world.

There are a few mountains off in the distance, but they look tiny compared to where we are. Lakes are scattered everywhere around us. Mount Katahdin stretches out wide, the rocky surface looking harsh and unforgiving. It feels like a different planet up here. I'm not sure if I'm more shocked by the view or the fact that I was able to hike up here.

"Finally," I say, coming to a stop.

Caleb laughs. "Not yet," he says, walking forward. He points to show the trail stretches onward, and without any more trees, it's easy to see thin lines on the mountain, showing where the trail stretches upward.

"This isn't it?" I say, moving to follow him. The trail is more level than it was before. It still continues in an upward fashion, but I'm able to walk at a regular stride again.

"Almost. The trail will be easier now."

And it is. I don't know if it's because it isn't as steep or that the view is so good it helps distract me from how much my legs hurt, but either way, it feels like we're going faster.

I keep my eyes on the rocky path of the mountain. The trail is mostly dirt, with the occasional boulder getting in the way. The farther I look, the more trails I see, hikers off in the distance, all heading in the same direction: up.

We don't have to walk for too long before I see the sign, and this time I know we're almost at the summit.

"There it is," Caleb says, confirming my thoughts. His face lights up, making me realize this is the thing he's been fighting for. It's time to cross the finish line.

Groups of hikers linger around the sign, and a few of them look over and see us.

"Chip!" a younger guy with long straggly hair shouts. "Time to finish!"

Everyone at the summit turns and watches as we approach the sign. One by one, they all start to cheer and clap. Caleb's pace gets faster, and he reaches for my hand again, pulling me alongside him.

The summit sign is large. It's assembled with two-by-fours that form a triangle with a large board that reads "Katahdin" in bold letters, along with information for trails and how many miles they are.

We're only a few steps away from being able to touch the sign when I tug on Caleb's hand.

"Hold on," I tell him, taking a step toward him and reaching into his backpack. I pull out my phone, which I zipped into one of the pockets. "Go ahead, I want to get photos." I hold up my phone.

He hesitates at first, not wanting to go on without me, but the cheering around us gets louder, and he takes his final steps to the sign. The grin of utter joy is unmistakable, and while I don't know any of the hikers at the summit with us, it's clear

Caleb does, and the family atmosphere among these strangers is uncanny.

There's a huge burst of applause when Caleb's hand touches the sign, and I snap a photo with my phone. He moves to walk behind the sign and then steps up to where another two-by-four is screwed into the triangle structure so you can stand behind the sign.

Caleb stands at the summit and throws his fists into the air. I snap another photo, smiling as I watch him take it all in.

When I imagined Caleb reaching the summit of Mount Katahdin and finishing his journey, I worried it was going to be anticlimactic. He'd get to the top, maybe take a picture, and then hike back down. But this is anything but.

Hikers continue to shout and clap as Caleb soaks it all in.

"Come on!" he shouts, gesturing me over.

I cross the small distance and move to where Caleb is. I step up onto the two-by-four so I'm standing behind the sign as well. Caleb wraps his arm around me, securing me in place.

The group of hikers erupts into another round of applause as Caleb kisses me.

Caleb passes my phone to someone, and we start taking photos with the sign, the smile never leaving Caleb's face. Right as we're stepping down from the sign, another hiker shows up in the distance, sporting a massive backpack like Caleb's. Even though I don't know who it is, our entire group begins to cheer again as they reach the summit.

It takes a couple minutes for the excitement to die down, leaving an aura of euphoria in the air.

"Oh, I've been meaning to ask," Caleb says suddenly.

I turn, still riding a high from everyone's energy. "What?"

"I just wanted to confirm. You said you were cutting back on college classes so you'd have more free time, right?"

I nod. "I already canceled some of my classes."

"So, you'd have time for a boyfriend?"

I grin. "Only if it was the right person."

He mirrors my expression. "Am I the right person?"

I look at the mountain stretching out in front of us, pretending to think about it. Caleb's gaze is locked on me, and I see him roll his eyes. When I turn back, smile wide, he already knows my response.

"You're exactly the right person."

Support the author!
REVIEW THE BOOK ON AMAZON!

Marly's road trip of a lifetime doesn't just check off bucket-list destinations, it forces her to face the grief and guilt she feels over her parents' death.

For most 19-year-olds, a cross-country trip is an offer you can't refuse, but for Marly, it's the last thing she wants after losing both her parents in a car accident. Nine months after their death, she would rather stay home working the retail job she hates, than deal with her loss. It's not until family and friends corner Marly into driving her mom's renovated 1978 VW bus across the United States that she's ripped from her emotional paralysis.

Marly goes on the trip, warily exploring the life her parents knew she always wanted — hiking mountain summits and living out her photography dreams. Her composure unravels when she meets a guy who pushes at the walls she's so carefully built around herself.

Will he be the one that causes her to face her deepest wounds and reclaim the life she thought was gone forever?

Meet Me at the Summit is the first book in the Road Trip Snapshot Series. If you like sweet romance, travel, and coming of age, then you'll love this story that will be sure to tug at your heartstrings.

Start your own road trip by reading Meet Me at the Summit today!

Subscribe to Mandi's Newsletter:
https://bit.ly/AuthorMandiNewsletter

**Subscribe to Mandi's YouTube channel
to watch as the book is created:
https://www.youtube.com/user/mandilynnwrites**

acknowledgements

This book has practically written itself. I've never experienced a story that has brought me such joy throughout the entire writing process, and I hope that joy comes across through the pages of the book.

However, I can't forget to thank all the people who helped bring this story to life. My illustrator, Warren Muzak. My editor, Natalia Leigh. And of course my mom, who doubles as my number one fan and proofreader.

And lastly my readers. Without all of you, I wouldn't be able to sit outside and type on my laptop all day and call it a job.

about the author

Mandi Lynn Bell is the author of sweet young adult romance novels with the perfect dash of adventure. Mandi spends her days writing and making YouTube videos about self-publishing. When she's not creating, you can find her exploring the outdoors to get inspiration for her next book.

WWW.MANDILYNNBELL.COM

@AUTHORMANDILYNNBELL

Subscribe to Mandi's Newsletter:
https://bit.ly/AuthorMandiNewsletter

Follow on YouTube to watch as the next book is created:
https://www.youtube.com/user/mandilynnwrites

www.ingramcontent.com/pod-product-compliance
Lightning Source LLC
Chambersburg PA
CBHW021218220726
48287CB00015B/1681